Una McCormack

WEIRD SPACE

STAR OF THE SEA

**ABADDON
BOOKS**

W W W . A B A D D O N B O O K S . C O M

An Abaddon Books™ Publication
www.abaddonbooks.com
abaddon@rebellion.co.uk

First published in 2016 by Abaddon Books™,
Rebellion Publishing Limited,
Riverside House, Osney Mead, Oxford, OX2 0ES, UK.

10 9 8 7 6 5 4 3 2 1

Editors: Jonathan Oliver & David Moore
Cover Art: Adam Tredowski
Design: Sam Gretton & Oz Osborne
Marketing and PR: Rob Power
Head of Books and Comics Publishing: Ben Smith
Creative Director and CEO: Jason Kingsley
Chief Technical Officer: Chris Kingsley
Weird Space™ created by Eric Brown

ISBN: 978-1-78108-482-3

Printed in the UK

To my family

Refuge in grief, star of the sea,
Pray for the mourner, pray for me.

John Lingard

CHAPTER ONE

THE WATER HAD been a constant worry. All through the hot summer, Yale had watched the fields around the settlement with an anxious eye, waiting for the water to disappear. Every morning, waking early, she would walk out beyond the fence and into the precious, hard-grown fields around the settlement to check that water was still flowing along the irrigation channels. The planet Stella Maris, for all that it provided a haven for the desperate and homeless of two species, was after all a hard world, where famine could easily take hold. Only by the grace of the Weird had the people of Stella Maris been able to feed themselves. The Weird—enemies of this dimension everywhere else, consuming humans and Vetch alike—here did no harm, but had succoured the settlement, nourished it, keeping the water running and the crops growing. But the Weird were gone now—had been gone for months, ever since Delia Walker had passed this way with her crew of runaways, in search of the portal leading to the Weird dimension. In Walker's wake had come enemies, pursuing her and the secret she brought, and the settlement had been attacked.

Those attackers were all dead now. Walker herself had disappeared into thin air, but the bodies of her crewmates had been found, up in the mountains near the portal. Also found there had been the bodies of the little band of people from the settlement who had led Walker to the portal. The settlement itself, which had endured a vicious attack from people without conscience, had tentatively begun to rebuild. But the Weird— who had for so long sustained them, clinging precariously to the thin soil of this desert world—had gone silent. Once a month, one of the telepaths would go up to the portal to try to speak to them, but there was nothing. The portal remained glassy and closed.

But the water had not disappeared. Not yet. Spring had passed, and Yale had watched in fear, certain that one morning she would wake to drying streams and empty wells, but that had not happened. Summer came, hot and radiant, and then the most abundant autumn that Yale could remember in her time on Stella Maris. Now the crops were home, and the first sniff of winter was in the air. And still Yale kept her vigil, leaving the settlement early each morning, beating the bounds, watching for any change that might signify news of the Weird.

Or of something else. Because Yale did not believe that the attack was the last they would hear from the Expansion. Not with the stakes so high. As well as her watch on the water, she had been busy over the summer taking stock of what weapons the settlers had, should a more sustained attack come. The settlers of Stella Maris were mostly runaway slaves from worlds within Satan's Reach, that lawless part of space where cruelty and exploitation were the rule. They had come to Stella Maris with nothing of their own beyond their lives and their hard-won freedom, but their recent visitors had supplied riches: two large land vehicles, some hand weapons, and some ground weapons too. Not much, but it was, thought Yale, at least the makings of a defence. And then there was the ship that had brought Walker: a battered old freighter that seemed unlikely to ever fly again, but with a little love and attention... The *Baba Yaga*. In its hold, Yale had found a small cache of sidearms, a treasure trove from former days, gun-running to border worlds during the Vetch wars. It was a good ship, the *Baba Yaga*. One to look after. Yale had got it under cover, away from any prying eyes in orbit. You never knew what the future might bring, and an escape route was invaluable. Now all she could do was watch, and wait, and hope that whatever came from the Expansion was not too brutal.

The day was drawing to a close; the sun was still bright on the horizon, but there was a bite in the air. A faint prickle of stars was starting to appear in the sky. Yale stood on the hillside and looked down across the brown fields towards the settlement. A small place, but always busy. She tracked people drawing water from the wells; saw the smoke of cooking fires rising from the long-houses; watched the children running about in play. This was no great city or spaceport, nothing like the places where Yale had spent her lost past, but the daily life that unfolded here was no less important.

Its tranquility had made the sudden interruption of the violence and fury of the rest of the known universe all the more shocking. Like many other inhabitants of Stella Maris, Yale had come here to escape that world; she was among only a few, however, who did not think that what had happened in the spring was the end of it. The other settlers might tell themselves that the attack had been a one-off, but Yale was sure that more would be coming to Stella Maris. The secret of their Weird portal was surely known now, and the opportunities would be too tempting for the kind of people that Yale knew inhabited the space beyond this world. Stella Maris would attract them now, like a beacon lighting up the sky.

She heard the crunch of footsteps behind her and turned quickly. Ashot, a friend; Vetch, but still a friend. That had been one of the many things to get used to about living on Stella Maris, along with the steady pace of daily life and the relentless, routine tasks—living alongside Vetch, and learning not to be afraid of them. The scars of the Vetch wars ran deep in the human psyche, and there was no getting past how physically imposing they were: huge, tentacled, with a strange, ungainly walk that put you on edge. But years of working alongside Vetch simply to survive had smoothed most of this away. Yale barely distinguished now between Vetch and human. And this Vetch—Ashot—was a member of her long-house, her home, someone she saw at close hand almost every day. Someone with whom she had debated and discussed all the decisions the settlement made, and someone who, despite Yale's privacy, knew when she was worried, and valued her enough to take those worries seriously.

Still, they were great hairy stinking beasts, the lot of them. Ashot had long arms and legs, and as he lumbered towards her, the long tentacles on his face swayed and shifted, tasting the air, tasting her mood. When he drew near, he nodded at her. "Thought I'd find you here."

She turned to look beyond the fields at the bare desert. "I'm a creature of habit."

"You're a creature of something. I'm not sure what."

Yale shrugged and took a sip from her water bottle, rolling the mouthful carefully around. One good thing about this world was that nobody asked you where you were from and why you had come here. Most people here were escaping pasts so painful that they never wanted to think about them again: histories of slavery, and cruelty, and great fear. Everyone worked on the principle that what mattered now was the new life, the life on Stella Maris, and that the past was best left buried.

Take Ashot, now—Yale had no real idea who he had been before arriving on Stella Maris. He was a medic, yes, and a good one, but she had no idea if his training was formal, or had been acquired in the field through hard experience. His shambling walk was clumsy even for a Vetch. There was an old injury there; old pain. She would never ask him about it and he, in turn, would pay her the same courtesy. But she saw him, sometimes, watching her, and she wondered, sometimes, what he guessed about her.

Yale offered Ashot the water bottle, but he shook his head and she put it away.

What counted was the life they shared on Stella Maris. Yale had been surprised to learn, this late in life, how it felt to be attached so strongly to something. It was not an emotion that had much troubled her in the past. She was surprised at how much she had come to care about this community, and this world.

Ashot was watching her with curious, clever, compassionate eyes. "Are you going to stay here all day?"

Yale shrugged. "I might."

"Seems a waste of time."

"Something bad is going to happen," she said. "I know it."

"You've been thinking that for months now."

"And each day brings it closer."

He grunted noncommittally. "Yet today is such a beautiful day."

"Watch out for the beautiful days," said Yale. "They don't last forever."

"What a way to live!" he said. "Never to enjoy the moment."

"Not at all! I *love* being the harbinger of doom."

"Come back down to the long-house, Yale. Nothing's going to change."

"You're wrong there," Yale said. "Everything is going to change." She looked up at the sky. "Beyond recognition."

"Nothing is going to change *today*." He snuffled—a gentle Vetch laugh—and the ends of his tentacles curled up in a smile. "The crops are in. We're safe for the winter—"

"Yes, the winter," Yale said. "But after that?"

"We worry about that when the time comes."

Yale sighed. She didn't, in truth, believe, so long after the attack on the portal, that the Weird would suddenly withdraw their help. But something called her out here still. She looked up at the steadily darkening sky. Was it that she could watch what was going on up there more easily?

"Not the Weird on your mind today, then," Ashot said. "Something else. Something from beyond." He waved upwards with his paw. "Do you know something? Have you heard something?"

That startled her. What resources did he think she had? "Heard something? How would I hear a damn thing out here?"

"You've kept your secrets closer than most on Stella Maris."

"Well, I've not kept an interstellar communicator tucked under the bed."

"There's one on the *Baba Yaga*."

"And it's been silent as the grave."

"Still," said Ashot, "if the message that Maria sent was received, someone will surely want to track it to the source. And I get the feeling you think these people might be worse than the ones that were here before."

Yale shuddered at the thought of the squad that had been sent to Stella Maris in the spring. "I'm not sure there could *be* worse, but there might be *more*, and they might be more effective." She scuffed the ground with the toe of her boot. "It's been months. Why aren't they here yet?"

"You're keen for them to come?"

"Not particularly. But I've never been good at waiting."

"You'd think you'd have learned that, living here." He grunted. "I know someone who shares your concerns. Maria Emerson."

Yale almost growled. Maria and her small child had come to Stella Maris with Delia Walker and, for reasons best known to herself but unclear to Yale, sent messages to people within the Expansion. She had surely given away the location of this world.

"Do you still not trust her?" Ashot said. "She's been a great asset."

Yale frowned. "I don't think she's duplicitous, far from it. I think she lacks experience. I think she doesn't know how the world works, and because of that, everyone here might suffer."

"I think you're doing her an injustice," said Ashot.

"Oh yeah?"

"She led a sheltered life, that's clear. But she got herself and her little girl here, even as people were chasing her."

"Yes, that's all very well, but what did she hope to achieve, sending out those messages?"

"She wanted to expose a massacre. Bring those guilty to justice."

"Well, there is no justice; not in the Expansion. All she's done is told the universe where we are. And I promise you that the universe is going to be interested. Because what we have here is unique." Yale looked up to the mountains, where the silent portal was hidden. "What we *had* here."

"We still have it," Ashot insisted.

Yale dug her toe further into the ground. "There's a long winter yet. Let's see what happens in the spring—if we get that far. The Weird have gone quiet after only one attack. Let's see whether more dedicated attention will bring them back—or drive them away for good."

MARIA EMERSON SAT on the step of her long-house, contemplating her new life. The day was fresh, the sweetest kind of autumn day, and she was busy peeling vegetables. *Kitzim*, a woody root plant; a little like a sweet potato, but with a peppery flavour. She had never eaten one until a few months ago. Now she had eaten them boiled, mashed, stewed, and even sweetened in a pudding. They were a staple crop on Stella Maris.

Once upon a time, Maria had been a military wife. Her husband, Kit, had been a sergeant in Fleet: hard-working, respected, a good provider. They had been childhood sweethearts and best friends. They had a little girl, Jenny. Life had been good. And then, in the middle of the night, Kit had come home, and told Maria to wake their daughter. They had packed only essentials, and they had gone on the run.

The handful of weeks that followed had been filled with chaos and terrible loss. Ripped from her safe home on Braun's World, Maria was dragged away from the safety of the Expansion to the lawless stretch of space known as Satan's Reach. She'd tried to make things as safe as she could for Jenny, to be the support that Kit needed. She never doubted that Kit had good reasons for taking them away from their lives, and she had been right. Kit had run because he knew a terrible secret, and, after he was murdered, Maria had carried on, first alone with Jenny, and then throwing in her lot with Delia Walker. That had, in time, brought her here, to Stella Maris. But the secret that Kit had died to expose, and which Maria now knew, had been too big, too terrible, not to draw enemies after them. A faction within the Expansion's intelligence Bureau had, to seize power, faked the opening of a Weird portal on Braun's World, and murdered millions of people to cover up their crime. The Bureau had given chase, sending a squad of assassins to track her down and kill anyone with knowledge of the secret. They had failed, but it had cost many lives on Stella Maris.

Not least, those of most of the new friends Maria had made: Kay Larsen, the kindly doctor who had helped Kit escape Braun's World and risked her own life to make sure the massacre was known; Hecate Heyes, the old priest who had known the route to the safe world; and, of course, Delia Walker herself—hard, resourceful, and intent on proving that war was not inevitable, and that humans could live in peace alongside the Weird. Of the crew that had come to Stella Maris on the old ship the *Baba Yaga*, only one other person remained: Failt, a little Vetch boy who had stowed away to escape slavery, and who was devoted to Delia Walker after she'd saved his life, an unlikely chink in the armour of someone so controlled.

Delia Walker... Was she really dead? The assassins had chased her all the way into the mountains, up to the Weird portal, and while their bodies, and those of Larsen and Heyes, had been found, there had been no sign of Walker. Failt did not believe she was dead, but Maria could not accept his explanation: that Walker, several months pregnant, had jumped into the portal, and gone wherever the Weird would take her.

Wherever Walker was, she had found a way off Stella Maris, and that was something Maria knew would not be possible for her. The *Baba Yaga* would not fly again. The pilot had died when the assassins came, and nobody here had the implants that would allow it to phase into the void and cross interstellar space. Besides, what was there to go back to? Kit was dead, and Maria was a wanted woman. Acting on Walker's instructions, Maria had sent information of the cover-up to Walker's contacts within the Expansion, in the hope that the news would break. Since then, there had been only silence, and Maria, grieving for her husband, her new friends and her old life, had tried to make herself useful, to persuade people to put aside their mistrust.

Jenny, only four years old, had proved resilient. With Failt beside her, she had thrown herself into this new life, and it warmed Maria's heart now to see her playing with the other children. She could see five of them now, swinging from a tree; Jenny laughing, and Failt clambering up amongst the highest branches, holding out a hand so that a smaller child could come and join him. When each child was comfortable in their own spot, they sat and shared the fruit amongst them.

Failt had been the key to being accepted. His cheerfulness and friendliness—and his willingness to work hard—had helped him settle in easily on Stella Maris. His love for Maria helped others permit themselves, every once in a while, not to hold her at arm's length. She had done her bit, too—helping the community clear the damage after the attack, taking more than her share of work in the fields, helping keep an eye on the children when others were called away by their tasks. It felt like a thousand years had passed since Maria's old quiet life with Kit and Jenny back in the Expansion. She felt older, wiser, hardier—but she was still afraid that her presence here on Stella Maris would bring trouble to her new friends.

She peeled a few more *kitzim* and tried to put it from her mind. She saw, walking along the path towards her, a huge Vetch, Ashot, one of the people from her long-house. Living in such close proximity to Vetch—that was something else that had gone from unimaginable to everyday. The long-houses on

Stella Maris housed fifteen to twenty people apiece, children and adults and the elderly, humans and Vetch alike. There was nowhere else in the known universe where this happened, and it *worked*. Everyone was here for a good reason—escaping slavery, mostly—and all were willing to accommodate each other. And so Maria had gritted her teeth, and told herself that she must learn to live alongside the Vetch, putting aside the prejudice and paranoia that had been a staple of Expansion propaganda all the time the two great space-faring empires had been at war.

In fact, it had not been hard to respect and even like Ashot. When Failt had been wounded in the attack, Ashot had taken care of him, and had been calm and kind as Maria fretted at the boy's bedside. She suspected that Ashot had influenced the other members of his long-house to take in Maria and Jenny, too, when they had taken in Failt. Life on Stella Maris was marginal, and the people needed these extended families in order to survive.

They greeted each other and Ashot sat down beside her on the step, taking up the remaining two-thirds of the space. He was broad, and compact for a Vetch, although still huge in human terms: nearly two metres tall. There was something of the bloodhound about him, with his long legs and arms, and a sorrowful look in his bulging brown eyes. His face was both fascinating and unnerving. Even after months alongside the many Vetch of the settlement, Maria could not help looking at the blood-coloured tentacles hanging from the centre of his face. He had a gentle manner she had not expected, and the famous "Vetch reek," a staple of the war vids and flicks that filled up Expansion entertainment channels, had turned out not to be true. Ashot smelled of wood-smoke. And *kitzim*. But they all smelled of *kitzim*.

He nodded his head at the pile of vegetables, which made his tentacles jiggle, then took out a little knife and began to help her with her task. His huge paws, hairy and six-fingered, were quick and dexterous. They fell into a peaceful rhythm. This life was good, Maria thought. There was much to commend it. Running from danger into danger palled rapidly. She could only wonder how long it would last.

"It's good to see them playing," Ashot said, after a while, nodding towards the children.

"Very good," Maria said.

"Jenny seems to be sleeping much better now."

There were few secrets to communal living. Jenny's nightmares must have been a trial for everyone, but none of the other members of the long-house had ever complained. "She is," Maria said. "And I am grateful to you all for the kindness you've shown her. Her father..." Maria trailed off.

Ashot sliced the peeled *kitzim* and put the pieces in the pot. "We are very good at looking after bereaved children here."

Bereaved. That was the word. Maria felt her eyes go damp. She and Jenny were bereaved. She turned inwards for a while— thinking of Kit and how much she longed for him, how much she missed him—but slowly the present reasserted itself: the crisp day, the routine task, the solid presence and smoky scent of the alien body beside her.

"I think you should go and talk to Yale," Ashot said.

"To *Yale?*" Maria frowned. She knew Yale, of course—they were members of the same long-house—but the other woman was elusive, to say the least. The first to leave in the morning, the last to return in the evening, Yale would stand in the doorway while decisions were debated and made, watching events with a slight, sardonic smile, only weighing in at the end to agree to whatever decision had been made. Something about Yale unnerved Maria; at the same time, something seemed familiar.

Yale did not seem to be like anyone else on Stella Maris. She reminded Maria of Walker. "Why on earth would I speak to Yale?"

Ashot pushed his peelings into the pile of scraps. They would use those as fodder for the beasts; nothing went to waste here. "Because I think she is worried about the same thing that you are worried about."

"That *I* am worried about? What do you think I worry about, Ashot?"

"You worry about Jenny, chiefly, of course. But also you are worried about the messages you sent. Whether it was the right thing to do. Whether there will be consequences. What they might be—and when they will come. You are worried that you did the wrong thing—or, perhaps I should say, that you did the right thing, but that it will come at a cost."

"You seem to be very sure about how my mind works."

"You are a good woman, Maria," he said. "Of course these things trouble you. You are not like Walker was, presuming on our help, demanding it. We have welcomed you here—as far as we have been able, given the harm that your arrival caused. And because you are a good woman, you feel responsible for us." He paused, thoughtfully. "You are not responsible for us, of course, except in the ordinary way that we each must take care of each other or die alone. But you should go and talk to Yale. I think you'll find you have more in common than you realise."

Maria fell silent. This was the first time, she realised, that anyone on Stella Maris had asked a favour of her. She supposed she should pay attention. "All right," she said. "I'll go and talk to Yale."

Ashot lifted one big paw and pointed beyond the fence. "She's out there. Staring at the water channels."

"You mean *now?*"

He put the last of the *kitzim* into the bowl. "This is done," he said. "Jenny is happy and loved. The day isn't getting younger. Why not?"

YALE WAS SITTING with her back propped up against a fence post and watching the stars when she saw Maria. Sent by Ashot, no doubt. "Bloody busybody Vetch," she muttered, but when Maria drew close, she stood up and greeted her cordially.

"Ashot said you were checking on the water levels," Maria said. "I'd like to come along, if that's okay."

Yale eyed her thoughtfully. Maria was slight, girlish, with big eyes. Someone's high school sweetheart, she bet; the kind of girl that attracted good men who wanted to protect her and provide for her. Yale had not been that kind of girl, and harboured some dislike of the type. She was frankly amazed Maria had got this far. Perhaps Ashot was right. Perhaps the young woman was steelier than she appeared.

"I *was* looking at the water levels," said Yale. "Now I am having a rest."

"Oh, I'm sorry."

Maria looked confounded and embarrassed, and Yale found herself regretting her tone. So *that* was how it worked. "Don't sweat it," Yale said. "I can't stay here much longer. It's getting cold at night now. Come on, if you really want to stare at irrigation channels."

She led Maria round the edge of the field. Beyond the fence, the ground was red and barren. On this side, it was markedly different: brown and bare after the *kitzim* had been brought in, but definitely fertile. The water seemed to come from nowhere. There were wells in the settlement, and then little springs bubbled up here and there around the cultivated lands, which the people of Stella Maris had channelled. Yale strode on, silently. Maria matched her step, but she cracked first.

"Ashot said I should come and talk to you."

"Yes?"

"He said that you and I are worrying about the same things."

"Yes?"

Maria frowned. "He didn't mention how uncommunicative you'd be, though."

"No?"

"No. I figured that myself."

Yale stopped walking and turned to face Maria. "What do you want, Maria?"

She was surprised by Maria's cool, direct gaze. There was something very open about her. Like Ashot had said, she seemed incapable of deception or subterfuge. Perhaps this was another reason she won herself so many friends and protectors. Walker had put herself out to protect Maria, and Yale suspected Delia Walker had not been in the habit of putting herself out for others.

"I'm afraid," said Maria. "Not about the lack of communication from the Weird—"

"You should be," Yale said. "We'll die if they go completely."

"Yes, I know... I mean, of course I'm afraid of that, but there's nothing I can do about it. It's the silence from the Expansion that worries me..."

Me too, thought Yale. "Maria," she said, "I know what was in the messages you sent out from here. I know about what happened on Braun's World. But I'm not quite sure *who* you sent the news to."

"Delia gave me instructions," Maria said. "I did what she told me—"

"You're not that stupid," Yale said. "Who did you tell?"

Maria was silent for a moment, as if trying to judge whether telling what she knew was some betrayal of trust. "Some major news channels, some high-level politicians. Some people I didn't know; I had to look up their names. Government officials, bureaucrats."

"That was the best Walker could do?" Yale shook her head. "Then we're both right to be worried about the silence from the Expansion. Because that suggests that they're taking their time to make a plan to deal with us—and our portal—once and for all."

Maria clasped her hands together. "I thought so, too. I've often wondered who those people were, that came to Stella Maris. The way they chased Walker; the way they attacked the settlement... They seemed so hardened. So *relentless*."

That, Yale thought, was because they were crimopaths. She concealed her shudder. Latent telepaths, experimented upon, augmented, until their moral compass was removed, and they were able to kill indiscriminately. The Expansion's worst weapon. Yale didn't volunteer any information, but she was aware of Maria watching her carefully. Yes, it would be easy to underestimate this woman. She'd gone through more than most and come out stronger. She had been loyal to Walker, but would she be as loyal to Stella Maris?

"Do you know who they were, Yale? Had you come across people like that before?"

"I'd heard things about them." This was no more than the truth. She had *seen* crimopaths in action, but there was no need to go into that. That was the past, thank Christ.

"What kind of things?" Maria pressed. "How did you know about them? I'd never heard anything, and Kit never mentioned anything like them—"

"Perhaps he didn't know about them," Yale said. "Perhaps they were kept quiet."

Maria pondered this for a while. Then she said, "Most people here, they're from Satan's Reach. But you're not, are you? You're from the Expansion."

Yale didn't reply. Maria gave a frustrated sigh, but Yale wasn't just evading her question; something had attracted her attention. "Look."

Maria sighed again. "Where am I looking?"

Yale pointed up the hillside. "See the road that comes down from the hills?"

"I wouldn't call it a road, exactly—"

"You see it, though?"

"Yes." Maria stared towards the hills. "Is there someone coming?"

Yale nodded. "Yes."

"There isn't anyone out on patrol up there, is there?"

"Not that I know."

"And you would know."

"Yes, I would."

"Could it be one of the..." Maria shuddered. "One of those killers..."

Yale frowned. That had been her first thought too, but surely not? The area around the portal had been thoroughly searched—she'd made sure of that—and nobody had been left alive. Everybody had been accounted for—except Delia Walker, damn her. Damn, damn, *damn* Delia Walker.

Maria drew a sudden breath.

"What is it?" said Yale.

Maria shook her head. "No, it must have been a trick of the light."

"What?"

"For a moment, I thought it looked like... Well, like Delia."

Yale didn't reply, but she walked along the fence and stood

facing the road, her hand shielding her eyes. Could it be Walker? Could they have missed her somehow in the search? She took a step forwards and squinted at the dark figure. Something about it did remind her of Walker. Yale, who had learned to control her reactions many years ago, felt a sharp stab of fury, an urge to violence that she thought had long been suppressed. What the hell had Walker been doing out here, all this time? How had she survived the crimopath attack when the others had not?

"Yale, is it her?"

"I don't know."

"What's she been doing all this time?" Maria whispered. "Why hasn't she come back before?" Her voice rose, excited. "Perhaps she has news from the Weird! Perhaps she can tell us why they're no longer speaking to the telepaths—"

"It can't be Walker," Yale said, savagely. "She can't have survived—"

"We didn't find her body!"

"Perhaps she fell off the mountain. Perhaps she fell in the *portal*—"

The figure was getting closer.

"Come on," said Yale. "Let's go."

"Go?" Maria said, with a frown.

"Back to the settlement. If Walker's back, I want the gates closed. If it's anyone else, I want the gates closed. Damn it, I want the bloody gates closed!"

Maria was standing her ground. "No. If this is Delia, I want to see her. I want to speak to her. I know that you all have no reason to trust her, but she was good to me. She saved my life— and Jenny's—and she protected us when we most needed it."

"She was a stone cold bitch."

"She was *loyal*," Maria shot back. "I owe it to her to speak to her. If she's been away all these months, there'll be a good reason. I want to hear what it is!"

"Maria," said Yale, through gritted teeth, "this is not just about you."

This was the test. Was Maria thinking intelligently? Or only of herself? The young woman looked up the road, and shook her head. "All right," she said. "We'll go back."

"Good choice," said Yale. "Come on. I don't like a mystery either, but we've got to be careful. We don't have much in the way of defences."

She set off at a jog, Maria a little way behind her. They reached the edge of the field, where the road from the mountains cut through the fence and headed towards the settlement. The figure was drawing nearer. Yale turned onto the road, and picked up her pace. Maria hurried behind her. After ten minutes or so, they drew close to the big fence that ran around the settlement. Yale slowed to a stop, bending over and putting her hands on her thighs to catch her breath. The gate stood open, and two people came out to greet her.

"Yale?" one called, a Vetch woman who towered over even the tallest human on Stella Maris. "What's going on?"

"Someone's coming," Yale said. "Down from the mountains. We need to bar the gate." She glanced back over her shoulder. Maria was a few hundred yards away. She hesitated, but then said, "Let her in first."

Once Maria was safely inside, the gate was closed and barred. "Who is it?" said the Vetch woman. "Who's coming?"

"No idea," said Yale.

"I think it could be Delia Walker," said Maria, to Yale's dismay. Soon the name was spreading like wildfire around the settlement. People began to come out of the long-houses and gather round the gate, muttering Walker's name and speculating.

"It can't be Walker," said Yale firmly, to the people next to her, but the idea had taken hold, and they would not be convinced. *Can you see her? Where's she been hiding? Does she know where the Weird have gone? Does she have a message from them?*

"It can't be Walker!" Yale insisted. She pushed her way through the crowd back to the gate. There was a little viewing hatch: she lifted this and watched as the figure drew closer. "It's not Walker," Yale said, after a few minutes. "It really isn't her."

She stood back to let Maria see what she had seen: a girl, no more than fifteen, at Yale's best guess. She heard Maria sigh in disappointment.

"Who can she be, poor girl?" Maria said. "She looks like she's walked a long way." She looked round at Yale. "Nobody's missing, are they?"

"Everyone accounted for, as far as I know," said Yale.

"Except Delia," said Maria.

"Except Walker. And that isn't Walker."

Yale moved back to look through the hatch. The girl came closer. When she was about ten feet away, she stopped. She was small, with long brown hair in rat-tails, and wearing a very grubby dress. She lifted her hand in greeting.

"My name is Cassandra," she said. "My mother was the Walker."

CHAPTER TWO

FROM ORBIT, STELLA Maris looked dry and inhospitable, but Eileen O'Connor was excited to be looking at it. Eight months ago, she had been teaching xeno-anthropology at the prestigious University of Venta, and then out of the blue came an invitation to a meeting with a representative of a large private charity, looking to spend some money in her area. O'Connor had been around long enough to know that one did not turn down such a meeting, and had gone by barge and boat to an impressive building just off the Greenway, the home of Parliament and many government departments. She'd sat in a big marbled office, answering questions about her research, her background, and her affiliations. Then she went home again.

After that initial contact, things went quiet for a while and then, suddenly, there had been a flurry of more meetings, and briefings, and tests (including a thorough medical), and even more meetings... O'Connor's office-mate, who had once applied for the civil service, said the process was familiar, but she could shed no light on which government body used the building

O'Connor had visited. Then everything went quiet again and, after a couple of weeks, O'Connor assumed nothing would come of it, and put the whole experience out of her mind.

Then the message came. *We are pleased to inform you that you have secured a place on our research programme. Please attend the following meeting...* The message gave very precise directions, including private transport to a large island on the western edge of Venta's main archipelago. She was told to expect to be away for several weeks. All had been arranged with her university; even her rent had been paid for the duration.

Those several weeks turned into several months, and were likely to extend to several years. When O'Connor arrived at the island, she realised that around thirty other scientists—some senior, some nearly as junior as her—had come too. They gathered that evening at dinner and speculated wildly as to why they had been brought together, and which super-villain was intending to exploit them, and to what nefarious ends. All was made clear the following morning, when (some of them rather the worse for wear) they attended their first full briefing, by a woman in dark navy suit who introduced herself as Director Woodley. They were some of the finest minds in the Expansion, she said, and had been brought together to study a new phenomenon: a Weird portal, on a distant world, where the population lived alongside the Weird and were not enslaved by it.

O'Connor would never forget the thrill that went around the room. Woodley smiled. "I'm sure you understand now the need for all this secrecy. You have all been very patient with our tests and interviews. You should understand that we have looked at over two thousand candidates while assembling this team. You are the people that we have chosen."

There was considerable pride around the room, and then a

hand went up at the front; an older man, clearly used to being heard. "May I ask—chosen for what?"

Woodley smiled. "A mission beyond Expansion space, beyond even Satan's Reach. The Weird portal lies on a world called Stella Maris. We will be going there to study it. You"— she gestured around the room—"all of you, will be coming with us."

O'Connor gasped in delighted shock. Everyone knew about the Weird, of course; about the damage that had been done on worlds across the Expansion. Most assumed that the government was working on a means of destroying them. But in her secret heart, O'Connor had yearned to study them at close hand. Her expertise was on alien groups that collectivised more holistically than her own competitive, individualistic species. The Weird, so far as she understood from the spotty reports that came through, were at the far, opposite end of the spectrum: a species guided by a single mother-mind, that followed its will slavishly, and could make humans do the same.

But this portal? This sounded different...

"You said the population lived alongside this portal," said the man again. Vincenze, O'Connor recalled; he had been sitting opposite her at dinner the previous night. "But haven't we seen that elsewhere? On World, for example."

Woodley shook her head. "On World, the humans were enslaved by the Weird, kept in a drugged state which made them pliable and allowed the Weird to consume them. Other encounters have also involved enslavement of humans—the mind-parasites, for example. Dr Vincenze, I know that you're an expert on these: perhaps you could explain."

Vincenze stood. "The mind-parasites are an invasive infection that leaves a host body intact, but puts their mind—their will— under the control of the Weird. Often the host does not even know that they are infected until very late on. I have been trying to create an antidote—a means of freeing the parasites' victims. We can test for it—but so far we can't cure. Right now it's a death sentence and, at the end, a hideous experience."

O'Connor shuddered. To lose one's mind in that way—to be slowly taken over, to the extent that you could no longer prevent yourself harming those around you... It really was hideous.

"Your work is vital," said Woodley. "But what is happening on Stella Maris is different. For one thing, the community there is unique, in that it is made up of human and Vetch. They live together peacefully. And, as far as we can tell, they are not drugged. We have seen evidence of art, creativity, industry—these are not slaves living in the thrall of the Weird. They are independent, but somehow succoured."

Many questions followed; it was noticeable, however, that everyone spoke as if they would soon be there. Nobody in that room said that they wanted out; indeed, it didn't even occur to O'Connor what might have happened if she had refused. What threat was needed? Every one of the people here wanted to see this extraordinary portal. After a full few days in which they received an intensive briefing about Stella Maris, they boarded the ship that would take them there.

The long journey had been conducive to collegiality. At Woodley's instigation, they held regular research seminars, explaining to each other their individual research, and learning about overlaps and how they could support each other. O'Connor was nervous as hell before her own seminar: there were some seriously eminent people in the room. But she did herself proud, getting a pat on the arm from the other young woman on the team, Palmer, and even a nod over supper from the self-regarding Vincenze. From Woodley, they learned more about the harshness of the environment on Stella Maris, and were assured of the resources and comforts that had been assembled for them. "There'll be no scratching a living out of the desert sand or sleeping under the stars for any of you," Woodley said with a smile. "We want your minds and bodies rested for study."

So the journey went on, for weeks, with everyone keen to reach their destination and aware they were involved in something very special. When they were at last told that they were coming out of phase, everyone gathered on the observation deck for their first sight of the world that would be their new home.

"Not much, is it?" said Vincenze, with a sniff.

"Miserable old bugger," muttered Palmer to O'Connor, who stifled a laugh. "It's not how it looks that counts," she added, more loudly. "It's what we'll do down there."

"Spoken like a true believer," said Vincenze, turning his back on the sight and walking off. O'Connor stayed for a while with a group of her colleagues, as they studied the world below, discussing what they knew about it and what they had planned. Eventually, even Palmer went off, leaving O'Connor alone.

"Still staring at the desert, Dr O'Connor?"

O'Connor looked up to see Vincenze. "We've been in phase a long time. It's good to see a world again."

He sat down next to her. "Hmm. And you think this world will deliver everything you hope it will?"

"I don't know," she said. "How can I, until I get down there?"

That earned her a genuine if avuncular smile, as if she was a clever student who'd surprised her teacher. "You're excited to be here, aren't you, Dr O'Connor."

"You can call me Eileen," she said.

"Eileen. I'm Paul."

"I know that, Dr Vincenze."

He smiled.

She turned back to the screen. "Of *course* I'm excited. I've been studying collectivised species for years. Not one has been as unified as the Weird. How many people get close enough to study them? The chance to observe the Weird first-hand is marvellous!" She could not control the tremor of excitement in her voice. "A *peaceful* part of the Weird—it transforms everything we know about them!"

Vincenze was smiling at her. "I'm glad your enthusiasm is unmarred."

O'Connor frowned. "What would mar it?"

Vincenze did not reply directly, but nodded slightly towards the soldier standing at the far end of the observation deck. O'Connor was not sure what he meant. Growing up in a militarised society, she was used to seeing armed men on every corner. "I don't know what you mean—"

"Not noticed how... ubiquitous they are?"

"No."

"It's just you and me here now," Vincenze whispered. "But that's enough. If there are two or more of us, there's at least one of them."

O'Connor frowned. "I supposed they're protection."

Vincenze smiled. "Protection. Yes. You're a terrible danger to me, Eileen. And I... Well, I am a terrible danger to *myself*, never mind to anyone else."

"I meant, when we arrived. We don't know if we'll receive a welcome."

"Protection, yes." Vincenze nodded. "And the army of administrators? What are they here for?"

"Somebody's got to make sure we're not wasting money," O'Connor said.

Vincenze was even more amused by that. "Yes, yes, it would be terrible if even a single grubby groat was wasted. A good job we do not count administration as waste. We would seem a very suspect outfit if that were the case."

O'Connor frowned. Her delight at the sight of Stella Maris was being tested, and now she felt the uncomfortable presence of the soldiers like a weight upon her shoulders. "If you didn't like the way the expedition had been set up, why did you come?"

Vincenze shrugged. "Several reasons. Not least that if a very secret expedition is mounted to a hitherto unknown world boasting a safe Weird portal—well, how could anyone refuse? I want to see the Weird up close too, Eileen—just like you." He gave a warm smile. "But the chief reason was that I was drafted."

"Drafted?"

"It's an expensive business, training in my field. Even more expensive, doing the research." He glanced again at the door. "And this was payback."

"But you're not Fleet?"

"We're all Fleet, ultimately."

She frowned. "I suppose it's a horribly dangerous time. This portal might be harmless, but that's hardly the case for any other portal we've seen."

"The Weird are not necessarily the most immediate danger," Vincenze said, his voice so low that he all but mouthed the words.

At first, O'Connor wasn't sure she'd understood properly. What could possibly be more dangerous, more destructive, than a Weird attack? "What do you mean by that?"

Again, his voice was very low. "You must have seen the news. On the blacklist channels—"

"I don't look at that kind of thing," she said quickly. "Full of rhetoric and conspiracy theories." And reading them was likely to get you black marks against your name when it came to promotion, loans, moving house, and so on.

"Not unlike the sanctioned news, then. Eileen—it wasn't the Weird on Braun's World. It was our *own people*—"

"I no more believe that than that the government created secret murderous telepaths to fight the Vetch." She shook her head. "You're an eminent man. I'm surprised at you, watching that kind of thing. I'm even more surprised at you believing it. You shouldn't be falling for that kind of rubbish. You should be concerned with evidence."

"Well," said Vincenze, "we'll see."

The soldier at the door was beginning to get restless. O'Connor suspected that he was bored of waiting for them to go join the others, more than anything else.

"You're working on communicating with them, aren't you?" Vincenze said.

"Yes."

"Do you think you can?"

"I don't know." O'Connor smiled. "Perhaps I'm being too idealistic in what I can expect from them—or from our visit here."

The soldier was right up next to them now. He was very young, and very serious. "You'll have to move on now."

Vincenze gave him a friendly smile. "Move on?"

"This area is now out-of-bounds for non-military personnel until further notice."

Now Vincenze wasn't smiling. "Out-of-bounds?"

"You know the score. Routine sweeps." He stared back at Vincenze. "You're working on the parasites, aren't you? You know the score."

O'Connor was startled. A direct challenge: telling Vincenze that even the lowliest soldier round here was at least as well informed as the scientists whom they were protecting. Still, he had a point. O'Connor laid a gentle hand on her colleague's arm.

"Come on. I'm sure we've both got plenty to do."

"We do," said Vincenze. They left the room together. Their guard watched them as they walked along the corridor. Just before they parted ways, he turned to her and said, "Did you know that this is one of seven ships on this mission?"

"*Seven* ships?"

"*We're* all on one ship," he said. "The scientists. What do you think are on the other six ships?" He smiled. "Perhaps we need a lot of protection," he said, and went on his way. "Or perhaps there's just money to burn."

MARIA REACHED TO unbar the gate, but Yale stopped her. "We don't know who this is."

"Did you hear her, Yale? She said the *Walker!* She knows something about Delia!"

"Maria, it's not possible—"

"We have to know more! We have to speak to her!"

Before Yale could reply, the crowd shifted, pulling them apart. The next thing Maria knew, the gate was open. Silence fell as the people of Stella Maris observed the girl standing outside. She was slight, and carried nothing with her. She was by no means a threat, or not visibly. There was a rumble of quiet discussion, and then, in that curious and opaque way that they had, the settlers seemed to come to a decision. The crowd parted, and Cassandra walked into the settlement.

She looked around her, anxiously, as if seeking out a friendly or familiar face. "Where is the *Baba Yaga*?" she asked. "I need to leave this world. Please, help me."

Again, there was that quiet susurration, and then a human woman stepped forwards. "Follow me," she said. "We will hear what you have to say."

The woman led the girl off, and Maria followed as quickly as she could, struggling to get through to see the girl close up. She saw Yale, too, working her way through the crowd, quickly and efficiently. They passed by low long-houses where people were standing on the steps, watching and talking as they came past. They soon came to a large, high building: the community's central gathering place, right at the heart of the settlement. Here many of the crowd hung back, and the people who usually spoke for their long-houses went through into the hall. Yale, reaching Maria, pulled her inside. "I want you here for this," she muttered.

Maria had not been inside the hall before. Most of the decisions taken on Stella Maris were day-to-day, concerning farming or cooking—getting by in the world—and most often taken within the individual long-houses. The last big decision had been whether to help Delia Walker in her mission, and Maria had not been there. So the hall was new to her: a high, wide space with room for many rows of seats. The seats were wooden and beautifully carved; between the windows hung tapestries in bright, startling, abstract patterns. This art alone was proof that the Weird here were something very different from other worlds where humans had encountered them. There, people were enslaved, dulled by the Weird's influence, kept alive only to be consumed. They could not have produced such pieces of art. Here, on Stella Maris, people were sustained.

The rows of seats were filling rapidly. Cassandra was brought in front of them, and left standing there alone, looking small. Yale pulled Maria to the front, and they stood to one side, at the end of the first row of seats. There were glances, and a couple of frowns.

"Are we allowed to be here?" Maria whispered.

"I'll go where I damn well like," said Yale.

Ashot, lumbering up behind them, explained. "Nobody is barred from coming in here, Maria. The chamber was big enough to hold everybody, once upon a time, but over the years the settlement has grown, and we designate people to speak on our behalf from our long-houses. If someone disagrees— they are not bound by the decision of the whole. The majority did not agree to help Walker, but some of us went to help her nonetheless."

Maria wondered whether she and Jenny had been the subject of such a discussion, and whether most of the people here had not wanted them to stay. That was a sobering thought.

The gathering settled into silence, and one of the Vetch at the front stood up. "Who are you?" she said to the girl. "Why are you here?"

Cassandra looked back at her, fearlessly. "I've told you my name. Cassandra. My mother was the Walker. Delia Walker."

The room muttered.

Cassandra looked around. "Where's Maria?" she said. "Maria will know that I'm telling the truth."

Yale gave Maria a little shove, and she walked forwards, slowly. Cassandra stared at her for a few minutes, like an artist trying to capture her face as best she could, and then she broke into a wide smile. "Maria! Yes! You're Maria!"

"I am," Maria replied. "But how do you know that? How do you know me?"

Cassandra shrugged, as if this was obvious. "Mama knows you."

"Where *is* your mother?" Maria said.

"She's part of the whole."

"Do you mean that she's with the Weird?" said Maria.

Cassandra pondered this, her young face screwed up in concentration. "I don't know what that means," she said at last.

"She is part of the whole. The whole is many. We are part of the whole."

The Vetch woman who had spoken first stepped forwards again. "I still have questions," she said. "If I may be permitted?"

Cassandra, seeing the huge Vetch, took a step back. "Maria?" she said, an anxious note creeping into her voice.

"I think it's for the best if you answer their questions, Cassandra," Maria said, gently. "The people here have no good reason to trust me, or believe what I say. I brought a great deal of trouble with me. So, I'm afraid to say, did your mother. Can you answer their questions?"

Cassandra frowned. "I'll try. But it's hard. And we don't have much time."

"What do you mean?" said Maria, but Yale, who had come to stand behind her, put her hand on her arm.

"Let the others talk for a bit," she whispered. "We can listen."

Maria nodded.

"What do you mean that we haven't much time? Are we in danger?" asked the Vetch. She frowned at Maria. "Is somebody coming to Stella Maris?"

Cassandra stood staring at her feet for a while. Then, just as the Vetch was about to ask her question again, she said, "I'm sorry. It's hard for me... I haven't done this for real before. Yes, something's coming. I'm not clear what. But I need to leave. There's a ship, isn't there? The *Baba Yaga*. Can you take me to it, please?"

The room began its murmuring again, and the Vetch woman lifted her hand to quieten it. "No," she said. "She cannot take you to it. Will you answer our questions?"

Cassandra shrugged. "Maybe. I don't know. But they're not important." She stared straight at Maria, and tilted her head. "Maria," she said, after a moment. "Maria, I have to leave this world. I have to get away. Can you help me?"

Maria looked around the room. Some of the faces looking back were hostile, most were neutral. She couldn't see a friendly face at all. "I don't know if I can," she said.

The girl looked fearlessly around the room. "Will someone help me leave?"

She certainly sounded like Delia, Maria thought: stating clearly what she wanted people to do and expecting them to fall into line and deliver. The murmuring around the room began again. "Wait," said the Vetch woman to Cassandra. "We must speak to one another."

The quiet talk soon rose into a louder discussion. Someone of a kindly disposition brought Cassandra a chair and a cup of water. The girl drank gratefully.

"What do you think, Maria?" Ashot said, softly. "Can she possibly be from Walker?"

Maria studied the girl closely. She had only known Delia Walker for a short time, but the woman had not only saved her life, she had *imposed* herself upon her. Walker had been intelligent, focused, and uncompromising. Could the mother be seen in the child? Perhaps there was some physical likeness, a gesture here and there, a twist of the head or a tilt of the chin... but what could you say with any certainty? Was it all wishful thinking?

"How can she be?" Maria replied. "Delia Walker was pregnant when she disappeared. This girl must be at least fourteen. It's impossible."

"Is it the same child?" Yale urged. "Did Walker mention other children?"

"We were hardly confidantes," said Maria. "But my impression was that this was her first pregnancy."

"So the girl is lying," said Yale.

"Perhaps," said Ashot.

"Perhaps?" said Yale. "There's no perhaps about it. You don't go from unborn to fifteen in a matter of months."

"You are not taking into account the Weird," Ashot replied patiently. "We have no idea what the Weird can do—"

"Accelerate time?"

"Who knows?" said Ashot. "But I was thinking more that perhaps time passes at a different rate in the Weird's dimension."

Yale frowned. "You think she went into the portal?"

"It's what Failt thinks happened," said Maria.

"We have all said many times that it's as if she fell into a hole in the ground," Ashot said dryly. "We seem to be wilfully ignoring the fact that she was standing next to one."

Yale shook her head. "No. No way. It's not a hole in the ground. It's a portal into another dimension. You don't just drop in and pop out again—"

"You're the expert on other dimensions, are you?" said Ashot. "Perhaps that's exactly what you do."

"Here are your choices," Yale said. "Pick one: Walker died and the crimopaths dealt with the body in such a way that we couldn't find it—"

Crimopaths, thought Maria. *Is that what they're called? I knew you knew about them, Yale. I knew you'd met them before. But how, and where, and when?*

"Or Walker didn't die, and she's been hiding these past months for reasons known only to herself."

"Didn't you lead the search of the area, Yale?" Ashot had a mischievous gleam in his blood-red eyes. "Are you saying you missed her?"

"I'm prepared to accept she might have got the better of me," Yale replied. "But I can see why you might think it's unlikely."

"And then what?" Maria said. "Somehow she found this girl out there and has persuaded her to masquerade as her daughter?"

"She might have come with Walker on the *Baba Yaga*—"

"She wasn't on the *Baba Yaga*," said Maria.

"How do you know?" said Yale.

"Because it's *tiny* and I would have seen her," said Maria. "Unless you think I'm part of the plot, too. Which I don't think I am."

"All right," admitted Yale. "That option is too complicated. Here's another one. This girl is our long-expected visitor from the Expansion."

Both Maria and Ashot looked at the girl uneasily. "This isn't what I expected," said Maria, doubtfully.

"I was expecting force," Ashot agreed.

"Well, I don't know what they might have planned," said Yale. "But isn't that more likely than that an unborn child walks out of the mountains as a fifteen-year-old after only five months?"

Just then, the door burst open and Failt ran in. He looked around wildly, and then he saw the girl sitting at the front of the room. He ran to Maria. "Is that her?" he said. "Is that her? Is that sister Cass?"

Maria looked at the Vetch boy anxiously. She didn't want expectations to be raised that could not be met. "I don't know, Failt."

But Failt was running towards the girl. "Sister Cass!"

She looked up at the name and—to Maria's astonishment—leapt to her feet and let out what Maria could only call a squeal. It was so natural—so *girlish*...

"Failt!" the girl cried. She threw her arms around him, as if he was a long-lost relative that she had not seen in years. This, more than anything else, convinced Maria of the truth of Cassandra's story. She didn't know how, and suspected she might never how exactly, but in that heartfelt reaction to meeting Failt, Cassandra had surely shown herself to be Delia Walker's daughter.

She turned to Ashot and Yale. "I believe her," she said.

"What?" Yale said.

"She's Delia's girl, I'm sure of it."

"You made up your mind quickly," Yale said.

Maria gestured helplessly towards the human girl and the Vetch boy holding onto each other, and giggling like old conspirators. "Look at them," she said simply. "You can't fake that. She knows him. She *loves* him."

"She can't," Yale said roughly.

"And yet there they are," Ashot said. "Now if we can only find out what she wants."

"You'll help me, won't you, Failt?" Cassandra said. "You'll come with me?" Her voice was so plaintive that Maria suddenly had the urge to look after her. Whoever she was, it was important they remember how young she was.

"Whatever you need, sister Cass." Failt looked at Maria. "That's right, isn't it, Mama Maria? Whatever she needs?"

"We can certainly try, Failt, but I don't know whether it will be possible." She turned to the girl. "Where are you trying to go?"

Cass looked back at her, with her strange distant eyes. "The Expansion. I have to go to the Expansion."

"See," muttered Yale. "I said they were behind it."

THERE WERE MANY things about Stella Maris that had tried Yale's patience over the years, not least the dearth of labour-saving technology, the relentless diet of *kitzim*, and the heart-breaking lack of ice, gin, and tonic. But few things exasperated her more than the length of time it took people to make decisions. The quickest way to get to the bottom of this would be to talk to Cassandra in depth, and in private, and Yale would not get the opportunity while the rest of the settlement went through the lengthy process of discussion, disagreement, more discussion, consensus-seeking, further discussion, and more discussion. She would need a miracle to get the access she needed.

"Itching to get your paws on her, aren't you?" said Ashot, in her ear.

"I need to know what's happening."

"Is it really the Expansion?" said Ashot. "Or the Bureau?"

Yale didn't answer, but gave her friend a canny look. Of course Ashot would know the difference. The Expansion was a catch-all name for humanity's great empire. Fleet was its iron glove. And the Bureau? Well, that was the fist the glove concealed.

"Please, Maria," begged Cassandra. "I have to leave."

"I'm sorry, Cassandra," Maria said, "but there's no way to leave Stella Maris. The planet is cut off—intentionally so."

"But you have a ship," said Cassandra. "The *Baba Yaga*."

Not for the first time today, Yale felt a deep sense of unease. How did the girl *know* these things? It was impossible that she was Walker's daughter. But why would the Bureau send a child? What possible purpose could be served by that? The Bureau, while made up of many brilliant individuals, was ultimately a blunt instrument. It didn't engage in baroque plots. For one thing, nobody there had the imagination; even the cover-up on Braun's World had been fairly straightforward when you got to the bottom of it—faking press coverage, destroying information, finishing up with the murder of some unlucky witnesses. Hardly subtle. Yale could not see what plan Cassandra might serve. But it still didn't mean she believed the girl was a messenger from Walker, speaking to them from beyond the grave. Or from another dimension... Yale shook herself. No. Not possible.

"Yes, there's the *Baba Yaga*," Maria said doubtfully. "But there's nobody here who can fly it." She looked around the hall and her eye fell on Yale. "Is there?"

Yale shrugged.

"It needed a pilot with implants," Maria explained. "But the man who flew us here is dead." Again she looked around. "There *isn't* anyone..."

Yale whispered, "Delia Walker would know that."

"But I have to leave," Cassandra insisted. "I have to leave *soon*. Or I might not be able to leave at all."

At the back of the hall, there was a sudden noise. The doors had been thrown open, and a few more people had run in. "Ships!" one of them called out. "There are ships in the sky. Seven of them!"

It didn't take a genius to guess whose ships. Fleet, at least; and in all likelihood, something else too. *Please, no crimopaths*, thought Yale. *Please, not that.* She strode through the hall, Ashot behind her, and out into the settlement's little square, and looked up into the dark sky. Seven bright shapes hovered high above, and, all around them, smaller sparks of light: landing shuttles.

"Well," Yale said to Ashot, "here comes trouble."

Ashot nodded. "I suppose the only surprise is that it's taken so long."

Yale glanced at Maria, who looked back at her in terror.

"Yale," she said, "what should I do? They'll kill me, me and Jenny!"

Consensus-making was all very well, Yale thought, but it took too long, and whatever time they had had for deliberation was now over. "We're done here," she murmured to Ashot. "Get Failt and the girl, will you?"

He nodded and slipped back into the hall. Yale turned to Maria. "Don't worry," she said. "We're going to hide you, Maria. You and Jenny and Failt—and the girl." She stared back up at the sky. "We don't want them catching up with her—or you. So it's time to go."

"Go where? Where can we hide? The settlement's not that big—"

Yale gave her a crooked smile. "I know plenty of places around here. Go and get Jenny, pack what you need, and be back here quick as you can."

Maria hesitated. "Why are you helping me, Yale?"

"Does it matter? Hurry up, will you? We've not much time!"

The woman set off at a run, just as Failt came out of the hall, holding hands with Cassandra. "Where's she going, Yale? Where's mama Maria going?"

"The Expansion are here, Failt," Yale said, bluntly, and he hissed. "I'm taking Maria away, somewhere safe, so that they can't get to her." She nodded at Cass. "You too."

Cassandra looked up at the sky. "Are we leaving? Are we leaving Stella Maris?"

"Not yet," said Yale. "We don't have time. We need to get you safe first."

"Don't worry, Cass," said Failt, "I'll be with you."

Gently, Ashot laid his paw upon the boy's arm. "You're staying with me, Failt."

"But I have to stay with sister Cass!"

Yale turned to him. "Listen, Failt. The people in those ships are here to kill Maria and Jenny, and will probably kill Cass if they find her and think she's anything to do with your Missus Dee. I need to get them away, but the more there are of us, the easier it will be to find us. So you're staying here."

"But—"

"You're staying here, Failt."

Ashot put his arm around the boy. "It won't be for long. Just until we find out what's going on. We have to get the others to safety as quickly as possible."

Maria was running back to them, a big bag slung over one

shoulder, Jenny's hand clutched in her own. "Got everything?" said Yale.

"Essentials," she said. "Where are we going?"

"To the *Baba Yaga*," said Cassandra. "We should go to the *Baba Yaga*."

"We can't," said Yale. "Those shuttlecraft are landing between us and it. We're going..." She hesitated, and then glanced at Ashot, who nodded. "We're going somewhere else. Somewhere safe. For a little while."

Yale led them quickly through the settlement towards the gates, where a big wooden building housed all the transport the people of Stella Maria had: a large and rather dilapidated lorry, and two big ground vehicles. The latter were new possessions, inherited from the crimopaths after they had been killed. Yale hurriedly directed Maria inside one of them, handing up Jenny to sit in the back, and helping Cassandra to climb up. She threw Maria's pack up after them.

Failt, she saw, was standing nearby, fists bunched, tentacles quivering in a mixture of grief and anger. "Failt," she said, "I promise it won't be for long. And I promise that if Cassandra leaves Stella Maris, you can go with her."

She closed the doors on the back of the vehicle, and went round to the driver's cabin, where Ashot was standing by. "I didn't think I'd get this far without someone stopping us," she admitted, and patted the side of the vehicle. "I didn't think they'd let me take this."

"You know what they're like," he said. "Takes them ages to decide anything. I don't think they realise yet what's happening." Ashot offered his hand, and Yale shook it. Quietly, so that only she could hear, he said, "Get away while you can. I don't want them catching up with you either."

She smiled. No real secrets on Stella Maris. She nodded, and hopped up into the cabin. Ashot opened the big doors and Yale drove out. A few people called out—*Hey! Where are you going?* and so on—but she pushed on. Glancing back through the rear-view mirror, she saw Ashot, standing with his hand upon Failt's shoulder. From the back, she heard Maria say, "We use that boy. I hope he doesn't suffer for it."

Yale didn't reply. She drove through the gates and accelerated up the road through the farmed fields. As soon as she could, she got off the road and onto the rough red ground leading up to the mountains. The settlement was soon a distant speck. The vehicle bumped on, and Yale took stock of her situation: not good, but not yet desperate. She glanced back at her passengers. Jenny had fallen asleep against her mother's shoulder, and Maria's eyes were shut. She looked weary; running did that to you. Cassandra was sitting staring out of the window, eyes unblinking.

Yale had misgivings. Hiding Maria and her daughter was one thing. But to take this girl with them? The jury was still out on Cassandra as far as Yale was concerned. It *could* be a coincidence that the Expansion ships and Cassandra had arrived on the same day—she had to admit it didn't prove any link between them—but it hardly filled her with confidence. And she might yet draw their enemies to them... Yale stared at the red land ahead. Who *was* Cassandra, really? Why was she here? These were questions Yale intended to have answered, as soon as she got the chance.

"Where are you taking us, Yale?" said Maria, from the back.

Yale looked up. Maria's eyes were still shut.

"Where do you think?" Yale said. "We're going to the portal."

Cassandra started in her seat. "No!" she said. "That's not where I need to be!"

"There's where you need to be," said Yale. "And where you have to be, so that you don't get killed."

"Mama will be cross!"

49

"Pleasing your mama," said Yale, "is your problem, not mine."

Maria laughed quietly, and then opened her eyes, and reached out to take Cassandra's hand. "I know this isn't what you want," she said. "I'm listening to you, and I believe you, and I promise I'll do everything I can to help you. But if we stayed at the settlement, we might be taken by the Expansion, and so we need to get somewhere safe. Is that okay?"

Cassandra looked doubtful. "I guess," she said.

"Thank you," said Maria.

Yale looked back. "Get some sleep," she said. "It's a long way."

"We will," said Maria, with quiet authority.

Yale drove on. Everything went quiet for a while, apart from the thump and bump of the tyres upon the barren ground. Then Jenny opened her eyes. She rubbed at them with her small fists, and looked up at her mother.

"Are we there yet?"

CHAPTER THREE

AFTER THE EXCITEMENT of that first sight of Stella Maris, everything went quiet. They saw shuttle craft emerging from the other ships and heading down towards the planet's surface, but still they received no instructions. The scientists, who had been expecting immediate landfall, waited, and waited, but nothing happened. After a day or two, they fell back into their old routines of formal discussion and informal gossip, all of them asking the same question: *When do we get to see the planet at first-hand?* Woodley, when pressed, had no answer; Vincenze was not surprised. "Don't look to Woodley for decisions," he muttered to O'Connor. "At the end of the day, she's not the real authority here. That's Fleet—or whoever the Bureau has picked from Fleet."

Altogether, they stayed in orbit for more than a week, with Stella Maris visible, but tantalisingly out of reach. Some of the scientists, particularly those used to running their own research and managing their own time, became restless. There were one or two loudly voiced complaints over dinner and in the rec room.

Even Palmer, who was generally easy-going, was heard to mutter about the delay.

"It's not like we're doing anything up here," she said. "No samples, no data—nothing. It's a long way to bring us without letting us anywhere near our object of study!"

O'Connor was content to wait. No doubt the powers that be had good reasons for delaying their journey down to the surface. It would be an equally long way to bring them all just to have them attacked in the night by hostile settlers.

Vincenze was not surprised. "We're the least important part of this mission," he said. "They'll want to scope out the area before having the bother of herding us."

"Our work here matters," said Palmer.

"Oh, yes, the *work* matters," said Vincenze. "But if they could replace us with drones or machines, they would. Nobody's indispensable. And people with expert knowledge are a threat to those who don't have that knowledge."

O'Connor let his complaints roll over her. Another day passed. Woodley, in great excitement, was sent down. As the mood on the ship became increasingly restless, O'Connor noticed the soldiers on board moving about in pairs. At last, eight days after they had begun orbiting Stella Maris, the order was given from above for the scientists to make planetfall.

"They've had a while down there, now," Palmer said, cheerfully. "Let's hope there's something left for us to study. I'm hoping for an award out of all this. Maybe even a promotion."

They crowded into their assigned shuttles, complaining about leg room, and secured themselves into their seats. They waited, and waited, and after about an hour, they heard the thrusters powering up. There was a lot of muttering—*at last* and *about time* and *I thought they'd forgotten us.* The shuttle journey was quick enough, falling precipitously through the atmosphere, and there was such a clean landing that not even this pampered lot could find anything to complain about. Excitement levels were rising; even another half-hour sitting in their seats waiting for permission to disembark couldn't dampen the mood. At last, the pilot gave the word to go, and there was the usual scramble to be first off. The hatch at the back popped open (O'Connor noticed two armed soldiers standing beside it), and the first gust of the air of an alien world swept through the cabin. It was dry, and sandy, with a bitter tang, and yet everyone on board gulped lungfuls as only people who have been breathing conditioned air for weeks can.

O'Connor, stepping out onto the surface, had to admit that the reality of Stella Marias was rather disappointing. Bare scrubland rising to rocky foothills that became bald hills—proof, as ever, that projecting one's romantic hopes on strange and distant worlds was often a mistake. "Not what I hoped for," she said to Palmer.

"Depends what you were hoping for," Palmer replied, then pointed off in the other direction. "That's more like it."

O'Connor saw, rising from the bare land, a clutch of solid-looking single-storey buildings. The soldiers had been busy in the time they'd had had before the arrival of the scientists, putting up the base camp in a few days.

"All praise to our boys," said Palmer, cheerfully. "I wouldn't much fancy camping out in this environment."

Eventually, all the scientists were on the planet's surface. There were three big ground vehicles waiting to meet them, and they were transported across to the base. O'Connor saw a high fence, thick wire and watchtowers, and they quickly passed through. The vehicles parked up in a sandy open area before a big squat building, and they all got out. There was much chatter and speculation, but then they heard Woodley's voice, asking them to be quiet and listen.

"It's good to have you here with me at last!" she said. "I hope you'll like what you find here. I think the boys have done a fantastic job getting this facility up and running in such a short time."

A couple of people started to clap, and a brief, polite round of applause followed. When it died down, Woodley turned to a tall, stern man in Fleet uniform standing next to her. His position was clear to everyone present: Woodley might be directing research, but this was the authority. Woodley introduced him as Commander Inglis, and he stepped forwards to speak.

"Welcome to Stella Maris," he said. "I won't keep you long, as I know you've been waiting some time now to make landfall. Feel free to explore the base. Obviously there are sections to which only Fleet personnel have access, but you'll see quite clearly which these are."

"What *can* they be hiding?" muttered Vincenze, and O'Connor shushed him.

"We'd ask you not to go beyond the perimeter, of course," Inglis went on. "There are known hazards here on Stella Maris, and no doubt there are also plenty out there that we don't know about yet. Otherwise, the space is yours. You'll find living quarters—solo, of course; we don't want you cracking up."

He smiled, and there was scattered polite laughter.

"There's plenty of recreational space. There's a gym, and our pride and joy, the swimming pool." He smiled again, somewhat more genuinely, O'Connor thought. He should be proud, really, of how quickly this had all gone up, a testament to the Expansion's discipline and organisation. "The pool isn't huge, so get your time there scheduled quickly. All living quarters and lab space has been assigned—your handhelds should be updating with that information now. I imagine Director Woodley has scheduled meetings with you all for later in the day. Come to me with any concerns you might have. In the meantime, welcome to Stella Maris. Be safe, work hard, and let's learn about the Weird together." He gave Woodley a brisk nod, and then walked away.

Woodley, stepping forwards, had little else to add. She asked them to make sure they knew when they were expected to meet again, and sent them on their way. O'Connor couldn't resist teasing Vincenze. "See?" she said. "If we'd come down earlier, it would have been exactly like Woodley said—we'd have been camping under the stars. Instead we have a swimming pool!"

"A swimming pool?" Vincenze smiled. "I think I'd prefer the stars. Particularly strange stars."

"Come off it," said Palmer. "You would've been the first to complain about your back if you'd been sleeping on bare rock."

"I'll be complaining about my back anyway," he said, gamely. "Have you ever slept on the bunks they bring on this kind of mission?"

Palmer laughed, and went off to explore her lab space. O'Connor walked through the base, map open on her handheld, until she found the scientists' living quarters. Another anonymous low grey building, built from strong, lightweight plastic. They all looked the same, but she was sure that she would soon get her bearings. The door opened when she presented her wrist chip, and she wandered down the narrow corridor until she found the door to her quarters. It was a small room, just big enough for a bunk, a desk, and toilet facilities, but single occupancy as promised, and that was what mattered. Vincenze, who had been following her, poked his nose inside and sniffed. "Monastic cells," he muttered, and then wandered off down the corridor to find his own space.

O'Connor opened her case and unpacked quickly: mostly hard-wearing clothes, and a few home comforts. She set up the com console on the desk, and then lay down on the bunk. It wasn't that uncomfortable, she thought with a smile, and in fact she was soon relaxed enough to drift off into a light doze. She woke refreshed a couple of hours later to a soft buzz from the console, alerting her that the general meeting of the scientific staff was an hour away. She showered, dressed, and went off to explore the rest of the base. Her explorations were quickly done: canteen, rec room, gym (and swimming pool, already busy with fierce-looking individuals she assumed were Fleet). Some of the soldiers had already scratched out a pitch and were kicking a ball around.

O'Connor left them to their games and went to find the room were the meeting was to be held. This was in one of three buildings given over to the scientists, holding meeting rooms, work spaces, and a bare common room she was sure would quickly become scruffy and homely.

But she could not find the work space assigned to her; there must have been some sort of glitch. With so much to do building the base, she was amazed there hadn't been more. It wasn't a problem, and she would raise it with Woodley later. She went outside for a sniff of the air, and then saw Palmer heading towards the meeting. She called out to her, and they went in together.

"Couldn't find a work space," said Palmer.

"Me neither," said O'Connor.

"Think they've forgotten us?"

They took their seats in a row at the middle of the room. Woodley was already at the front. There were two soldiers with her, and two more at the door. "I doubt it," O'Connor said, thoughtfully. "I doubt they miss anything."

Things progressed unusually quickly for an academic gathering; Woodley reiterated the instructions that Inglis had given them all to remain within the confines of the base, and not to stray into restricted areas. Just before she opened up for general questions, she looked down at her notes, and said. "One or two of you will have noticed that you don't have work spaces assigned to you. If you're one of these, could you come and speak to me after the meeting?"

There were some questions, mostly to do with getting specialised equipment, and then the meeting ended. Palmer and O'Connor hung back, as did two or three others. Vincenze, passing by, said, "You're in favour. I wonder why."

"Out of luck, more like," said O'Connor. "I bet all the best spaces have gone."

"It's our positive attitude," said Palmer. "You should try it, Vincenze."

He grunted, and went off. Palmer and O'Connor joined Woodley at the front.

"First, let me put your minds at rest," said Woodley, with a wry smile. "We haven't forgotten you. You don't have work space yet because we don't intend for you to be working here. Don't worry!" she said, seeing the worried looks going round. "You've hit the jackpot. We want you down in the settlement. Our intention is to embed a handful of people there: to get to know the settlers, to work with them, and to get their help in finding the Weird portal."

Now there was enthusiasm. It made sense, thought O'Connor, glancing round the group. They were mostly younger members of the group, and all working in the softer end of science: anthropologists and linguists, all with expertise in alien species.

"Have we made contact with the settlement yet?" asked one of the young men.

"Not yet," said Woodley. "We've scouted out the area—it's about six miles from here—but when Inglis and I discussed first contact, we decided we didn't want to go over there simply as Fleet. So we needed to wait for you all to be down here. A party is going over tomorrow—there'll be myself, Inglis, security, and..." She glanced at O'Connor. "You'll be part of the group, Dr O'Connor."

"Me?"

Woodley smiled. "Don't sound so surprised. You're a friendly face."

"I'm very junior."

"That just makes you less threatening."

Everyone laughed. "I'll take that as a compliment!" O'Connor said.

"It's meant as one," Woodley said. "This meeting is crucial: if we don't present a friendly face to the locals, we'll struggle ever to get them onside. I'll free up some work space for you all if you're really eager, but assume that you're going to be embedded in the settlement, and that that's where your real work will be happening." She smiled at O'Connor. "If we play our cards right tomorrow."

Woodley dismissed them, and O'Connor and the rest went off to get something to eat, discussing the opportunity ahead. O'Connor left early to get some sleep before her trip the following day. Just after she had entered her room, however, there was a buzz at the door. Vincenze was outside. She sighed, and stepped back to let him come in.

"Well," he said, perching himself on the edge of her bunk and peering around, "you really are in favour. So you're off in the morning? I'll come down and see you there when you're settled." He looked glum. "Although I imagine it won't be long before you're back."

She sat back in her chair and laughed. "Really, you're impossible! A brand new world. Fantastic facilities. Everything we need—even consultation and participation! Why did you come along if you didn't want to be here?"

"You know why," he said. "The same as you. To learn about the Weird." He lowered his voice. "Be careful, Eileen. Things here aren't as straightforward as they seem. There are other agendas at work here, and your good nature might well be used."

"I'm not an idiot, Paul."

"No, you're not. So use that fine brain of yours—to its fullest capacity."

"I'll take care," she said. "I promise."

He nodded and left, and O'Connor lay down on her bunk. She slept well and rose early, and packed quickly, ready for the adventure ahead. She and Woodley, with Inglis and five soldiers, took one of the vehicles that had brought them from the ship. They trundled through red desert, before reaching a stretch of clearly fertile land, through which a road cut straight through to the sole settlement on this harsh world. But when they reached the gate, it was barred against them.

FAILT HAD HAD a hard life. Born into slavery, he had never known either mother or father. His earliest memories had been of scrabbling around for food along with the other piglets, as they'd been called by their overseers, those bloody bastards. They'd liked to throw the food in and watch the bigger kids push past the small ones. Failt used to hide food for the tinies and pass it to them. But most of his memories were of his time underground, working in the mines on Shard's World. He'd been sent down there one day, and not come back up again for years. The day he'd been let out, he'd run.

Like many runaways before him, he had found Stella Maris.

With its wide skies and wild land and space to roam, Stella Maris was paradise to Failt. From the depths of his huge, passionate heart, he loved everything about it. He loved the people, he loved the life, and—born into slavery and having only escaped by the skin of his teeth—he loved the freedom that he had never experienced until Delia Walker arrived in his life. To her, above all, he had given his love, and eternal gratitude that she had brought him to this wonderful world, where he could live in peace and harmony.

There was much about Stella Maris that still puzzled him, nonetheless. As a slave, on Shard's World, Failt had been used to having orders barked at him, and jumping to obey them, in case of big trouble. That had always been the nature of things, although Failt tended to catch it more often than others. Delia Walker—Missus Dee—showed him a different way. She would ask his opinion, sometimes, and even for his advice. He knew that she would make up her own mind, and not always take that advice, but what mattered was that she listened. This— the simple demonstration of respect—had transformed Failt's world as much as his escape. He was respected here on Stella Maris too, he knew, despite his close association with Walker. He was not sure why, but he was glad to have found the home and family for which he had longed his whole short life. Nevertheless, the way that the people of Stella Maris made decisions confused him.

There were no orders, shouted and to be obeyed, and not even the direct questions and swift action of Missus Dee. Instead, there was slow deliberation, conversations that took place over days, over meals or work or leisure, from which a consensus slowly emerged. In peaceful times, and for everyday decisions, such as which field to work on next, which piece of work needed prioritising, it worked. If a consensus did not emerge, and the matter was grave enough, the long-houses would each hold more formal discussions, presenting their positions to a wider meeting of the community. This would, sooner or later, lead to some kind of consensus. It brought every single person into the fold, and in a place where many people had once been enslaved, that sense of being heard mattered.

But it took time. It was not good in a crisis. And this was surely a crisis.

The gates were barred when the visitors from the ships arrived. Failt wove his way through the crowd, right to the front. There was some discussion, and then Failt watched as Ashot put himself forwards, and a human woman from another long-house agreed to go with him to speak for the settlement. The gate opened, and Failt got a good look at the visitors. Three people stood at the front: two women, one quite young, and a man who was clearly someone used to giving orders. The boss, Failt thought; he was good at identifying who was boss. Behind these three, and standing at the ready near their vehicle, were five soldiers, armed and helmeted, weapons close to hand.

The man walked forwards. "I am Commander Inglis," he said. "I am in charge of the mission here." He opened out his palms. "We're here in peace, from the Expansion. We mean you no harm."

Ashot shifted his weight slightly so that his huge bulk barred the open gateway. "That remains to be seen."

Inglis frowned. "I hoped we might start on a friendly footing—"

"You've brought soldiers with you," Ashot pointed out.

"You'll have to forgive us. We know nothing about you—"

"We know about you," said the woman. "People came from the Expansion only a few months ago. They attacked our settlement and caused the death of many people." She paused.

"We killed them all."

Failt watched closely. The younger of the two women had covered her mouth in horror. Her older colleague was frowning, and was looking at the commander as if for confirmation. He, meanwhile, had acquired a steely expression which suggested he had not been party to this information, and was not pleased with superiors who had kept him out of the loop.

"I see this comes as news to some of you, at least," said Ashot.

"It comes as news to all of us," said Inglis, quietly. "If anyone came to you from Expansion space, it was not with my knowledge. *If* anyone came—"

"They came," said the woman. "We are not liars."

The older woman stepped forwards. "My name is Woodley," she said. "I'm here to coordinate the scientific mission. On behalf of my government—or whoever sent those people—I apologise. But we are not here to cause harm. We want to learn about the Weird, and to discover whether we can make peace with them in some way. As for the soldiers—there's a Weird portal here. Several worlds within the Expansion have suffered devastating losses as a result of Weird incursions—"

"Yes," said Ashot. "We know about those. Rocastle. That was one." He paused, then added, pointedly, "Braun's World."

Failt looked at each of them, hard, but there was no reaction from their visitors at that last name. Failt tugged at one of his tentacles. Had Maria's messages got through? Didn't everyone in the Expansion know now what had really happened on Braun's World?

Suddenly the young woman lifted her hand. "Please," she said to Woodley. "May I say something?"

Woodley looked unsure, but the commander gave a nod. The young woman stepped forwards. Failt sniffed. She seemed honest enough. Her smell was friendly, non-hostile. Still, you couldn't trust even your tentacles these days. Delia Walker had often smelled of fury.

"My name's Eileen O'Connor," the young woman said. "I don't know anything about the attack. I absolutely believe you that it happened and I'm appalled that people from my home would do this to you. We are not all bad. The work I do—I study other species. I listen to them—other cultures—and I try to understand them. Not on my own terms, but on theirs." She smiled, openly, without hostility or malice. "I'm so excited to be here! I want to understand the Weird. That's all I ever want to do—listen and understand. If people from my home have hurt you, I'm sorry. We're not all the same. That's what my work is all about. Learning about the differences between species. So that we can understand each other better."

She took a step or two forwards, coming to stand in front of Ashot, and looking directly at him. "I'm scared of you, you know. Because you're Vetch."

There was a low rumble around the crowd. She lifted her hand, asking them to carry on listening.

"No, that's not right, is it?" she said. "It's not right to be scared of someone just because they're Vetch. I want to get past that. It's prejudiced, and it's wrong. That's how I feel about the Weird. If there's a way of living with them, I want to help find out what it is. Because otherwise people will keeping acting out of hate and fear, and that will only harm us all." Suddenly she blushed, and looked down at her feet. "I'm sorry if I'm speaking out of turn."

Ashot was eyeing her thoughtfully. "What do *you* want?" he said, in a gentler voice. "Why have you come here?"

Woodley intervened. "We want to learn from you. We'd like to spend some time with you—a few scientists, myself and O'Connor amongst them. We want to learn about the Weird."

"I have not said that the Weird are here," said Ashot.

"No," said Woodley. "But we know that they are."

Ashot turned away. He and the woman spoke together in quiet voices. Ashot was shaking his head, vehemently, but the woman seemed to be pressing him to agree to something. Eventually, he gave a curt nod. The woman stepped forwards and spoke once again to Woodley and Inglis. "We have listened," she said. "We will take your messages back to the community, and hear from them what they have to say."

She and Ashot came back through the gate, which was barred again behind them. Failt did not hang around, but scampered off quickly to the meeting hall. He wanted to make sure that he had a place for the debate that was about to happen.

He would later think of this as the saddest day he had spent on Stella Maris. Losing Missus Dee had been bad enough, but Failt assumed that she would come back for him eventually, and when sister Cass arrived, he knew that his faith had not been ill-founded. But watching the discussion that afternoon in the central hall, Failt knew that whatever had held the community here together, whatever bond the Weird had supplied, was no longer strong enough. The humans wanted one thing, and the Vetch wanted another. Worse than that: as the afternoon went on, those positions became more entrenched, and Failt struggled to see how they could ever be reconciled.

At last, he crept away, unhappily. He knew now where the meeting was heading, and he wanted to think about what he ought to do next. He sat hunched up on the great wooden steps outside the hall and stared at the ground. He thought about Missus Dee, and how she would have stopped all this. He thought about sister Cass, who needed his help but was far, far away. He thought about the Weird, and how, once upon a time, they had helped the people of Stella Maris live in peace and harmony. He thought about soldiers, and slavers, and other bad people, the kind of people who would send him back to Shard's World, where he had worked for years underground and where he would die before he was full grown if his owners got him back again. He felt a large hand come to rest upon his shoulder, and jumped.

"It's all right," said Ashot. "It's only me."

Failt looked at him with big scared eyes. "They're coming, aren't they?" he said. "The people with the guns. They're coming here."

Ashot nodded. "Nothing I could do."

"I thought we were all friends," Failt said. "I thought we lived in peace and harmony."

"We were," said Ashot, "and we did. Soldiers complicate everything." He sighed. "We have to look out for ourselves now, Failt. When it comes to it, I'm not sure we will be able to rely on the humans."

Failt thought of Missus Dee. "Some of them," he said, stoutly. "We can rely on some of them."

YALE HAD TAKEN a circuitous route through the back country, fording the river far south of the place where Delia Walker had crossed it many months before, and coming up into the mountains by a different route. The journey had taken a couple of days, and her passengers had, on the whole, been patient. Only sometimes, as Maria and Jenny rested in the back, Cassandra had come up front to sit beside her in the passenger seat, and the girl would sigh, as if some great mistake was in the process of being made. *I'm doing my best*, Yale would think, when the weight of Cassandra's silent disapproval became too much, and then she would wonder why she felt she had to justify herself in this way. It was like she had been brought up in front of a superior, and was being called to account for her actions.

On the second day out from the settlement they drove high into the mountains along the route of the river, going as far as they could before the track narrowed to a stony pathway, and their vehicle could go no further. Yale made them take all they could carry, and they hid the vehicle under the cover of a clutch of trees that stood on the riverbank. They went the rest of the way by foot. Little Jenny did her best for an hour or two, but eventually stopped, exhausted; Yale passed her pack to Maria and carried the child on her shoulders the rest of the way.

The trees were patchy, but gave them some cover. Yale led them through, upwards, until they reached a rocky outcrop from which three distinct paths led. "I'm sorry," she said, "but I have to blindfold you now."

Maria looked at her in amazement. "What do you mean?"

"Where we're going—it's a secret refuge. There are only half a dozen people on Stella Maris who know where it is." And there were at least a hundred more people that Yale would tell before she shared the information with Maria, and at least another hundred before Cassandra.

"Do you still not trust me?" said Maria, quietly. "What do I have to do?"

"It's not about that," said Yale. "It's about..." She glanced down at Jenny, leaning against her mother's leg, tired, but wondering what this new game of the adults was all about. "Maria, if you were taken... You might not want to tell, but they have telepaths..."

Maria sighed. "All right. I understand. But we can't go all at once, can we?"

She was right, and it was a long, slow process, carrying Jenny on her shoulders as she led Maria up the path, and then turning back to get Cassandra. Yale had half-expected the girl to be gone when she returned for her, as weirdly and as inexplicably as she had arrived, but she was there, and patiently let Yale cover her eyes and lead her up to the others.

Their destination was a large cave that cut back into the mountainside, overlooking the river. The sound of running water was very strong within, but the cave itself was dry, and there were supplies up there: bedding, firewood and a brazier, some dried foodstuffs. Maria made herself busy, getting some food together. "*Kitzim*," she said, grimly. "Dried. That's new."

Yale went to the back of the cave, where a small storage area was set off behind curtains. A large wooden box held an ancient communicator, stored out here for the people using the refuge. She switched it on.

It didn't work. She pulled at switches, jabbed at dials, opened it up to examine the interior, and after fifteen fruitless minutes began—fluently and with increasing volume—cursing the day that she had ever set foot on this benighted world, with heat, and its *kitzim*, and its lack of a good stiff drink. Eventually she became aware of Maria, standing behind her. "Yale," she said quietly. "There are children here.

"If the worse they hear over the next few weeks is me swearing, I'll be pleased."

"I don't care about your bloody swearing," hissed Maria. "I mean, you're frightening them."

Yale looked round. Sure enough, Jenny was sitting on a mattress near the little brazier, eyes wide and staring. Cassandra had an arm around the child, and she too looked worried, chewing her lower lip and tugging at a long strand of brown hair.

Yale took a deep breath. "Sorry," she said. "I'm sorry. It's just..."

"I know," said Maria. "Come and eat something."

But she didn't know, Yale thought, as she sat, bone-tired and silent, eating the makeshift meal. She couldn't possibly understand this helplessness, this frustration, this *terror*—that the Bureau was almost certainly here on Stella Maris, and there wasn't a damn thing Yale could do about it. When Yale finished eating, she went straight to bed, turning only briefly to address the others.

"I can't stop you from leaving," she said, "but please—respect this place. Don't try to find your way back. We may be glad of the secrecy, one day."

When she woke the next morning, she felt more rested and able for the day ahead. All three of the others were still there; barring serious complications, she assumed they would be staying. She got up, fetched fresh water, washed, and ate the breakfast that Maria had prepared. Bloody, bloody *kitzim*. "I think I'll go hunting," she said.

The days fell into a steady pattern: fetching water, hunting, cooking, clearing up, sitting quietly and wondering out loud what was going on back at the settlement. Cassandra often paced, but she did not go beyond the refuge. Every so often, she would ask Maria when they could leave. "Ask Yale," Maria would say, but Cassandra never did.

Every day, Yale tinkered for as long as she could with the communicator and tried to get it to work. She allowed herself a couple of longer forays, ostensibly to get more of the contents of the ground vehicle, but also in the faint hope of learning something of what was happening back at the settlement. But there was nothing, only the whispering silence of a world mostly devoid of sentient life. If great events were unfolding in the universe, they did not seem to be troubling the mountains of Stella Maris.

Late one night, as Maria and Jenny slept safely under cover, Yale went out to look for Cassandra. She found the girl sitting under the stars and looking out over the river. She sat down beside her. They were quiet together for a while, making no demands upon each other. At length, Yale said, "I know you want to leave. I promise I'm working on it."

Cassandra turned to look at her and gave a thin smile. "Mama's grateful. So am I."

"Can you tell me why you have to leave? You said you have to go to the Expansion. Can you say why?"

Cassandra lay back and looked up at the sky. "Do these stars have names?"

"Probably," said Yale. "Numbers, more likely. Does that mean you can't tell me?"

"No," said the girl. "I can't."

"Can't? Or won't?"

"Can't," said Cassandra. She turned her head to stare at Yale, that direct look that seemed to pierce right to the back of the head. "You don't tell people everything, in case they're taken."

Taken? Yale left her to the stars. The fact was, the girl creeped her out. She went back inside and spent the night tinkering with the communicator. The next night, she was able to send a message. To her intense relief, Ashot's voice back in response. "*You've taken your time,*" he said. "*What have you been doing?*"

"Equipment failure. Bloody communicator!" Maria, standing behind her, tutted at the language, and Yale reined herself in. "It's good to speak to you. What's happening? Has there been any contact from those ships?"

There was a pause.

"Ashot? Are you still there?"

"*Yes, yes, I'm here. Yes, we've heard from the arrivals. They've put up a base a few miles from here.*"

"Soldiers?"

"Plenty of soldiers. And scientists. They say they've come to study the Weird."

"I'm sure they have. But it's the soldiers we need to worry about."

Again, that pause. Yale frowned. "Go on, Ashot, what are you not telling me?"

"You're not going to like this, Yale. A small group came to the settlement. They asked to come and live amongst us."

"I assume you sent them packing." Yale waited for him to reply. And waited. "You didn't send them packing."

"The community discussed it. They allowed them to come."

Yale felt Maria's hand on her shoulder. *Remember,* she thought, *there are children here. Don't show them how afraid you are.*

"Failt thinks that without the Weird we can't live in peace and harmony."

Yale frowned. Failt believed a lot of strange things. He believed Delia Walker was without sin, for one thing. "Who's there? Soldiers?"

"Yes. Some scientists. Some administrators." Ashot gave a dry laugh. *"They're doing medicals on us all."*

"I bet. You know what's coming, don't you?"

"I do. They're putting up a fence, Yale."

She felt cold terror for her friend—for all the Vetch still in the settlement. "Come and join us, Ashot. Bring whoever you can."

"I won't leave the settlement. Not yet. I can't bring everyone, and I won't leave anyone behind."

"It's going to get dangerous."

"I know. I'm working on it. I've got to go. I'll be in touch."

There was a crackle, and then silence. Yale sat back on her heels.

"What does he mean, a fence?" said Maria.

"What do you think?" Yale shot back. "A prison. It's what the Expansion does best."

"For us?" Maria glanced fearfully at Jenny.

"For the Vetch first, I should think."

"At least it's not been a bloodbath," said Maria.

"Not yet," said Yale. "We have the first round to go through yet. Not blood, but bureaucrats. Death by administration. Death by committee." Death by Bureau. She glanced over at Cassandra playing with Jenny, and, as if she sensed Yale's eyes upon her, the girl looked up. She seemed to be saying: *I told you we should leave.*

CHAPTER FOUR

O'CONNOR WAS NOT what anyone in the Expansion would call wealthy, but she enjoyed a comfortable way of life. Rents were high around Venta, and the cost of commuting was a constant grumble for everyone trying to make a life in the huge city of islands. But there were compensations. Food was very cheap, and even if off-world travel was completely out of O'Connor's reach, there was plenty of entertainment in Venta itself. Once a year she and a couple of friends made it out to some of the more remote islands to enjoy the sun and the sea, and even a little glamping. There were a few super-rich on Venta—really grossly rich—but for the most part people were comfortable. And you didn't see poor people. Vagrancy wasn't tolerated, or even permitted, by law: depending on your circumstances, it landed you in jail, in hospital, or with a one-way ticket to a world with a labour shortage. The settlement on Stella Maris was the poorest place O'Connor had ever seen, and she was finding the reality of poverty a shock.

There was no lighting, beyond candles, which people made

themselves. The only heating was from wood-fires. Water was drawn from wells around the settlement, and was not on tap. Heating water meant making a fire. Cooking meant making a fire. Eating anything at all meant grubbing around for hours in the big fields beyond the fence, day after day after day. Everyone worked, hard, all the time, just to make sure that there was enough food. She was sure that there must have been times during the history of this settlement when people had gone hungry. She and her colleagues, Palmer included, discussed it on their first night at the settlement.

"How do they live like this?" O'Connor said,.

"I guess we have to remember where they've come from," one of the young men, Dixon said, uncertainly. "Didn't Woodley tell us many of them were from Satan's Reach? Slaves?"

"I've been to some of the worlds in the Reach," one of the other men said. "There was nothing like this."

"Perhaps you were only shown the respectable bits," said Palmer. "Does anyone show off their slave quarters?"

"They're so *poor*," said O'Connor, softly. "If we want to win trust, we need to show that we can make a real difference to their lives."

From that it was a short step to them deciding to set up a clinic, and O'Connor and Palmer spoke to Woodley the following morning. She listened to their ideas and agreed to take them to Inglis. He gave the okay after a few days; more than that, he welcomed the idea, and offered whatever help they needed. The soldiers that had come with them from the base had already commandeered space within the settlement, and were putting up some of their light, robust buildings to serve as accommodation. Adding another unit for a dedicated clinic was no problem. Medical supplies, and simple instructions for common procedures, arrived the following morning from the base, with Inglis' blessing. Within three days, O'Connor and Palmer had their clinic open for business.

Nobody came. Late in the afternoon, some of the humans (no Vetch) came to look at what they were doing. O'Connor came out to speak to them, to explain their purpose, but when she approached they moved on without saying a word in reply. She and Palmer closed up in the evening without having seen a single other soul. The following afternoon the weather took a turn for the worse, and the sky went dark, and, without giving the matter a second thought, O'Connor turned on the lights.

When she sat down at her desk, she nearly had a heart attack. Four small, grubby faces were pressed up against the plastic window. Children, drawn to the light like moths. It took O'Connor a few minutes to work out why. Born on Stella Maris, they had never seen electric light before. That someone could light up a dark day seemed nothing short of miraculous. O'Connor invited them inside to come and see. Two of them ran off, but the other two, bolder, came inside. O'Connor let them play with the switch—on and off, on and off—and they loved it. Palmer, studying them as they played, saw a bad case of conjunctivitis. She called the little boy over, wiped his eyes, and gave him some antibiotics. After half an hour, as if working on some internal clock, they ran away back to their long-houses. That was all the contact they had on the second day.

On the third day, it rained heavily and nobody came. On the fourth day, which was dry but cloudy, a human woman came up to the clinic and demanded to speak to them. O'Connor and Palmer gave each other a worried look, and went out to meet her.

She glared at them. "What did you do to my boy?" she said. "You did something to his eyes. What did you do?"

Palmer stepped forwards. "I washed his eyes clean. And I gave him some ordinary antibiotics. They can't do him any harm—"

"I know what antibiotics are," snapped the woman. "I'm not an idiot! I came to say thank you. He's better. Next time, ask permission. We're none of us stupid, you know." She peered inside over their shoulders. "What else have you got in there?"

And that was that. The clinic was open for business. After a hectic fortnight, it was clear that their work was winning the trust of a significant proportion of the human contingent of Stella Maris. There had not yet been a Vetch patient through the door, which O'Connor knew frustrated Palmer. "We've got to convince *all* of them," she said. "It's not enough if we only persuade the humans."

O'Connor nodded, but was privately relieved. Like every Expansion citizen, she had been fed from birth a steady diet of anti-Vetch propaganda, and while she kept a healthy scepticism about such things, the reality had been nearly as frightening as the stories. They were so big... so ungainly. They rocked about when they walked and you weren't quite sure they weren't going to topple over and land on you and crush you. There were so—well, *big*.

At the start of their third week, the visitors from the base had all their buildings up and running. O'Connor ran the clinic every morning, and, in the afternoons, she handed over to Palmer and tried to get to know the settlement better. She knew a large number of the humans by name, and some even greeted her in a friendly manner. Gritting her teeth and suppressing her fears, she would nod and smile at the Vetch, who looked back with big, bulging eyes and twitching tentacles. She had no idea whether this was hostility or friendship. Most evenings she spent with her colleagues, swapping stories and notes, or else in her little room recording her impressions of the day, noting down her conversations, laying the groundwork for her research. She had not failed to notice that nobody—neither human nor Vetch—had said a single thing to them about the Weird.

During that third week, new supplies, foodstuffs and medical, were sent over from the base. Perched on top of the vehicle, peering around him with ill-disguised distaste, was Paul Vincenze. When he saw O'Connor, he gave a dry smile. "I said I'd visit," he said. "But dear lord, Eileen, you poor creature! What an unspeakable dump! I hope your jabs are up to date."

She smiled and took him on a tour, showing him the new buildings they had put up, the administrators' offices, the mess, and finishing with her pride and joy, the clinic. He sat and watched, and even helped them out with some simple procedures. When they were finished, she took him back to the tiny mess. He drank tea (she stuck to water), and she got him something to eat. He took a bite and screwed up his face. "What on earth is this stuff?"

"It's called *kitzim*. It's the staple crop here. They do everything with it. I've even had it sweet." She took another mouthful. "You know, I wouldn't be surprised if they used it on the buildings. It dries very hard. We'll rinse the dishes as soon as you're done."

"*Kitzim*," he said, thoughtfully. "Did you know that's a Vetch word?"

"No?"

"It means 'stew.'"

She laughed. "I didn't know that."

He ate the whole bowl, helped her with the washing up, and then leaned back in his chair. "Does this whole set-up not bother you, Eileen?"

"What set-up?"

He gestured round. "*This*."

She looked out of the window onto a bright winter's day. "The sun is shining," she said. "I am doing good work, and I have the chance to do further work that might save the lives of billions. Why would anything about that bother me?"

"Yes, that's what our work is—or should be. Work that might save the lives of billions," he agreed, and then he gave her a canny look. "But you've not yet got to the Weird portal, have you? I imagine I'd have heard if you had. My guess is that you haven't even had a mention of the Weird from your grateful patients."

It was true, but O'Connor wasn't surprised. There were good reasons for many of the people here to mistrust the Expansion, and the work she was doing at the moment was building bridges. "No—"

"So chiefly what you've been doing here the past few weeks is administer jabs."

"We have to establish trust," O'Connor said patiently. "There are a lot of people here with good, personal reasons for doubting us. I imagine you've heard the story back at the base. This isn't the first contact they've had with the Expansion. Some rogue agents came here at the start of the year and caused some havoc."

"Rogue agents, eh?" Vincenze stared outside again. "How are you getting along with the Vetch?"

"Not well. They don't really come to the clinic." She thought about that. "One or two, in the last couple of days. But I wish more would come."

"You sound disappointed."

"I am, but I'm not really surprised. The war was very bitter, wasn't it?" She shook her head. "You know, they all live side-by-side, the humans and the Vetch."

"As I recall, that was one of the chief reasons our government was so interested in Stella Maris. A unique arrangement, I was told, enabled by the Weird."

"Up close it's quite hard to understand," she said. "I've been watching them together, trying to see how it works. I have a feeling that some of the humans here aren't really all that comfortable with the arrangement. I wonder whether if it would be better if they didn't live side by side."

"Hmm." Vincenze finished his tea. "So you've been busy, at any rate."

"There's been so much to do! The people here have almost nothing—you must have seen as you came through. Some of the cases I've seen would have ended in blindness. Children, going blind. Can you believe it?"

"Almost impossible to believe," said Vincenze. "And as we certainly can't countenance blind children, I must conclude that it's lucky for the people of Stella Maris that we're here." He stretched. "I imagine the database is well underway. Full documentation of everyone living here."

"Well, yes, I suppose so. I don't know."

Vincenze sighed. "Oh, Eileen," he said. "What do you think all those administrators are for?"

"Someone has to be counting the grubby groats," she said, waspishly.

"You're so *naïve*."

"And you see conspiracies where there are none. It would have been wrong for us to sit up in the hills and deny them access to the facilities we have."

"And does this kindness extend to the Vetch?"

"I told you, we've tried! The Vetch don't want it!" She sighed. "Look, everything is fine. You don't need to worry. Tell me what's going on back at the base."

"Not much. As we still have no idea where the portal is, we can't start doing any serious work as yet. The patrols are out, surveying the area, but so far it's proving elusive. We thought the clue was in the irrigation channels in the fields—if we followed those, we'd find the source. But they're leading nowhere. I'm certain that the water here is because of the Weird; that they're supplying it in some way. When you test the water, there are compounds in it, traces of... well, something..." He shrugged. "But the water doesn't lead back to them. It's as if the Weird are everywhere and nowhere."

"I'm sure the telepaths will discover something," O'Connor said.

Vincenze blinked at her. "The telepaths?"

"They're hoping to do scans on the Vetch."

"Telepathic scans?"

"It's just a precaution—"

"Yes, yes, just a precaution."

"Look, Paul, if you were living alongside two thousand Vetch, you'd want to know that you were safe too!"

"I thought we were allies these days," he said sharply. "Against the Weird."

"Maybe back in the Expansion," she said. "But we're in the middle of nowhere here! There's no surveillance, no ID chips. Anyone can do anything!"

"I imagine that's the appeal of the place, for some."

"Maybe, but it's not safe. There are children here—"

Vincenze sighed. "Yes, that always helps. Do you know what a full telepathic scan is like, Eileen?"

"I don't, and I bet you haven't had one, either."

"No, I'm glad to say I haven't. I gather it's like having your brain unravelled, at speed, shredded, and the bits shoved back inside."

"Then I'm sure they're only hoping to do the same partial scans that we all had when we signed up for this mission. If people have nothing to hide, they'll be happy to answer questions. Scans are quicker, and they make more sense. It's easy to forget things, forget details."

"Spoken like a true Expansion citizen," Vincenze said, and smiled. "Look, let's not talk about this any longer. Take me for a walk. I can see grey walls like these back at the base. Show me some of the settlement itself."

They walked out beyond the Expansion buildings, and out into the settlement. The afternoon was lengthening, and low amber lights were coming on all around. "There weren't lights here before," O'Connor said. "Candlelight, that was all."

"Electric light," said Vincenze. "A true marvel of our age. People have sold out whole civilizations for less." When he saw her expression, he said, "I'm sorry. Let's not quarrel. I am interested in anything and everything that you might show me. The truth is, I'm thinking of relocating down here. I'm interested in seeing what long-term exposure to the Weird can do to a population."

She turned and smiled at him. "You'd be very welcome! I'd love it if you came here!"

"I'm a miserable old bugger, Eileen," he said, with a smile. "But I appreciate your courtesy."

They walked on. O'Connor pointed out the long-houses, explaining how they worked: that the settlers lived in big groups of mixed species and ages, sharing the work and the care of the children. She showed him the central hall, and he stood for a while staring at the carved doors. "Amazing," he said. "No, no—there was nothing like this on World." He looked around. "Do you think we could get a peep inside?"

She shook her head. "We haven't been invited, and I wouldn't presume. This could be their most sacred place, for all we know."

"It could also," he said, dryly, "be the location of the portal."

Suddenly, from over by the Expansion buildings, a siren sounded. Three short blasts, then silence.

"What's that?" said Vincenze.

"I don't know," said O'Connor. "We should go back."

They hurried back to their own zone. As they drew closer, two soldiers approached them. Both were helmeted, and carrying their weapons cradled in their arms. "Dr O'Connor. Dr Vincenze. Please come back inside," one of the said. "I'm afraid the settlement is off-limits for non-military personnel for the moment."

They hurried into the mess, finding Palmer and one or two of the others there. Palmer came over to them, a worried expression on her face. "We've got a case of *teltis* fever, Eileen. One of the Vetch came in today. It's definitely *teltis*."

Vincenze said, "What does this mean exactly?"

She turned to him. "*Teltis*, Dr Vincenze. It's a common enough malady in Vetch, and easily curable. Nothing more than a high fever and a few aches and pains."

"Sound like a common cold," said Vincenze.

"It is—in Vetch—although not common. In humans, it can mutate into something more deadly."

"Ah," said Vincenze, nodding his head. "I understand."

"I said that humans and Vetch shouldn't be living together," said O'Connor.

"Yes," said Vincenze. "That is surely the best thing all round. Well, I can't say that I'm surprised. I'm not surprised in the least."

CASSANDRA AND JENNY were playing a clapping game together. Watching them, it struck Maria how young Cassandra was. She had all the awkwardness of adolescence, and still, sometimes, had some of the gaiety of a child. But what, really, could her childhood have been like? She had tried asking, a few times, but Cassandra would say nothing. Or perhaps *could* say nothing? She claimed, sometimes, when pressed, that she had few memories of being a child, and that she remembered little before finding herself walking along the road to the settlement. But she clearly remembered her mother well, and she often talked about Delia as if she was present. Certainly she believed her mother was alive somewhere. Maria shook her head. The Weird were beyond her comprehension. Could anyone ever understand them? Delia Walker had thought so. But Delia Walker was not here, only this odd child, giggling away like a little girl with her Jenny.

Yale came to speak to her. "They look like they've made good friends."

"Cass is very good with her."

"I wonder..." Yale hesitated. "Would you be okay leaving them together for a while? Do you think Cass could cope? I want to show you something."

Maria glanced anxiously at her little girl. "How long?"

"The afternoon? If you don't think it's safe, that's okay. But I really do want to show you this."

"Is it important?"

"Yes," said Yale. "I think so."

Maria thought. She wouldn't have hesitated to leave Jenny with a trusted baby-sitter, back in the old days. But the old days had been a Fleet base, with mothers like her. Not a damp hideaway halfway up a mountain, with her enemies at her heels. But Cass and Jenny had got wind of the conversation, and Jenny begged to be left for a few hours with Cass. Cassandra listened gravely while Maria pressed on her the great responsibility of looking after the little girl.

"Oh, lay off her, Maria," said Yale, at last. "She seems smart enough to me."

Finally, they left the refuge, Maria still looking anxiously over her shoulder. "You know," said Yale, "if she really has come from the Weird, chances are she'll be able to cope. She must have seen things we couldn't even begin to imagine."

"But can she cope with a four-year-old?" said Maria. "It's not as easy as it looks."

She was expecting to be blindfolded again, but Yale made no move to cover her eyes, and they did not go back down the route along which they had come. Instead, Yale led her up the pass, higher into the mountains. "You aren't stopping me from seeing where we're going," Maria said.

"No," she said. "I'm not. And I'm taking you somewhere even more secret, even more precious than the refuge. You wanted me to trust you, Maria. This is me proving that trust."

The path was rocky and steep, but Yale was sure-footed and quick, and Maria had to concentrate to keep up with her. "Do you trust Cassandra a little more now?"

Yale frowned. "I don't mistrust her. I don't necessarily believe everything she says. *She* might believe it, I'll give you that. She certainly seems to."

"So why keep doubting her?"

"Maria, it isn't *possible*!"

"Would you have thought that the Weird were possible?"

Yale sighed. "No. Not really."

"I want to help her," Maria said. "I want to help her leave."

"Oh, yeah? How do you intend to go about that?"

"I don't know. Could we steal one of the Expansion ships?"

Yale glared at her. "You're on your own with that. I'm not into suicide pacts."

"If only someone could fly the *Baba Yaga*!" Maria said.

"Yes, well, we'd still have to get to it," said Yale. "And I'm not sure we could get there without the Expansion spotting us, never mind get it into orbit. And away into phase. And out—"

"Yes, all right, I get your point." They walked on in silence, upwards, and then Maria said, "You're taking me to see the portal, aren't you?"

"Yes. Or what's left of it."

"You *do* trust me!"

"Yes, Maria, I trust you."

After about an hour's walk, the path came out near the top of the mountain pass. Maria looked down on the river below. "I guess that Delia came this way," she said. "With Kay and Hecate..."

"They came along the river," Yale said. "But they met this path here, yes." She led Maria onwards, and soon they came to the mouth of the cavern inside of which the Weird portal lay. Yale pointed. "The portal was that way."

Maria frowned. "Aren't you coming with me?"

"What's the point? It's gone."

"It'll come back."

Yale shrugged. "Are you going in there, or not?"

Maria went off alone down the narrow passage. Step by step, she thought, she was retracing the last moments of her friends... She heard footsteps, and turned to see Yale coming up behind her. "I thought you weren't coming?"

"Better not to be alone," Yale said.

"Hoping to see something to your advantage?"

"Always, Maria. Always."

They walked on, in single file. After about five minutes, they came out into the cavern where the Weird portal had once been. Maria had heard descriptions of an open portal, and seen the faked footage from Braun's World, the awful blood-surface, rippling and congealing as Sleer and other monstrosities were formed. She shuddered. She was glad not to have to see that here; even if this portal was friendly, the basic biology would surely be the same. But nothing like that was happening here. The surface was smooth, as still and opaque as a piece of frosted glass. Again, she thought of Heyes, whose body had been found here, and of Walker, who had simply disappeared. Heyes, Maria thought, might have liked her to say a prayer for her here, so she did: a small request for the repose of the old woman's soul. And what about Walker? Maria thought of old tales of ghosts wandering, their spirits restless and unavenged.

Yale said, "I guess we'll never really know what happened here."

"Cassandra, perhaps, could tell us. If we asked."

"Cassandra barely knows what day it is."

"Are you starting to think she is who she says she is?"

Yale sighed. "I've honestly no idea. Perhaps, if she came up with something, I'd be more inclined to believe her."

"Or perhaps less."

Yale shrugged.

"Failt thinks the Weird supplied us all with a bond, you know," said Maria. "I always thought he was making it up. He can be so fanciful!"

Yale gave a grudging smile. "Yes, he's romantic about the Weird. The reality was, well, rather more shocking."

"You came here when the portal was open?" Maria looked at her in amazement.

"Once. Never again."

"And you felt nothing like Failt said?"

"I was bloody terrified."

Maria looked back at the glass. "Standing here, looking at this—I can *feel* it... Feel what he means. Or, rather, the *absence* of it."

"I have no evidence either way," said Yale. "A feeling isn't enough."

"Perhaps it is with the Weird."

"Hmm." Yale sounded distinctly unconvinced. She was scuffing her toe against the stony floor. "Anyway, you know where the portal is now. Not everyone on Stella Maris knows that. It's a secret we keep even from ourselves."

"Why are you trusting me with this, Yale?"

"I'm not really sure myself." She sighed. "Maybe because you were never really part of us—not before the Weird left. If the Weird *did* make some kind of bond between us, you weren't..." Yale frowned. "'Assimilated' isn't right. It was definitely consensual. I mean, I know a lot of people here were desperate, but it was still consensual. And you weren't yet part... What does Cassandra say? Part of the whole. You would have been, if the Weird had stayed, but they didn't. So you didn't have the chance. You didn't become part of the whole. And I think you're coping better now. You have a clearer head."

"You *do* feel it, don't you?" said Maria. "The absence."

Yale didn't answer. "I'm going to have a look round. Make sure no-one else has been here. If you want a good hard reason for bringing you here, it's this. Someone needs to know where this place is, so that it can be defended, should the time come." She stared down into the closed portal. "I'll tell you something, though, Maria. Feeling or not, I'd be happier if the Weird came back."

Maria nodded. She turned to follow, looking back over her shoulder one last time at the empty, glassy surface that would keep its secrets for a while longer. Yale looked around for a while, and then they started on the long walk home.

Maria heard Jenny's voice, raised in laughter, before she entered the cavern, and her heart lifted at the sound. She heard

Cassandra too, chattering excitedly, and thought perhaps spending time with Jenny might have done some good. Then she heard a third voice: familiar, rising and falling. She stepped inside the cavern. "Failt! What are you doing here?"

He ran over to throw his long arms around her. "Oh, mama Maria!" he said. "Had to come. Ashot asked, so I came. It's all gone wrong. Everything's going wrong."

FAILT WAS SAFE inside his hideaway near the gate before the trouble started. Failt had a lot of hideaways in and around the settlement. Even here on Stella Maris, where he was the safest he had ever been in his short life, he liked to know that he had a few boltholes. A slave could never be too careful. He was glad, now, that he'd trusted his instincts and taken precautions.

And the truth was, he'd been on the alert for a while now. Trouble had been brewing between the Vetch and the Expansion soldiers for some time. Take last week, for example. It had all happened out of the blue. One of the Vetch had tried to enter his long-house. There were a handful of children playing outside— all human, as it happened, not that anyone would notice under usual circumstances—watched over by one of the old men. The Vetch, a huge hairy creature who everyone knew to be as gentle as a summer breeze, had come back to the house to collect some tool he needed. On his way back out, and with one huge foot still on the steps, he stood chatting to the old man. Then one of the soldiers ran up, his weapon held up against his chest.

"You!" he shouted. "Get away!"

Everyone looked round. Nobody was sure at first who was being spoken to. Then the Vetch realised it was him. "Do you mean me?"

"You, yes, you!" said the soldier. "Get away from those kids!"

The Vetch looked at him in bewilderment. He pointed at the door. "This is my long-house," he said. "We share these spaces. We live together, human and Vetch."

The soldier gave an unpleasant laugh. "Not for much longer."

The Vetch had laughed back and walked away. Failt too had slipped away, to think about what he had seen and what he should do. Mama Maria wasn't here to tell. Delia Walker was long gone. And he knew—he absolutely knew—that things were going wrong. He was small and clever, but he was still a child. A Vetch child, surrounded by humans with weapons. Who would protect him now? That evening, at supper, he looked around his long-house and considered each of the adults in turn. He discounted all the humans. After supper, when the clear-up had been done, he went to Ashot and told him what he had seen.

The big Vetch medic didn't seem particularly surprised. "It's coming," he said. "I thought it might. Time for us to make some real preparations, Failt."

Failt wasn't sure at first what Ashot meant by that (preparation for what?) but on Ashot's instructions, he started to hide a few things here and there, mostly in his secret places just beyond the gate. This was an old toolshed, rather tumbledown, sometimes used as a shelter by the field-workers on hot days, but left alone during the winter months. Slowly, Failt began to store things that might come in useful. Food, medical supplies, a communicator retrieved some time ago from the *Baba Yaga*. Very late one night, he carried out his most audacious plan. He slipped out from his long-house when everyone was asleep, and he pulled the plug on the amber lights that now shone all around the settlement. Under the cover of the darkness and the confusion, he purloined the other vehicle left from the crimopaths' attack and hid it inside his shed.

All that remained now was to make sure that he was hidden

away when the time came. Ashot told him when to go. He said that he was sending a couple of Vetch to visit the clinic, and that he thought the soldiers would come soon after. He was right.

A siren went off. Three long blasts, and then all the Expansion civilians disappeared inside their buildings. All the people in the settlement—human and Vetch—stood looking round, asking each other what was going on, unable to provide each other with answers. Failt saw Ashot dashing towards him from the Expansion clinic. "Time to go, little one," he said.

"What's happening, Ashot?"

"They've found a case of *teltis* fever. They're going to move now."

Failt didn't understand. "But that's hardly anything—"

"It is for humans." Ashot growled. "Not that it's true. There's never been a case as long as I've been here, and if there is now, the Expansion have brought it with them." He looked down at Failt. "Hurry up! No time to waste; they'll be here before you know it. Get away! Get to Yale. Tell her what's happening. Tell her to look out for our signal!"

And Failt—ever trusting, ever obedient—ran.

Just in time. A few scant minutes later, the soldiers came out of the Expansion buildings, armed and helmeted. They went in groups of four to each of long-houses, hammering on the doors of each building and asking for all the Vetch to present themselves. Where the Vetch refused, they barged inside and brought them out a gunpoint.

Other soldiers moved in formation through the crowd, moving the Vetch away from the humans. They were met with a great deal of confusion. Some of the humans tried to intervene on behalf of their friends and house-mates; others stood back in bewilderment, and mostly out of fear of the guns. Then the word *infection* was whispered, and before long it had passed around everyone there, and the humans stood back as all the Vetch were led away to three long-houses on the edge of the settlement. Later that afternoon, the wire went up.

Failt watched all this from his hideaway near the gate. When the humans stood back, he cried a little. This, more than anything, convinced Failt that the Weird had abandoned Stella Maris. Yes, the water was still here; yes, the crops still grew—but the bond that the Weird had nurtured, that strange consensual force that had allowed the two-species community to live in peace and harmony: that was surely gone.

Failt puzzled over this, and over what Ashot had said about the Expansion bringing *teltis*. This fever couldn't have come accidentally, could it? All these new arrivals had come straight from the core worlds, and must have undergone rigorous medicals before being allowed to come on the mission. Did Ashot mean that the Expansion had deliberately risked infecting the humans on Stella Maris with this fever? Who knew? Failt suspected he would never get to the truth. What mattered was the consequence of the story: here the Vetch were, all gathered together on one side of the settlement, while the humans all huddled fearfully on the other side.

But he had no time for such mysteries. He had to do what he'd promised. In the dead of night, he slipped under the fence out of the settlement and went to his old toolshed. The vehicle was packed up, ready to go. Well before dawn, he was on his way up to the mountains.

MARIA LISTENED TO Failt's account with mounting fear. When he finished, she shook her head. "They've built a prison camp. An *internment* camp." She turned to Yale. "You don't seem very surprised."

"Well, no, I'm not," Yale said, "although it happened quicker than I was expecting. It confirms what I suspected: the Bureau are here on Stella Maris, and they're the ones running the show."

"There's been lots of questions about Missus Dee," said Failt. "And about you, mama Maria. They know who they're looking for."

"But why are people allowing this to happen?" Maria said. "They sound nothing like the people I met when I first arrived here. Everyone was so dogged, so determined. It was clear how strong the bonds were between you all. Human and Vetch, living in peace and harmony. Everyone was so strong, so certain! What's happened? Why aren't people fighting back?"

"It's easy to say 'fight' when you're not in the crosshairs," Yale replied.

"But these are their *friends*. People from their own long-houses. They've lived and worked alongside them for years."

"Most of the people here were brought up in captivity," Yale said. "They're afraid of reprisals."

"They weren't afraid to help me send those messages out about the massacre on Braun's World," Maria pointed out.

"Perhaps if they'd known what was coming, they would have been."

"It's more than that, I think," said Failt sadly.

"What do you mean?" said Maria.

"It's the Weird. The Weird are gone."

"What difference does that make?" Yale said, harshly.

"The Weird was the bond," said Failt. "The way we were all safe here. Safe with each other. The way we knew each other."

Maria gave this some thought. "Like some sort of low-level telepathic field."

"That sounds like rubbish to me," said Yale.

"You felt it too," said Failt, with more than a hint of reproach.

"I know it. You know it. You felt it too, whatever you say."

"Maybe," said Yale, grudgingly. "Perhaps I liked people here more than I generally do. But this is all conjecture. The Weird aren't coming to help us. They've left the water supply switched on, but that's all we're going to get from them."

"If only we knew what was happening with the Weird," said Maria. "If only they'd *communicate* with us."

"Well, they have, haven't they?" Yale nodded at Cassandra. "Only she doesn't say very much. Hey, Cassandra! Any word yet from the Great Beyond?"

Failt growled. "Leave her alone!" He hopped over to sit next to her. "The Weird are gone. Isn't that right, sister Cass?"

She took his paw in her own small hand. "Not gone. In hiding."

"Or in retreat," said Yale.

"I said in hiding," Cassandra replied, sharply. "That's not the same thing." She gestured around the hideaway. "Are you in retreat?"

"Actually, yes, I am," said Yale. "There are bastards with guns down there coming after me. After you. After us."

"Then help me. Help me leave Stella Maris."

"Could we leave?" said Maria.

"Why would we want to?" said Yale. "Who out there gives a damn about us?"

Maria frowned. "Perhaps we shouldn't count on the people of the settlement continuing to keep the secret of this hideaway, after what's happened."

"You know, you have a point there," said Yale, and she sat in thought for a while. Eventually, she said, "All right. We'll leave on the *Baba Yaga*."

Maria stared at her. "The *Baba Yaga*? Is she flightworthy?"

"Yes."

"You seem very sure of that."

"I've made sure of it," Yale said. "I've not spent the summer unprofitably, you know. I knew we'd get visitors sooner or later."

"But about flying it?" said Failt. "Yershov had the things in his head, the implants..."

"I know," said Yale. She gave Maria a guilty look. "I have them too."

Maria stared at her in disbelief. "*What?*"

"Yes, yes, all right! I know! I've not been entirely straight. I haven't lied, though—"

"Yale..." said Maria, through gritted teeth.

"Look, I did what I thought was best. They were coming. Their shuttles were between us and the ship. But you're right. We might not be safe here anymore—"

"*You* might not be safe here anymore, you mean," said Maria, bitterly.

"I said I was sorry. But I can fly her, if we can get anywhere near her. That's a big *if*. They might spot us heading there. And they'll definitely know when I lift her from the ground. They might they send a ship after us. She's not got much firepower."

Failt waved his hand. "Ashot said to look out for his signal."

"What does he mean by that?" said Maria.

"I think..." said Yale, "I think he means that the Vetch are going to make a stand."

"What?" Maria said.

"Distract the soldiers. Let us get through."

"But they have no weapons," said Failt, "no means of defending themselves—"

"We beat the last invaders," Maria said.

"Half a dozen of them," said Yale. "And we got inside help in the end. How many of us did they kill? If they do this, it's going to be a bloodbath."

They sat in silence for a while, contemplating this. "So we'd better move when we have the chance," said Maria. "We'd better not waste their sacrifice—if that's what it's going to be. It's long past time we took Cassandra to the *Baba Yaga*. Yale, it's time to go."

CHAPTER FIVE

OVER THE NEXT couple of days, a slow trickle of people arrived at the refuge in the mountains, all Vetch. Like Failt and Ashot, they had seen what was coming, but they had not made such meticulous preparations. They'd had a hard journey, covering the desert between the settlement and the mountains without much in the way of supplies. They were exhausted and distressed. Maria welcomed them as best she could, but she was starting to worry about their supplies, particularly if, as the group thought, there would be more refugees on the way.

Yale was less enthusiastic, and seemed even to be angry to see them. "You do realise this place is meant to be secret, don't you?" she said. "Do you even have any idea whether or not you were followed?"

"We were not followed," said their leader, a Vetch woman named Isilt.

"The Expansion could be on their way right now. They'll have done a head count, you know. They'll know if anyone is missing—particularly Vetch."

"We were not followed," Isilt repeated, and Maria laid a warning hand upon Yale's arm.

"We've gone to a lot of trouble over the years to keep this place safe and secret—"

Isilt rose, all two-and-a-half metres of her, from where she had been sitting. She was so big that she had to stoop in the cave.

"Woah," said Yale, tilting her head back slightly.

"We were not followed," said Isilt, one paw tapping ominously against the other. "How many times do I have to say that, Yale? And what do you mean to do with us now that we are here? Send us away? That would certainly be the human thing to do."

"Hey, now, that's not fair—" began Yale.

"No?" Isilt leaned in. Yale leaned back. "Do you know what's happened? No, you were not there. You got yourself away as soon as trouble reared its head—don't think we didn't notice, Yale."

"That really isn't fair," Maria protested. "She was keeping me and Jenny safe—"

"She was saving herself," spat Isilt. "Like all humans, she puts herself first. Do you know what they did? They stepped back. They let the men with guns take our brothers and sisters, our friends from our long-houses. They stepped back and they let it happen. It didn't have to be that way! But we know better now. Never trust humans! They will not help us when we need it. So we must look after ourselves. We have come to the place where we know that we will be safe. We have as much right to be her as you." She jabbed a huge thumb towards Maria and Cassandra. "More right than those two!"

At this, Failt leapt forwards, his eyes bulging and tentacles waving, and put himself between Isilt and his sister Cass. He waved his arms around, ready to fight, and growled at Isilt.

"You leave them alone, you hear? You try to touch them, Failt will stop you!"

Failt had spent his childhood spent underground labouring in the mines of Shard's World. He never had the growth spurt that took most Vetch males to nearly three metres, and in all likelihood he never would. He was small, with gangly arms and legs that promised a much taller person that would never emerge. Isilt stood for a while, contemplating him, and then her tentacles twitched, and she began to whiffle with laughter. She reached out to rest her huge hairy hand, lightly, just for a moment, on the top of the boy's head. He snarled and pushed it away, but she just laughed.

"You're a brave one, Failt," she said. "I won't fight you. Not you! But do those two know," she said, glancing over at Maria and Cassandra, "what a champion they have in you?"

"We know," said Maria, firmly. She put her arm around Failt's shaking shoulders, and he grabbed her hand, clutching it to him. "We know very well."

Whatever Failt might have intended by his intervention, it had taken the heat out of the moment. Maria pulled him gently aside, leaving the Vetch to lick their wounds and eat their supper. Yale came to join her. "Bloody cheek," she muttered, glaring back over her shoulder at Isilt. "I'm only trying to make sure we're all safe."

"You asked for it," said Maria. "They've all obviously had a dreadful time of it."

"That's not my fault! I wasn't there!"

Maria gave her a steady look. "Would you have stood back, Yale? Or would you have fought for them?"

Yale gave her a crooked smile, and gestured around her. "I wouldn't have been anywhere near the fight in the first place."

"And you're not going to be anywhere near it in future.

But this is going to keep causing us trouble," said Maria. She frowned. Yale was leaving the following morning. "Causing *me* trouble."

"I think you'll cope," said Yale.

"I won't have Failt to intervene for me."

"But you won't have me putting my foot in it," Yale said.

They both smiled, wryly. Maria thought, *I am going to miss you. For all that you're only telling me half of the truth about yourself, I know I can rely on you.* "For what it's worth," she said, "I think you would have been first into the fray if the soldiers had come for the Vetch. For Ashot."

"Well, thanks for that. Look, try not to worry about Isilt. She's tired now, and angry, but I've had dealings with her in the past, and she's fair-minded. She'll come round. And I promise I'll come back as quickly as I can," said Yale. "Once Cassandra is on her way to—to wherever she's going, I'll come back. I'll bring help, if I can."

Maria sighed. What help could come to Stella Maris that would be enough to see off a concerted invasion from the Expansion? Only the Weird could help—and she doubted Yale had the power to make them materialise. They had sent their help—Cassandra—and that was going away. The Weird, clearly, had other priorities than the odd little settlement they had once succoured on Stella Maris.

Yale, Cassandra, and Failt set off before dawn the following morning. Maria went with them down to the place where the pathways forked, and she watched as Yale uncovered the ground vehicle. Turning to Cassandra, she took hold of the girl's hand, and then, unable to stop herself, hugged her, feeling the girl's thin body within her arms, wishing that she had been able to give her more love, more attention—more mothering. Cassandra stiffened at first within her grasp and then seemed to understand, and respond, holding Maria tight with her thin arms. "Thank you, Maria," she said. "Thank you for believing me. Mama is grateful."

"I didn't just help you for your mother's sake," Maria said. It seemed important that she let Cassandra know that she was something other than Walker's daughter. "I did it for yours, too. Take care of yourself, Cass," she said, relinquishing her hold. "Wherever you're going."

Maria and Failt said a quiet, sad goodbye. Maria had come to love the Vetch child as much as her own girl, she realised. He was quaint, and loyal, and madly courageous, and she wasn't sure she was going to see him ever again. "Please come home to us," she said, holding his strange body close to her. "Please come home to me and Jenny. You're part of the family now."

He twitched his tentacles up at her in his Vetch way. "I'll miss you too, mama Maria. And don't worry, I'm coming back. Missus Dee—she won't forget me."

The goodbye between Maria and Yale was considerably less effusive, but still respectful. "I guess it's up to you what you do now," said Yale, "and I trust your judgement. For what it's worth... protect the portal, as best you can."

Maria nodded. Yale knew too, that really this was their best hope. Beyond Stella Maris, nobody cared about the trials and sorrows of their small settlement.

"There'll be reprisals coming," Yale went on. "All it needs is a deep telepathic scan on the right person and the Expansion will know everything about this place. Where to find you, how to get here..." She ran her hand across her brow. "What am I doing? I should be here, not gadding about the Reach on the say-so of some weird teenage girl—"

Maria put her fingers to her lips. "Ssh! It'll be all right! I know what I'm doing!"

"Really?" Yale sighed. "I'm glad somebody does."

And then they were gone. Maria watched the vehicle reverse down the hillside, and then turn and go on its way. Yale stuck her hand out of the side window and waved goodbye.

Maria stood for a while, watching them fade into the gloom. Then she walked back up towards the refuge. She stood for a while on the pathway, wondering whether she should check on the portal, but the thought of that high lonely place, where her friends had died, filled her with fear and horror. Who knew what would come out, when the portal opened again? Would it be that same part of the Weird that had protected Stella Maris for so long, or that other part, that aspect that only wanted to consume? What would she do, if the portal opened, and she was there, all alone, and the Sleer poured out? What could she do?

She went back into the cave, and lay down on the mattress she shared with Jenny, holding her little girl for a while. She slept for an hour or so, before the other occupants of the refuge, stirring, woke her with their movements. And a new day began: cooking, hunting, fetching the water, waiting for news. The next day passed, and the next. On the third day, one of the Vetch came up from the path to say that people were coming.

"To harm us?" asked Maria, fearfully.

"I don't think so."

Still, they put a watch on the path, and were prepared to fight, if necessary. But the people who came were not enemies. They were a small band of exhausted and wounded people, bringing news of the defeat of the Vetch in the settlement. At the rear, making sure nobody fell behind, was Ashot. He looked around, wildly. "Did they make it?" he said. "Yale. Cassandra. Did they make it?"

* * *

ALTOGETHER, THE SCIENTIFIC team at the settlement spent eight days holed up in their own buildings. They were encouraged to remain indoors as much as possible during this time: *teltis*, they were constantly reminded, was airborne, after all. Not that they needed much persuading. The miracle was that any of them remained at all: most of the administrative team had requested evacuation rather than quarantine and, on the second day, a large vehicle arrived to take them all back to the base. One or two of the scientists talked about going back with them, but Woodley discouraged the attitude, as against the whole purpose of their mission.

"We came here to work with the settlers and gain their trust. If any of us leave now, it's signalling that we're not serious about our work. Anyone who chooses to leave now," she gave them all sharp looks, "can remain at the base for good."

None of the younger members of the team suggested leaving again. Going back to the base would mean the end of any serious research for them, and it was a long journey to have made to spend the whole time twiddling paper clips back at the base. But Vincenze was not awed by Woodley. "Earn their trust?" he laughed. "I think you'll find that moment has passed."

O'Connor, catching the older man at a quiet moment, said, "Why didn't you go back to the base when you could, Paul? There's no reason for you to stay."

"Two reasons," the older man. "First of all, I'm concerned for you."

"That's kind of you," said O'Connor, with a smile. "Now the real reason?"

"Let's just say that I'm curious to see how all this pans out."

It was a tense time. After the administrative team left, they received little contact from the wider world. The soldiers were busy beyond their zone. Sometimes they saw figures in hazmat suits passing by, and Palmer wondered out loud whether a full-blown epidemic was underway. "We should have left when we had the chance," she said eventually, not caring now whether or not Woodley heard her. "If there's an epidemic, we're all at risk. I don't want to die here of some stupid Vetch plague, just because I missed the last damn bus out."

Woodley had grown pensive and quiet, and didn't take Palmer to task. It must have been a shock to the director, O'Connor thought, to have demonstrated so clearly how little authority she had over this mission. When it came down to it, when a serious situation arose, the soldiers were the ones running Stella Maris, and Inglis reigned supreme.

On the eighth day, the soldiers gave them permission to leave their buildings. The *teltis* had been contained; there had been no cases among the humans, and no further cases among the Vetch. "Permission to leave our buildings?" asked Vincenze. "What about permission to leave the zone?"

The soldier who had come to brief them looked at him impassively. "You can go out into the settlement if you want, sir, but I don't advise it."

"There's no risk of infection, is there?" Vincenze asked.

"There's no risk of that," the soldier agreed. "But the area can hardly be considered safe."

"I wonder what he means by that?" said Palmer.

"Only one thing for it," said Vincenze. "Let's go and have a look round."

Leaving their own buildings, they walked out into a settlement that was much changed.

"Where is everyone?" said Palmer, looking around the silent town. She walked to the nearest long-house, and saw a face peeping out of one of the windows. She waved her hand in greeting, but they quickly darted out of sight at her approach.

O'Connor was struck by the difference: the settlement had hardly been what you could call a buzzing metropolis, but it had always been busy with life: people working and talking; children running and playing. Now there was quiet, and very little movement outside.

Vincenze, meanwhile, had walked on ahead. O'Connor followed to find him standing, arms folded, in front of a high wire fence. There were three long-houses behind the fence, which he was studying with a frown upon his face.

"What do you think this is?" said O'Connor.

He gave her a sorrowful look. "Oh, Eileen," he said. "You know what this is!"

She peered through the fence. The three long-houses were quiet, and there was no movement between them. She said, "This is where the Vetch are, isn't it?"

Vincenze nodded.

"But why?" she said. "If there's no longer any risk of infection, they can come out now. We don't need them in quarantine."

"You said it yourself," Vincenze said.

"What? What did I say?"

"It's better if humans and Vetch don't live side-by-side."

O'Connor looked at him in horror. "I didn't mean *this!* Not behind barbed wire!"

"No?"

"No, of course not! This is awful!" She looked helplessly at the little prison. There were easily over a thousand Vetch. Was there even room for them all, in so few houses?

"What did you imagine, then?" Vincenze said. "'Separate but equal'?"

"I don't know what I thought—"

"No, I don't think you did. If it's any consolation, I should imagine that separating the humans from the Vetch was the intention before this mission even arrived."

"But *this?*" O'Connor said. "How does this help us find the portal?"

"Look around you, Eileen," Vincenze said, and he waved his hand around the emptied streets. "A cowed population—a divided population—is unlikely to cause trouble. I doubt there was ever a case of *teltis* fever here." He stood for a while, deep in thought, staring into the prison. "You do have to wonder," he said, more to himself than to O'Connor, "exactly what's happening behind that wire."

O'Connor tapped his shoulder. A soldier was heading towards them, and his approach was enough to encourage them to move on. They walked back to the Expansion zone in silence. O'Connor was struggling to reconcile what he had said with what she believed the mission was trying to achieve. After a little while, Vincenze spoke.

"I think I'll return to the base. I gather there's a vehicle heading back that way tomorrow." He shook his head. "There's nothing I can achieve here now. And I think that if you want to find the portal, Eileen, you'll have to try new methods. You'll learn nothing from these people now, unless you use force." He stopped in his tracks, and turned to her. "Please," he said, taking her hands within his own, "take care of yourself."

"What do you mean, Paul?"

"I mean that there is a great deal of fear here now. Many of the people here, as I understand it, were once slaves. They must be terrified that that's what the future is going to hold for them. Slavery might not exist within the Expansion, but there's plenty of precedent for handing back slaves to their owners within the Reach. People know that. If they think they're heading back to slavery, if they're desperate enough, they'll fight back."

"You mean the Vetch?" O'Connor shuddered. "I'm glad they're in there, in that case."

"Not just the Vetch. The humans, too, if they're frightened enough." He eyed her thoughtfully. "Perhaps you should think about coming back to the base, too."

"No," she said firmly. "I came here to work with these people. We can start again; try to earn their trust again."

He shook his head. "Eileen," he said, "that's not going to happen."

He was right. Over the next few days, O'Connor and Palmer tried to re-establish their clinic, but none of the humans came. They rarely saw people about, and those who did have to go outside, to get water or food, hurried away when anyone from the mission drew near. They tried a few visits to the long-houses, but the doors were barred to them, and people who had once been friendly were now at best sullen, at worst openly hostile. Many, it was clear, saw the clinic as the root of all the troubles. Eventually, by tacit agreement, they gave up. The clinic closed, and the space was taken over by new arrivals from the base. More soldiers. Another two long-houses next to the Vetch zone were commandeered, and the wire fence extended. *Zones,* thought O'Connor; *when did we start to think in terms of zones?* But that's how the settlement was mapped now, with the human settlers on one side, the Vetch behind their wire, and the Expansion slowly encroaching, as more soldiers came from the base. Perhaps Inglis was expecting trouble, too; or seeking to head it off with a display of force. If that was the plan, it didn't work.

The disturbance started around midnight. O'Connor was woken by shouting, and for a moment she thought she was back at her apartment on Hennessy's World, and the students next door were partying again. Then she heard hammering at her door, and became aware that Palmer was calling out her name. When she opened her door, she found her wrapped in a dressing gown and trembling with fear. "Eileen, they're coming. The Vetch are coming."

O'Connor pulled on some shoes and a coat. "What do you mean?" She went over to the window, and saw soldiers running past. A few shots were fired, close by. Then a flare went up, turning the night sky orange. Palmer flinched. "Christ," she said, "it's all going to shit! We've got to get away from here!"

But O'Connor couldn't move. She was mesmerised by the violent colour of the sky. As she stood, staring, a face suddenly reared up at the window: huge and hideous, with blood-red bulging eyes and vile, pulsating tentacles.

Vetch.

O'Connor screamed; Palmer screamed. Both women turned and fled, coming eventually to Woodley's office, at the centre of the Expansion zone. They slammed the door, locked it, and shoved a filing cabinet in front of it for good measure. Then they sat in uncomfortable plastic chairs and listened to the fighting outside. Gradually, as the night wore on, the noise began to die down and, a little before dawn, O'Connor felt safe enough— and exhausted enough—to fall asleep, with her head against Palmer's shoulder.

Palmer woke her, mid-morning. "It's over," she said. "We're safe."

She had been awake for some hours, it transpired, and, unable to hear any more fighting, had risked moving the cabinet and unlocking the door. In the next room, she had found Woodley and the rest of the science team. They all gathered together now, and waited for news. It took a little while to filter through to them, and few of the soldiers were forthcoming, but eventually they formed an idea of what had happened that night. The

Vetch had broken through the barriers. Some of the humans had helped them, although most had remained hidden inside their long-houses.

The battle that followed had been short, but extremely fierce. More than thirty Vetch were dead, along with two of their human supporters. There were no Expansion fatalities, but several of the soldiers had been injured. Most of the Vetch were now back behind the wire, although some had taken the opportunity to escape the confines of the settlement. There were patrols out in the surrounding countryside to track them down and round them up. Some of the humans had tried to get away, too, and yet another of the long-houses had been commandeered to hold them, along with the humans who had fought against the Expansion.

"What happens now?" said O'Connor. "Are we safe? Should we go back to the base?"

Palmer, visibly shaken, said, "I'm not going anywhere until they're all under lock and key. Angry Vetch on the loose—it's the stuff of nightmares! They'd kill us all in our sleep if they had the chance. Those creatures are *beasts*."

Only because they'd been treated that way, O'Connor thought. Still, the propaganda ran deep, and she shuddered at the thought of that Vetch face at the window.

"Inglis tells me they're planning more stringent measures to keep the Vetch interned," said Woodley. "They'll be documenting everyone here on Stella Maris now—humans too. I suspect that ultimately the plan will be to repatriate the Vetch."

"Repatriate?" said O'Connor, in alarm.

"Good," said Palmer fiercely. "Good." She shook her head. "I don't understand the people who helped the Vetch against us. How could any human side with the Vetch?"

Woodley nodded her agreement. But O'Connor found she

couldn't join in their conviction. Repatriate? Where to? Most of them weren't Vetch citizens. Why would they be taken in there? Did they mean return them to their owners? And then she heard Vincenze's voice in her head: *Why so surprised, Eileen?* But she wasn't surprised, she realised; not at all. She was horrified.

THE FORMER OWNER of the *Baba Yaga* had been, by all accounts, a pretty vile drunk named Yershov who had used the ship for gun-running during the Vetch war. When that business had dried up, he had slowly become addicted to painkillers as his pilot implants had slowly decayed. He had also, in his feud with Delia Walker, betrayed Stella Maris to the Expansion and brought the crimopaths down on them. Yale had heard nobody say anything good about him (except Maria, but she seemed to see the good in everyone, even where there wasn't any), and now she was cursing the dead pilot herself.

She had good reason. Yershov, hired by Walker to bring the *Baba Yaga* to Stella Maris, had landed the ship bang-slap in the desert, miles from the settlement. Job done, he refused to budge the ship again. Then he'd gone and died during the crimopath attack, leaving his ship out in the open. A great ugly decaying hulk of metal, it was not hard to see on the scrubland around the settlement. Yale had done her best to conceal it over the summer months, in anticipation of the arrival of the Expansion, but the ground between them and the ship was open, and the Expansion base was nearby. There was a risk that patrols might discover them, and Yale was pretty certain that patrols from the settlement would be frequent and wide-ranging right now, on the hunt for runaways.

The ground vehicle, although a faster option, was also noisier, and liable to cause a dust storm. So, with a sinking heart, and wondering whether this was the best choice, Yale decided that they should abandon it, and make their way to the *Baba Yaga* on foot, under cover of darkness. If trouble came, they wouldn't be able to get away, and she was worried about her travelling companions: Failt would be fine, but Cassandra was... not frail, exactly, but not strong. Slight. Still, Yale admitted, as she watched the girl trudge on beside her, there was a focus about her. Determination. It certainly brought to mind Delia Walker... Yale stamped that thought down firmly. This was *not* Walker's daughter.

They took cover in the foothills overlooking the Expansion base, and Yale took the opportunity to take a closer look. It was rather bigger than she had expected. Seven ships had been seen in orbit, and she had counted at least ten shuttle craft. Was it all scientists and their kit? How many soldiers were there, exactly? Why? They hadn't needed soldiers to take the settlement, had they? By all accounts, the settlers had rolled over and let them in. So why so many? They didn't think they could use them to fight the Weird, did they? Or was there something she didn't know about, couldn't know about? There were some clever people in the Bureau. Had they come up with some means to destroy or at least cripple the Weird? Yale sighed. She knew so little, and had no means to find out. She glanced at the small pale girl hunched beside her. If she knew anything, she wasn't telling.

When night fell, they set off on the last leg of their walk. They reached the ship, squat and solid in the darkness, a little before midnight. Cassandra, with a sigh of relief, walked up the hull and patted it. "Hello, old girl," she said. "I hope you're ready for another adventure."

Failt gave a throaty laugh, sounding excited. Yale shivered; it gave her the creeps when Cassandra acted like she knew these things. Either she was a pathological liar, or... Well, the alternative was that everything she said was true, and that scared Yale even more. "Let's get on board while we can," she said. She opened the hatch and, one by one, they climbed on board.

Inside the *Baba Yaga*, there wasn't much to see: a single corridor, with the engines at one end and the flight deck at the other. The corridor had two doors on each side, which led to tiny cabins, and there were hatches below their feet that led down into the hold. They all knew the layout (Cassandra included, Yale noticed), heading straight off towards the flight deck. This, when Yale had first come on board, had been a greasy and unpleasant space, rather like its former owner. Over the summer, however, Maria had cleaned the ship from top to bottom. Yale had at first thought that it was a pointless exercise, before she realised that it was giving Maria something to do that wasn't simply grieving for her dead husband and her dead friend. Now that Yale was facing a journey on board this ship, she found herself glad of Maria's efforts. The *Baba Yaga* would never be a luxury cruiser, but she was sturdy and solid, and looked ready to enter the fray once again. More or less.

Yale took up her position in the pilot's sling. Cassandra sat down next to her and started playing with the controls. "What the hell are you doing?" Yale yelled, grabbing the girl's hand. "They'll have scanners on that base! They'll know when we power up!"

Cassandra, turning her head, gave Yale a cold, very grown-up stare. "I'm not an idiot," she said, sounding for all the world like a senior Bureau officer disappointed with an underling. "And I know how the *Baba Yaga* works. Yershov knew a trick or two. Mama watched and learned." Confidently, she worked at the controls. "Look," she said. "Shielded. We can keep an eye on them—and the settlement—quite happily. What are you looking for?"

Yale breathed out. "Ashot is going to let us know when it's kicking off at the settlement. I guess we'll see flares go up."

"We could probably see that by looking out of the window," Cassandra said dryly.

"All right," said Yale, "don't get too clever. I wouldn't mind knowing how the ships in orbit are configured, if you can manage that."

Cassandra busied herself at the controls. Yale turned to Failt, who was still hovering near the entrance to the flight deck. Yale had long had a hunch about Failt. Time to find out if she was right. She gestured to the boy to come closer, and he bounded across to stand beside her. "Right," she said. "You're to watch everything I do. But first, hold these."

She passed him two long leads, each with a jack at the end. Then, pushing her hair back from beneath her ears, she fumbled around until she found the sockets. She reached out a hand to Failt. "That one, please."

He handed her one of the long leads. Carefully, she pushed one of the jacks into place. "Wow," she said. "That packs a punch."

Failt was watching her, goggle-eyed. She reached out her hand for the other lead. "Wow," she said again, then, as soon as she had gathered her wits: "Fancy trying this one day, Failt?"

He stared at her. "You messing with me, Yale? I don't like it when you mess with me."

"I swear I'm not messing with you. Do you fancy trying this?"

"There a chance of that, Yale?"

"Maybe."

"Now you're messing with me."

"I'm not messing with you. Do you want to fly or don't you?

Failt laughed his throaty laugh. "Think I'd like to fly."

She smiled. "What you're about to see is even better than

flying, Failt. Flying has got nothing on phasing. Any idiot can fly. Flying is just flying. But this?" She reached out for the controls. "This is pure *being...*"

Failt was watching her carefully. "I'd be happy just to fly, Yale, if it's all the same with you."

"You'll see," she said. "You'll understand."

"Yale," said Cassandra, "the ships are placed equally in orbit."

"Oh, well," Yale said, "we might get through. And then again, we might not."

"What do you mean?" said Failt.

"If they'd been grouped together, we'd have stood a better chance," she said. "Got through at the farthest point away from them. With this?" She shrugged. "Chances are they've got the whole planet covered between them. Oh, what the hell. Nothing ventured."

"I think that the scanners on the base might have picked us up," said Cassandra. "Yes, they have. They know we're here, Yale. They'll be sending someone to investigate. If we're going to leave Stella Maris, we need to leave soon."

"What we need now," said Yale, "is for someone to distract them..."

There followed a tense twenty minutes. Yale used the time to get the ship—and herself—ready for phase, all the while willing Ashot to make his move. Time was of the essence. They needed to lift the ship from the surface and into phase before the ships in orbit had enough time to lay in a course to come after them. She flipped switches, coaxing the old ship back into life. "I wonder how quickly this ship can move," she said. "I wonder how *long* it will be able to move."

"She's old," Failt said, "but she did all right by us."

"We can all hope for an epitaph like that," said Yale.

Then, across the desert, the flares went up over the settlement. "Poor bastards," muttered Yale. "Oh, well. Here goes nothing."

Her hands danced across the controls. It was so long since she had flown a ship. They said it never left you, and she'd never believed that kind of thing before, but as she sat here now, working her way round the controls, she found that the reflexes began to kick in, and procedures long forgotten and unused were coming back to her. The past was always there, wasn't it? Waiting for you to summon it up, like a ghost that just wouldn't lie down and die. *But that's what I'm most afraid of, isn't it? That's what I need to watch out for...* Still, it was good to fly again, to loosen the bounds of a world, even one as free as Stella Maris. Under Yale's increasingly confident guidance, the old ship pushed up through the atmosphere. It creaked somewhat ominously around them, and then punched through into the black. Next stop, the void. Yale checked that the jacks were secure, and then fell back into the sling, feeling pulses of energy waving through into her synapses.

She felt like she was one drink short of a blistering hangover. "Christ," she said, to nobody in particular, "this is a terrible ship." Then: "Hey! Look at that. That's it! That's the void!" She laughed out loud. "Bloody hell! I think I'm going to pull this off! I didn't think I would!" She glanced at her passengers. Failt was whimpering, out of a mix of fear and sheer delight. Good kid. Cassandra, meanwhile, was silent, gripping the sides of her seat with white-knuckled hands.

"You know what, kids?" said Yale. "I'm bloody amazing. Remember that. And stick it on my bloody gravestone."

The ship lurched, terrifyingly. Failt yelped. Cassandra screamed. Yale was still laughing. Then the *Baba Yaga* burst into phase, and Yale became part of infinite space.

CHAPTER SIX

MAXINE LEE WAS working late. This in itself was not unusual: Lee was a night owl, and had reached a level of sufficient seniority at the Bureau that her superiors indulged some flexibility in her working hours. It worked out well for the Bureau: Lee was usually first in, and often last out. She had, for most of her time here, enjoyed the work (she was an information analyst), being of a cast of mind that liked looking for patterns in complex sources, and then writing reports of great clarity. So the sight of her swinging back in her chair, sipping water and nibbling at fruit and salad, was nothing new. A few of her colleagues joked that she would be there when the building was decommissioned, filing one last report about how effectively the lights had been switched off.

What was different these days was that Lee did not have the place to herself. The Bureau was on high alert, and had been ever since the portal opened on Braun's World and Delia Walker disappeared from Expansion space. Correlation was not causation, as Lee often reminded herself (and her colleagues), but surely these events—so shocking, so momentous—had to be connected in some way. Certainly her superiors thought there was some connection, and that was one of the reasons why everyone was working so hard these days, hunched over their desks and forgetting to eat.

Lee and her colleagues were now working as part of an Information Task Force, monitoring mainstream media and blacklist channels alike for discussion of the events on Braun's World. You'd think that a Weird portal opening would unite people in revulsion and horror, but that was not the case. The problem was, that someone out amongst the general population, who had not much grasp of how the Bureau worked, had also made the connection between the Weird attack on Braun's World and Walker's defection. In a mad, imaginative leap, they had come up with the crazy idea that there had *been* no portal on Braun's World, and that the whole thing had been cooked up by the Bureau to make people afraid and justify their grab for power. It was the kind of story which, if provable in court, would probably bring down a government, and end with a large number of important people behind bars.

It was, of course, nonsense. This kind of conspiracy theory was nothing new: the Expansion's ordinary citizens, without any real news sources that they could trust, had a habit of cooking up their own stories and passing them around, like infectious diseases. Usually they flared feverishly and then burned out before they could cause much trouble, but this particular story kept popping up again and again. The message from upstairs was clear: the story was a lie that had been manufactured and passed around by Delia Walker after she was fired from the Bureau, the vicious revenge of an embittered former employee. They wanted the story killed, and they were devoting resources to it. As ever, those resources were not quite enough. And so

Lee, and many of her colleagues, were stuck in the office late one beautiful spring night, tracking down the story as it turned up, and then arranging for the people spreading it to be brought in for interview—and, if necessary, a telepathic scan. It was tedious work, unrewarding, and other tasks were going neglected: Lee's console was buzzing with little red lights from messages and deadlines demanding attention.

"Oh, God," said Lanyon from the desk opposite, with a weary sigh. "Another one from the Night Watchers."

They all had particular blacklist channels that were their specific concerns, and Lanyon had drawn the short straw with the Night Watchers, a particularly unhinged bunch of "watchful and concerned citizens" who had, hitherto, been left to scream their fantasies into the dark. Last week, however, they had got their teeth into the Braun's World story, and they wouldn't let go.

"Bloody Delia Walker!" Lanyon grumbled. "I'd fire her myself if I had the chance. Out of the window. Into orbit."

Lee made a sympathetic noise. She largely felt the same way, and that was one of the great tragedies of this case, as far as she was concerned. Delia Walker had been greatly admired around the Bureau, particularly amongst the younger women. It was heartening to see a woman reach the upper ranks. She wasn't the kind to slam the door shut after her either. Many women told stories about how a conversation with Walker had led to a move away from an unhelpful superior, or a shift to more appropriate position for their talents, and so on. Delia Walker had not so much broken through the glass ceiling as smashed it with one fist and then made her enemies eat the shards. She had been tipped as the next Bureau Head, the first woman to take the role.

The news of her defection had come as something of a shock, and many people in the Bureau had taken it personally. And instead of Walker, they had got Adelaide Grant: efficient, yes, but cold. Ex-Fleet, and so a transplant into Bureau soil, rather than home-grown. Keeping them at their desks well into the night.

Lee leaned back in her chair. Lanyon was thumping at her console with one hand and snacking with the other. Lanyon snacked all day; Lee wasn't sure she had seen a bite of proper food pass the other woman's lips in weeks. Months. It was all very well doing that in your twenties, Lee thought, and she had been guilty enough in her youth, but after thirty you were asking for trouble. Lee wasn't sure that Lanyon would pass a medical at the moment. "Do you want me to go and get you something to eat, Gem?" she said.

"What? Oh, no, Maxie. No, I'm fine. I'll get this one logged and under scrutiny and then I'm going for a kip. Thanks anyway."

She wouldn't go home to rest, Lee knew. She would go up to the one of the little anonymous rooms on the ninth level—the sleep cells, they called them—and lie down on one of the cots for a few hours, and then she would come back down here and do it all over again, snacks included. A little light flashed blue on the console. Lee stood up and did some stretches. Then, in an attempt to deal with some of her backlog, she opened one of the messages that had been hanging around for a few days.

It said: *EVERYTHING YOU ARE AFRAID OF IS TRUE.*

"What?" Lee muttered.

EVERYTHING YOU ARE AFRAID OF IS TRUE.

The message flashed a few times. And then it disappeared.

Lee sat down. She looked round the room to see whether anyone was giggling: this was the kind of prank that sometimes went around the analysts' room, particularly when they were working on cases like this. But everyone was hunched over their work, frowns in place, shoulder muscles locked and forming the basis for severe lower back pain in years to come. Lee stood up again. She fiddled around with her comm, but she couldn't find the message anywhere. It had slipped away into the ether. "Gem," she said. "Have you—"

Lanyon thumped her hand against the screen. "I don't believe it! The story from the Night Watchers has been picked up! Twelve more channels. This bloody story! It just won't lie down and die. It's like a bloody Weird portal itself!"

The room went suddenly silent. Lee looked up and, to her dismay, saw, standing at the entrance to the analysts' room, imposing in an expensive dark blue suit, with her long hair swept up, Commander Adelaide Grant. She had clearly been there for some time, watchful as a spider, and had certainly heard Lanyon's last few words. Under the table, Lee kicked Lanyon's ankle. She watched as Lanyon become aware that something around her had changed. She looked back over her shoulder, and saw Grant.

"Fuck," she muttered.

"Agent Lanyon," said Grant, speaking in a clear voice across the room. "Can you repeat the last thing that you said?"

Lanyon cleared her throat. "I was just saying that the Night Watchers had been discussing the Walker story, and that twelve other channels—"

"Agent Lanyon, I asked you to repeat the *last* thing that you said."

Lanyon looked across her desk at Lee, who gave her a sympathetic look. "I... I honestly don't remember, Commander."

"Let me say it for you," said Grant. "You said, more or less, and I remove the expletives, which are inappropriate for a professional environment: 'This story won't lie down and die. It's like a Weird portal itself.' May I ask, Lanyon, do you think that the Weird are a laughing matter?"

Lanyon closed her eyes. She was exhausted; she hadn't left the building for several days and surely hadn't had a decent meal for longer than that. "No, ma'am," she said. "Not in the least. I'm sorry, ma'am, I just—"

"Just thought you'd make a joke anyway." Grant looked around the room. "Perhaps it's time for a reminder of what exactly we're fighting."

A room full of tired, overworked people looked back at her, sullenly.

"Lanyon, open the files from Braun's World. Put them up over there." Grant pointed to a big bank of screens that covered one of the far walls. "Maximum magnification, please."

And then the room full of exhausted junior civil servants sat and watched the horror of a Weird attack on a large urban centre. At the start, the mood was mutinous. After five minutes, most were in tears. After ten minutes, many had their heads in their hands or down on their desks. And, after fifteen minutes, when the footage ended, everyone in the room was defeated. Only Grant had watched the whole thing from start to finish. Lee had spent the last ten minutes doing ankle rolls and humming under her breath to block out the screams.

The screens went blank. There was a deep silence. Then Grant spoke.

"This is what we're fighting. It's not funny, not in the least. The Weird want to destroy us. And this is how they'll do it. Imagine that, here on Hennessy's World. Imagine it in Venta, or here on the Greenway itself. If they can do it, they will. And worst of all—they might be amongst us right now. There might be infection at work here in Venta right now. People serving the purpose of the Weird who don't even know it." She looked around the room thoughtfully. "There's something going on in this room I don't like," she said. "I'm bringing forward your scan schedule. You'll all be scanned again next week." A rustle of dismay went round the room, quickly smothered by Grant's stare. "If you don't like the work, people, report for relocation in the morning."

She turned and left the room. Everyone groaned. "Thanks, Lanyon," someone called.

Lee wasn't having that. Nobody had wanted to see that footage, and nobody wanted a telepathic scan—but they were mandatory, and Grant could compel them whenever she liked. As for relocation: well, minor data entry was probably very restful, but the problem was that when you had been this deep in the Bureau, you couldn't be permitted too much freedom afterwards. You ended up stuck out on one of the rim worlds with your information privileges zeroed, and a blanket ban on travel permits. You might as well just climb into the coffin and be done.

"Lay off her," Lee snapped. "We've all said things like that." She looked over her console at Lanyon. She had put her head down on her arms, and her shoulders were shuddering. "Come on, Gem," she said. "I'll finish logging those Night Watcher cases. Let's get you to bed." She stood up, glancing through habit at her console to make sure that nothing too sensitive was showing. And the message popped up again:

EVERYTHING YOU ARE AFRAID OF IS TRUE.

She slammed the cover of her console shut and went round the desk, plucking Lanyon from her chair and dragging her out of the office. They walked down the corridor to the dropchutes, and she took Lanyon up to one of the sleep cells, where she left her curled up on the bed. Then she went back downstairs to her desk. She worked on into the night, chasing her own leads and keeping up with Lanyon's. After a few hours, she thought she had done enough to mean that she wouldn't finish tomorrow any further behind where she was now. She took the dropchute herself up to the sleep cells and, after a salad and a pint of water, did some slow stretches, and then lay down on the cot and slept.

She woke ready for breakfast. She exercised, showered, drank water, and then went down the corridor in search of Lanyon. She was planning to take her down to the canteen for breakfast and make sure that she started today properly. But when she reached the sleep cell where she had deposited Lanyon the previous night, she found the door standing open and the room empty. Lee, with mounting fear, went over to the console and checked against her colleague's ID. There was no-one matching it in the building.

That was it, thought Lee. She wouldn't see Lanyon again. Perhaps it was for the best. The woman had surely been on the verge of a breakdown. Lee walked slowly down the corridor. She could only hope that someone upstairs would exercise a little judgement—if not compassion—and not give Lanyon a deep scan before sending her onto light duties somewhere. Lee wasn't convinced Lanyon would come through even a low-level scan intact.

She felt her handheld buzzing in her pocket, and sighed. The day's work was already accumulating. She lifted the handheld out and looked at the screen.

EVERYTHING YOU ARE AFRAID OF IS TRUE.
EVERYTHING YOU ARE AFRAID OF IS TRUE.
EVERYTHING YOU ARE AFRAID OF IS TRUE.

She deleted it all. There was a pause, and then:
MAXINE MAXINE MAXINE.
YOU CAN'T IGNORE THE TRUTH.
EVERYTHING YOU ARE AFRAID OF IS TRUE.

*　　*　　*

FOR AT LEAST a week after the uprising, life for the scientists still stationed at the settlement on Stella Maris remained subject to sudden disruption. The three sharp alarms would sound, and all the scientists (and the one or two remaining administrators) would dutifully leave their desks and make their way to the central building, where they would remain until they had the all-clear. They were not usually told what had caused the alarm, and they had the sense not to ask. O'Connor assumed that more runaways had been rounded up; in her darker moments, she wondered whether these interruptions were as much to keep her and her colleagues on edge and glad of the military presence.

After about a week, things began to settle down, with only the occasional interruption. But life did not go back to the way it had been when they had first arrived. The human settlers' numbers were depleted, many of their friends and neighbours now interned behind wire. With numbers down, and with no Vetch at all, the productive capacity of the settlement had been worse than halved. By necessity, they would become more and more reliant on supplies from the Expansion to bride the gap. The situation soon became clear to the settlers, leading to grudging interaction with the Expansion base, but no more than was strictly necessary. The Vetch, and the criminal humans, remained hidden behind the high fence. None of the civilians from the mission had access to them, or even caught a glimpse of them. O'Connor assumed that there were interrogations going on, or telepathic scans, but she tried to put these thoughts aside and focus on her work.

That was not as easy it sounded, not least because she was struggling now to see what she could achieve here in the settlement. Every so often, a communication would arrive from Vincenze asking after her health, and she would think about returning to join him up the base. Woodley had made it clear that the option was now open to them all, and two of their group had gone back. Then, one afternoon, Woodley came into her office, looking over her shoulder, and closed the door after her. "A quiet word?"

O'Connor nodded and waved her to a seat. "What's the matter?"

Woodley ran her hands through her hair. She looked very tired, and O'Connor's heart went out to her; the mission must have been a greater disappointment to Woodley than to any of them. "You must have guessed that we're finished here," Woodley said. "We'll never persuade the locals to tell us where the portal is now."

"Well, no," said O'Connor. "Handouts aren't going to buy their trust, only make them begrudge us more. But I'd assumed there were other plans underway?"

Woodley gave a non-committal shrug. "Between you and me," she said, "I don't think they're getting anywhere. I think," she lowered her voice, "that there's some kind of low-level telepathic field in operation. Do you know what a ferronnière is?"

O'Connor shook her head.

"It's a device that can amplify telepathic abilities. It can boost range, or allow a deeper scan. It can also help people *block* scans."

O'Connor frowned. "Surely people here wouldn't have access to such technology?"

"No," said Woodley, "but it's possible that the Weird could be able to simulate the effects. Whatever's happening, our telepaths are having no success. And they're trying, Eileen," she said, with a haunted look. "They're really trying."

O'Connor shivered at the thought of suffering a deep scan under duress—and there could be no doubt that's what was happening. No wonder the Vetch and the criminal humans were being kept out of the sight of people like her. "A telepathic field over a whole population, though? Is that even possible?"

"With the Weird? *Anything* could be possible."

"So what are we going to do? Are we going back to the base?"

"I don't know yet," Woodley said. "Inglis is keen to keep us here, for some reason known only to himself. But I, for one, don't have the stomach for it." She stood up, wearily. "I wish I'd never come," she said. "There's nothing for us here."

After she left, O'Connor sat at her desk and pondered the puzzle of the Weird. That there was some presence here was obvious: from orbit, it was clear that this was a bare world, and only the country around the settlement was fertile. Samples taken from the soil had demonstrated the presence of compounds associated with previous Weird portals. It could not be doubted that the Weird were succouring the fields in some way, nurturing them, and thereby allowing the people of Stella Maris to thrive. Until the Expansion had arrived, that was.

O'Connor put that thought aside. There was nothing she could do about that.

All she knew was that the whole time they had been here—even now—the water still flowed into the settlement.

But where did it flow *from?* She decided she would have to go and see the famous irrigation channels.

The next morning, she got permission to take one of the vehicles beyond the fence into the nearby area. She drove along the road to the edge of the farmed fields, and was startled at how suddenly the land became desert. Fertile land gave way to red rock and thin, gritty, lifeless soil. Low hills began to rise. She drove up into the foothills; standing and looking back at the settlement, the difference between the desert and the land around the settlement was startling, even in these winter months. How precarious life was on Stella Maris, O'Connor thought. How quickly this settlement would fail if the Weird ever went away. O'Connor guessed that the humans who had not stood in the way would be offered Expansion citizenship and relocated; the others would be returned to their former worlds in the Reach, or else left here. As for the Vetch... Who knew? But it would be a sad end for this unique place. O'Connor hoped that contact could still be made with the Weird, and that some kind of peace could be negotiated; but that decision was not hers, and if the Weird remained as hostile as they had been, her government would not hesitate to wipe them out entirely, if they could. One small settlement clinging on precariously at the very edge of known space would not stand in their way.

She climbed back into her vehicle. The afternoon was still beyond the conditioned air of the cabin, and she quickly dozed off. Sleep, as it so often did, let her mind work at its own pace, and when she woke, she realised what she had been missing. They had all assumed that the portal must be near the settlement, because the water seemed to arise from near the settlement. But would the Weird need to do that? Could their influence be felt at range? If so, the portal could be anywhere: it could be miles from here; even on the other hemisphere. How the hell, she thought, could they possibly find it, if that was the case?

She thought of other places where other stable Weird portals had existed alongside human populations. The people on World had had complex rituals related to their worship of the Weird; there was nothing of that here. There had been regular, physical contact with the portal, but would that have been necessary here? Did the people of Stella Maris go on pilgrimage to their portal? If that was the case, then there would be physical evidence on the land. Perhaps not roads—they didn't have the resources—but something smaller. Tracks, campsites, *something*.

She checked the time: it was getting late. She was expected

back that day, and she would cause unnecessary concern if she was late. Besides, there were still rumours of Vetch bandits roaming the countryside, and she had no desire to be out here if that was the case. She thought about what she should do next. She could still make it back to the settlement before nightfall, but the base was closer. While she was there, she could talk to Vincenze, and see what he thought of her ideas. It was her instinct as a scientist: to shape the hypothesis as quickly as she could, to work with someone else to bring it into focus, testing for flaws in the premise, developing ways in which it could be tested. She started the vehicle, and sped off towards the base.

It rose above the rough land as she approached, solid against the stark countryside. At the gates, she was stopped by the guards, who checked her identification and waved her through. She left the vehicle at the central pool and hurried through the base, eager to see Vincenze. He would be glad, surely, to know that there was still a chance of finding the portal. Behind his cynicism and pomposity, she knew that in his heart, he wanted to see peace between humanity and the Weird.

The workspaces were empty and silent, but that didn't strike her as odd; it was quite late in the day, and even this dedicated team needed to stop to rest every so often. Reaching Vincenze's workspace, she hammered on the door.

"Paul! Paul!"

No answer. She tried the handle, but the door was locked. She frowned.

"O'Connor!" someone called from down the corridor. She turned and saw Mackay, another of her colleagues, heading towards her. Her heart sank. She didn't like him much, and she certainly didn't want him hanging around when she wanted to talk to Vincenze.

"Why are you here?" Mackay said. "Have you heard?"

"Heard what? Where's Paul? I want to talk to him."

Mackay frowned. "So you haven't heard."

"Haven't heard what?"

Mackay put a finger to his lips. With a shock, O'Connor realised that he was white-faced and obviously very frightened. "Keep your voice down," he said. "Paul... They came for him three days ago."

"Came for him? Who?"

"Who do you think? The soldiers. They came to his lab around midday. Took him off. The next morning..." He stopped and rubbed his hand across his eyes. "Eileen, they shot him. Paul's dead."

"You want to go to Hennessy's World?" Yale sat up in her sling. Cassandra was lying back comfortably in her seat, her hands resting upon her lap, as if she had no idea what was involved in the request she had just made.

"Yes," Cassandra said, "and quickly. We've wasted too much time already."

"Yes, and you're wasting *my* time. Cassandra, what do you know about Hennessy's World?"

Cassandra tilted her head down and to the side, that odd movement she sometimes made, as if she was listening to something. "Well," she said slowly, "it's the central world of the Expansion, isn't it? Mostly water, but there are thousands and thousands of islands. Archipelagos. The capital of the Expansion is there. It's called..." She tilted her head again. "Venta. It's where the Council and Parliament meet. It's where the headquarters of the Bureau are located."

Yale stared at her. "How the hell do you know about the Bureau?"

Cassandra laughed. "Everyone knows about the Bureau!"

That was true, Yale thought, but what Cassandra said next wasn't generally known.

"There's a huge building on an island," the girl said. "It goes down and down and down underwater, and on the very lowest level there's a big room where the senior staff meet and make all the decisions that really matter. The Council doesn't really run things in the Expansion, and neither does Parliament. The Bureau does, from here, deep, deep underwater. The walls are see-through and you can look out into the ocean." She laughed girlishly. "The fish are funny!"

Yale's skin was crawling. Delia Walker would know these things, of course. Delia Walker had been as deep inside the Bureau as it was possible to get. She pulled herself together and said, "If you know all this, then you'll know that getting to Hennessy's World is more or less impossible. You don't have any documentation. Neither do I, and neither does he." She nodded at Failt, who was sitting cross-legged next to her sling, listening to this conversation closely. "There's more surveillance on one square mile of Hennessy's World than there is on whole planets outside the central worlds. You can't get in and you can't get out—"

Failt piped up. "Missus Dee got out. On this very ship." He patted the gunmetal floor. "The *Baba Yaga* can do it. The *Baba Yaga* did do it."

"Maybe, but I've no idea how," said Yale. "I suspect that drunken pilot she brought with her had a trick or two up his sleeve." She thought about what she'd learned about the pilot, Yershov, from listening to Maria. A gunrunner during the Vetch wars, and before the tech in his head had started to decay. The kind of person who knew how to slip unnoticed out of tight corners. "Anyway, that was getting out. Even someone like your pilot could get out. Getting in?" She shook her head. "You don't just turn up on Hennessy's World. You need passports, documents, sponsors. You need to be an Expansion citizen. You need to be on the books." She laughed. "I've never seen two people who look less kosher than you two."

"How about you?" Cassandra said. "Aren't you 'on the books'?"

Yale looked her. Cassandra was staring at her as if she trying to read what was going on inside her head. "If you're trying to scan me," said Yale, roughly, "stop it. Stop it now!"

Cassandra shook her head. "I can't read you," she said. "Not without really hurting you. And I wouldn't do that." She thought about that for a moment. "Not unless I was desperate."

"Oh, well, that's a relief! Don't try to scan me. Don't *ever* try to scan me."

"All right," said Cassandra, sulkily. "I won't."

Failt laid a paw on Cassandra's knee and said, "I'll help you, sister Cass. If you want to go to Hennessy's World, we'll find a way."

"Failt," said Yale, "there's no way you'll get to Hennessy's World. You're Vetch!"

He shook his head, sending his long tentacles twitching. "Doesn't matter. If sister Cass wants to go, I have to her help her."

"I want to go," said Cassandra. "I *have* to go." She smiled at Failt. "Failt and I will find a way."

Yale rubbed her temples. Her head was still sore from the jump into phase and her mind was still reeling from the glimpse of the void that she'd seen. She had no doubt that Cassandra would try to get to Hennessy's World: she was smart, that was clear, and certainly she was determined, and she clearly knew things that most people in the Expansion didn't. But she was very young, and between her and the Expansion lay Satan's Reach, the lawless space where the vulnerable became prey. Failt was smart too, and canny, but there were people in the Reach smarter and cannier, and who would look at these two and see an opportunity to make money. And if they made it across the Reach, what then? How would they cross the border into the Expansion? Since the Weird attacks, it was surely more policed than ever before. "It would help me," Yale said, "if you told me *why* you want to go to Hennessy's World."

Cassandra dropped her head, and her long, fair hair covered her face. After a moment, she looked up. "We'll find a way," she said.

"In other words, you're not telling."

"I don't *know!*"

Failt hissed quietly.

Yale sighed and leaned back in her sling. What could she do? Cassandra was like a force of nature—she'd got Yale to leave Stella Maris, hadn't she? But there were forces out there stronger even than a teenage girl, and Cassandra didn't have a clue about them. Everything that was good in Yale said that she couldn't—*shouldn't*—abandon these two children. But Yale had her limits, and the border between the Reach and the Expansion was one of them. Unhappily, she said, "There are plenty of stations on the border. I can take you to one of those. Shuloma Station is the biggest."

Failt and Cassandra looked at each other. "Not Shuloma Station," said Failt. "We made enemies there on our way through."

"Not Shuloma," said Yale. "All right. We'll find another. And once we're there, I'll help you find passage into the Expansion. But it won't be easy, Cassandra. It might not be possible for you, and it's certainly not possible for Failt—"

"We have to find a way."

"Yes," said Failt. "We'll find a way." He looked at Yale thoughtfully. "Why the border?" he said. "Why won't you go any further?"

She didn't answer. "If you want to see me set a course, Failt, you should come and watch." He padded over, and watched her hands dance over the controls.

"So where are we going?"

She sighed. "Well, Shuloma was the obvious place—anything can be bought there. But since we can't go there, we're going to try Capital Station."

"Capital Station?"

"It's nice. Like a luxury hotel. Comfortable. We won't get hassled."

"Sounds good to me."

She set the course, talking him through the process, and then she got out of the sling. "I'm going to get some sleep," she said, rubbing the back of her neck. "Forgotten how much phasing takes it out of you. You two should get some sleep, too. It's a long time before we get there." She hesitated at the door. "I know you know more than you're letting on, Cassandra," she said, "but please don't muck around with the controls. We're going to Capital Station, I promise. Once we get there, we'll think about how to get you across the border."

The girl gave her a curt nod. Yale left, and headed towards the cabins. She was aware of Failt padding after her, to get some sleep himself, she assumed, but when she reached her cabin door, he stopped too, and hung around. "Did you want something, Failt?"

"Why won't you come with us, Yale? Why won't you go into Expansion space?"

She sighed. "I can't tell you that, Failt. It's much better that you don't know. The fact is I'd be a liability." She studied him. "You know you can't go with her, don't you?"

His tentacles tensed, curling upwards, giving him a sulky air. "I'm going anyway."

"You can't," she said. "You wouldn't get across the border. They'll arrest you, and they'll torture you."

His big eyes bulged at her. "Torture me?"

"Because you're Vetch. Because you're connected to Walker—they'll find that out. And then they'll torture you because you're with her daughter—if she *is* her daughter—and then they'll torture you some more because some of them are sick bastards and they like making people scream. Anyway, they'll find out everything about her. I'd be a liability, and you'd be a liability."

"All the more reason to go with her," he said. "So they don't harm her."

Loyalty was one thing, stupidity another. "Why are you so sure that this is Delia Walker's daughter, Failt?"

"Looks like her. Smells like her, too."

"Okay..." She forgot, sometimes, that Vetch could read smell the way a human could read body language.

"She knows what she wants. Missus Dee was like that."

Yale looked at him thoughtfully. "You really do miss her, don't you?"

He looked at her sadly. His tentacles hung slack, disconsolately. "More than anything, Yale. She saved my life. I hid here, on this ship. Yershov, that bloody bastard—he wanted to throw me out into space. She wouldn't let him." He gave a low cackle of laughter. "She was his boss, no mistake! She saved my life. Didn't have to; nobody cared about my life before. But Missus Dee did. Yes, she was hard and she could be mean—I'm not stupid! I could see that! She made poor Hecate come with us when she didn't want to. But she was on the right side. She wanted us all to live in peace and harmony. And that one"—he twitched his head towards the flight deck—"that's her girl. My sister, sister Cass. Missus Dee knows what she's doing, Yale. If Cass needs to get to the Expansion, there's a good reason. So I'll help her. She's famblee."

Yale looked at the boy. She liked him and trusted him, even if she thought he was deluded. Perhaps there was no trap here, no scheme—just loyalty and the desire to do the right thing. But the past was the past, and Yale would not—could not—go into Expansion space. "All right. We'll go to Capital Station, and I'll try to help you both go on." She looked guiltily at him. "But that will have to be goodbye."

Rather sweetly, he patted her hand with his hairy paw. "That's all right, Yale. If you can't come with us, you can't. And back on Stella Maris—they'll need you, won't they? They'll need the *Baba Yaga*."

"Yes, they need me. I'm pushing my luck, you know, going as close to the Expansion as Capital Station. And you need to ask yourself too, Failt—what help would you be to Cassandra in Expansion space? Or would you only cause her trouble?"

He blinked at her with his big, goggly eyes.

"Sometimes, Failt, it's better to let people go."

CHAPTER SEVEN

IN THE WEEK following the *Baba Yaga*'s departure from Stella Maris, Maria found she had little time to reflect upon the departure of her friends, or to worry about what they were doing. A single, crackling communication had been received from the *Baba Yaga*, as it reached orbit around Stella Maris. After that, there had been nothing. Perhaps the Expansion ships had come immediately afterwards, blasting the little ship to smithereens. Perhaps Yale's old implants had faltered, and they were now stuck in the void, doomed to a lifetime of wandering the grey space. Perhaps the old ship, after so long on the ground, had not been flightworthy after all, and had slowly crumbled, or come down on a hostile world in the Reach. Or perhaps they were safely sailing towards whatever destination Cassandra had chosen. Maria had no way of finding out, and so she couldn't let herself worry. She had more than enough to worry about.

Each day seemed to bring more runaways to the sanctuary in the mountains. By the end of week, the group was about thirty strong. Most of the new arrivals were Vetch, but a handful were human. Amongst them was a telepath, and Maria and Ashot fell upon her. She went every few days up to the portal, to try to contact the Weird, to elicit some response or receive some aid. But each time she came back sad and disappointed. The portal remained implacably shut.

There was little in the way of good news from any quarters. One of the humans, a young man from the long-house adjacent to the one where Maria had found a home, thought that the settlement's days were numbered.

"Before I left—before the uprising—the humans were offered citizenship by the Expansion authorities. They said they would provide safe passage: documentation, transport, the promise of a home and work at the other end." He looked around sadly. "I think a few people were tempted."

The Vetch growled and muttered amongst themselves. Clearly no such offer had been made to them.

"How many?" asked Maria.

"Nobody from our long-house, I'm glad to say," said the young man. He eyed the Vetch worriedly. "But some of the other houses are discussing it. They say that whatever Stella Maris provided in the past, those days are over. A lot of people were saying that Stella Maris will never be the same again. The Expansion are here and they want the portal; and as long there's a chance of getting it, they will never leave. There'll be more ships, more scientists, more soldiers... People have been saying that Stella Maris is never going back to the way it was, that we should take what we can, while we can. Because the Expansion aren't going to share the portal. At some point, they'll move us on anyway, and they won't care where we go."

Isilt snorted. "Didn't take you people long, did it?"

"What do you mean?" said the young man.

"Humans aren't to be trusted," she said. "Happy to be friends as long as times are good. But soon as there's trouble—we're on their own."

The young man quivered with anger. "That's not true!"

"And what has been happening to us while this offer has been made?" Isilt's tentacles were shaking in rage. "We've been rounded up, pulled from our homes, locked up. Who is going to offer us 'citizenship'? Who is going to offer us work? Many of us *can't* leave Stella Maris. We were slaves—bought and sold! If we're forced to leave, we will have nowhere to go. People in the Reach will gladly take money to return us to our masters. They'll take us and make us suffer for running away. Do you know what happens to runaway slaves on some worlds? Do you know what could happen to us?"

"I know!" said the young man. "I was a slave too! Why do you think I'm here? It's the same for many of us—I don't believe a word these people say! Expansion citizenship?" He spat on the ground. "We'll find ourselves dumped on some border world and left to get on with it. We'll have to throw ourselves on the mercy of anyone who can take us—and that means selling ourselves, our bodies. We'll be bonded again before we know it! And what about the children, the old people? Who will take care of them?"

Isilt looked ready to carrying on arguing, but Ashot intervened. "That's enough," said. "Isilt, I understand your anger, but this doesn't help us. All we do is serve the purposes of the Expansion. They want us divided." He turned to Maria. "What do you think? Do you believe this offer?"

Maria was surprised. She knew that many on Stella Maris still regarded her with suspicion, and that not a few blamed her for the arrival of the Expansion. "Does it matter what I think?"

Ashot's strange face twisted in what Maria had come to recognise was a smile. "Of course it matters. You know the Expansion better than any of us—for better or worse."

Maria thought about this. She had been happy in her old life, of course, and she knew that given the chance, she would have remained where she was—Kit's wife, Jenny's mother, happy to watch her husband progress and her child grow. She hadn't wanted to leave Expansion space; she'd been forced. But would she go back now, knowing what she knew?

"I don't believe a word they say," she said. "Or rather, perhaps they mean what they say right now, because it suits them. But if it became expedient for the Expansion to sell every soul on Stella Maris back into slavery, they would do it without a shot. They would probably do it to their own people, if the need was there."

She looked around the people gathered here—not even three dozen people, frightened, hungry and cold—who had discovered that their friends could not be relied upon in need. She thought, *I don't need to frighten them more. They're frightened enough. I have to give them something to do...*

"I know you have no reason to trust me. You must be thinking—she's from the Expansion too! And I won't lie to you—I would have stayed there, and I'd be there right now, at home, with my husband and my little girl, if I'd had the choice. But they took that choice away from me, and I ended up here. You have all been good to me, better than I deserve. I know it's mostly been for Jenny's sake, really, and Failt's. Who wouldn't do anything for Failt?"

There was a ripple of gentle laughter across the whole group. *I might pull this off yet...*

"Failt worried about us all, you know," she said. "He was worried that while the Weird were no longer talking to us, we no longer had the bond that kept us all together. He worried that we would no longer be able to live in peace and harmony. Well, he's been right so far, I'm sad to say. So here's what I think.

We have to prove him wrong. He's gone now, gone on the *Baba Yaga*, but he'll be back, I know it. He said he'd come back. And I want him to come back to peace and harmony. Not to anger and disappointment. Peace and harmony."

She stopped speaking. She felt Ashot behind her, and she was glad of his solid support.

"I think Maria is right," he said. "Look around you. Look how few of us there are. Thirty? Thirty-three? Out of three thousand people. There are hardly any of us! We've all us been harmed, and I know that we've all got excellent reasons to mistrust each other. But that way lies death. We must trust each other."

"What shall we do?" someone called out. "What do we do, Maria?"

"I don't know, yet," said Maria. "I think we have some decisions to make. But most of all I think we have to learn how to live together again."

"So," said Ashot, "here we are. We've been conquered, without even realising what was happening. To all intents and purposes, our friends and families are enslaved again, and the rest of us—down here—are the only free people left on Stella Maris. For some, the situation is more critical than for others." His eyes darkened in fear, and Maria had to wonder what lay in his past. "Some of us know that there are people out there willing to return us to bondage, and punish us for the temerity of believing that we could we free. Others, down at the settlement, have perhaps not yet realised the danger they are in. So what do we do? Do we talk to our brothers and sisters back at the settlement? Do we try to persuade them of the danger they are in? Is this easy to do? The Vetch amongst us cannot return to the settlement without being imprisoned. But can humans slip in and out?"

The young man who had quarrelled with Isilt shook his head. "I wouldn't go back. We've all been logged and tagged—I had to cut out my chip before leaving." He showed them the bandage on his arm.

"People are afraid," said another of the humans. "So many of us were slaves, once upon a time. It's not easy to put that aside when faced with guns."

"I think," said one of the Vetch, recently arrived, "that they have even shot some of their own number. When we were passing through the desert, we heard weapons fire in the night. In the base."

"It could have been practice," someone else pointed out.

"But we can well believe that they would turn on themselves," Ashot said.

"If it serves their purposes, they won't stop at shooting any of us," said Maria. "I won't make that mistake again."

There was silence. After a little while, Ashot gently prompted her. "What do we need to do, Maria?"

Maria stared at the ground. How had she ended up here, on this world? She was nobody special. She was Jenny's mum. All she had wanted was to live in peace with her little family. And now this place, where she had begun to construct some kind of replacement for her lost life—now this was under threat. But what could they do? There were no weapons on Stella Maris other than those brought by the Expansion. What could they do, in the face of that? Nothing.

But here, tonight, she could take heart again. This discussion, right here—this was like the old Stella Maris, the one where people pulled together, heard each other's views and tried to accommodate them. Whatever was happening at the settlement, all that was good about Stella Maris was still alive right here. Despite the losses, and the betrayals, and without any need of the Weird to make them pull together. This, Maria thought, was worth keeping. Worth defending.

"What do we do?" She looked Ashot straight in the eye. Her friend; her ally. "We have to find a way to fight, don't we? Because if we don't fight for ourselves, who will do it for us?"

There were a few mutters around the refuge: "How do we do that?" "How can we?" "What can we do against the Expansion?"

"We can make it not worth their while to stay," said Ashot. "That, we can surely do."

"Here's what I think we need to do," Maria said. "Protect the portal. Fight back. And most of all—most of all—stay free."

LEE WAS BACK in her apartment trying to sleep when the message came again. "Shut up!" she hissed at the handheld. "Whoever you are—shut up! Go away! I don't want to know!"

It had to be a joke. One of her colleagues, trying to freak her out. But it hadn't been funny before Lanyon had been zeroed, and it was even less funny now. Lee was tired, and unhappy, and she wanted to sleep. But here she was, lying in the darkness, thinking: *What am I afraid of?* With a sigh, she rolled over in her bed, and tried to put some order to her thoughts.

She was afraid of the Weird, of course: who wasn't? The idea that such horror could erupt from nowhere and consume everything in their path was horrible. But the idea of the Weird was so huge, so abstract, and so impossible to prepare for, that you had to put it out of your mind or you wouldn't be able to function. Perhaps that explained some of what drove Adelaide Grant. It was her job to live with the thought of what the Weird could do every second of the day. Yes, Lee thought, that would explain a great deal about Grant.

So what else was Lee afraid of? The usual: sickness, pain, poverty. The latter wasn't such a problem for someone like her, Lee knew. The Bureau wouldn't let her go. And that was something else to be afraid of: Lanyon's fate; being zeroed; finding herself exiled from the centre, sent away from Hennessy's World to some backwater to sit for the rest of her life monitoring shipping traffic. Would that be so bad? She shook herself. Of course it would. Being zeroed was a punishment for mistakes made and weaknesses shown. They didn't send you to garden paradises for a quiet retirement. They sent you to polluted mining worlds, or struggling farm worlds, and they left you there to rot.

But these were the kinds of fears that everyone had, or everyone that Lee worked with. This message, this had been for her, and her specifically. *MAXINE MAXINE MAXINE...* So what was *she* afraid of? She, Maxine Lee, twice middle-distance women's champion at college, and still a fine runner (whenever she got the chance), excellent vegetarian chef (again, whenever she got the chance), and above all, a very tired, stressed, frightened, and, yes, somewhat paranoid junior information analyst information at the Bureau...

Her handheld buzzed again. "Oh, bloody hell!" she cried. "Leave me alone!"

She picked up the device to delete the message, but it was something quite different. Confirmation of her appointment for a telepathic scan, in two days' time. Bloody Adelaide Grant. She'd said she'd do it, and she had. Talk about micro-management. And to send it out in the middle of the night, too. Couldn't she leave her exhausted operatives alone to struggle with their job?

That was something else Maxine Lee was afraid of. That her mind wasn't her own. That battling the Weird, even as small as the battle she fought from her desk, was already pointless, because they were already here, inside her head, and worming their way in deeper and deeper, splitting her apart as she fought, on some subconscious level, to stop them taking her mind and making it their own. And even if she was free of infection, she was afraid—she was terrified—that she was the only one, and that everyone around was already infected, serving a different master, and looking at her through cold Weird eyes that saw her only as a threat... Yes, thought Lee, sitting up in a cold sweat. She was afraid of that. So that was that what the message meant? That she was infected?

The handheld buzzed again. She read the message.

ARE YOU FRIGHTENED YET? YOU SHOULD BE.

"You bastards."

YOU SHOULD BE FRIGHTENED, MAXINE LEE.

"Wait till I get my hands on you. I'll give you frightened—"

DO YOU WANT ANSWERS TO YOUR QUESTIONS?

"Of course I do!"

COME.

A new message arrived, contained directions to... what? A drop-off? A rendezvous? There was a place, and a date, and a time. Later that night. Typical. Caught between Grant and whoever was playing this sick game, Lee hauled herself wearily off the bed.

She followed the directions to the letter. This took her on a rambling journey around several of the inner islands and, at last, by foot, along some pretty odorous canals. Eventually, she found herself walking down a dark alley, where, eventually, she found herself looking at a wall. And that was where the directions stopped. She was at a literal dead end.

She thumped her hand against the wall. "You bastards!" she muttered. "You fucked-up, time-wasting, thoughtless bastards!"

She stood there for a while, staring at the wall, and contemplating ways in which she would punish her tormentor, if she ever got a chance. Eventually, she realised what she was looking at. On the wall, someone had painted an arrow, pointing down.

Lee looked down. There, by her foot, was a tiny datapin.

She reached down and picked it up, turning it round her fingers. Her handheld buzzed. The message said: *YOU TOOK YOUR TIME.*

"Ha-bloody-ha," she muttered, as she shoved the pin into the socket on her handheld. Letters and figures and symbols scrolled past, and Lee was experienced enough to know quickly that she couldn't decrypt it herself. She needed an expert. The good news—the only good news in what had otherwise been a remarkably shitty day—was that she knew one.

Mercy Grey.

Lee left the alley and headed back down to the shuttle stop on the pier. Mercy Grey was an old friend from college, one of those brilliant but fragile people who were never going to fit into what was laughably called the real world. She lived at the top of a ramshackle building on a small island in one of the outer suburbs, which required at least three separate boats to get to, even when you weren't starting from the back of beyond. Mercy had come to Hennessy's World from a backwater planet to study mathematics, with a side interest in encryption, without a penny in her pocket. In her first year she had invented something that Lee didn't even pretend to understand, but which had made Mercy very rich and, not incidentally, of huge interest to a number of powerful and influential people.

Once she'd graduated and polished off her doctorate in the time that it had taken Lee to complete her first degree, Mercy had bought this building, on this quiet island, and perched herself at the top, a lofty but generous landlady to the tenants below, who quietly made sure that she ate and washed and went outside sometimes. It was a responsibility that Lee had taken upon herself at college, and, when she took her job at the Bureau, Lee had surrendered her brilliant, if unusual, friend to their care with relief. She'd long made it a point to visit Mercy once a month and take out her for a walk, but in recent months, the pressure of work had meant she'd missed a few visits.

When Mercy opened the door, she was frowning. "What? What do you want now?"

"Hi, Mercy. How've you been?"

"How do you think I am? I'm no different—"

"Mercy," Lee said, as she weaved her way inside. "I haven't seen you in three months. Look," she said, lifting up the bags she was carrying. "Supper."

Mercy closed the door, turned, and blinked. "Huh. I was sure we'd just spoken. Oh, never mind. How are you, Maxie?"

"Fine, fine," Lee lied. She went over to the table, and started dishing out the rice and curry she'd brought with her. Mercy sat down, fork in hand, and started eating voraciously when the plate was in front of her. Lee (given the chance) loved to cook. Mercy saw food as fuel. As Lee leisurely ate seconds, Mercy filled her in on the work she'd been doing over the past few months. Lee listened happily and understood about a quarter.

Then Mercy said, "All right, Maxie. What's the problem?"

"Hmm?"

"You look tired, and you don't look well. You, of all people. You're an advert for healthy living. You're not allowed to look tired and unwell. So what's going on?"

Lee thought for a while. "A lot of things."

"Well, it must be something. Although really," said Mercy thoughtfully, "you've not been the same since..." She stopped, as if thinking better of what she had been about to say. "Well, since."

Lee started to gather up the plates. There had been three of them at college, all friends together. And now there were two. "Actually," she said, "what's worrying me is that I think someone is trying to embroil me in a conspiracy theory, and that I have a telepathic scan at work in two days' time that I think might result in me being sent to a mining world, never to see the sunlight on Venta again."

Mercy took the pile of plates from her and threw them into the sink, where no doubt they would languish until the next time her cleaner came. "Yes," she said, "I can see how that might be a worry. A conspiracy theory, huh?" She smiled. "I love that kind of thing."

"Be my guest." Lee reached into her pocket, and handed over the datapin. As Mercy examined it, Lee explained, in laconic terms, how she had come by it.

Mercy gave a snort of laughter. "Well, they're doing it with some panache, you've got to admit."

"If they've something to tell me," said Lee, "I'd prefer less stylish panache and more concrete information."

But Mercy was already becoming absorbed in the datapin. "I can get this done tonight," she said. "If you *want* to know what's on it tonight."

"What do you mean?"

"Well, you might want to wait till the scan is done before you start filling your head with anything potentially incriminating."

Lee sighed. Obvious, really. Yes, she was tired.

"In the meantime," said Mercy, "I think you should go home, get some rest, and try not to worry about it. Maybe go for a walk or a swim. A run, I'd suggest."

Lee smiled. "You're stealing my best lines."

Mercy looked up and smiled. "Go home. And here"—she reached into her own pocket and pulled out some tablets—"these will come in handy."

Lee shook her head. "I don't pop pills, Mercy. You know that."

"No? A shame. Not only do these help you sleep, they can also help block a telepath."

Lee looked at the packet of pills. They looked like ordinary painkillers. "No way."

"Honestly. I got them from a man who knows about these things. I hate telepaths. I hate the *idea* of telepaths. I hate that I might be going about my business, and there's some telepath passing by, having an idle rummage in my head—"

"That's not really how it works, Mercy."

"So they'd like us to believe. Trust me. Put one of these in your mouth before you go into the office," Mercy said. "Pop it just before the scan. It should work."

"*Should* work?"

Mercy was playing with the datapin. "Nothing in this world is certain."

O'CONNOR STAYED ONE night at the base, and left early the next morning for the settlement, her life transformed. The news of Vincenze's death preceded her, and her friendship with him seemed to mark her in some way, like a leper's bell. She was now suspect, in some way not entirely clear to her; whatever was sticking might too easily be passed on. Palmer seemed to make excuses not to spend time with her, and these days Woodley was barely to be seen.

It suited O'Connor down to the ground. She worked alone, poring over the few maps the mission had made, and sending requests up to the ships in orbit to capture more aerial images of the planet.

One bright morning, nearly two months after the Expansion had arrived on Stella Maris, O'Connor left the settlement. Her efforts had revealed a wide river some distance from the settlement and, beyond that, a range of mountains. Her study of the aerial maps, scant as they were, had also revealed what seemed to her to be paths—nothing as grand as paved roads, but what she believed might be tracks over the river and up into the mountains. O'Connor intended to drive out this way and see what she could find.

She did not announce the purpose of her mission in so many words. She said simply that she wanted to go and see first-hand some of the area that she had mapped. Woodley was happy with her going; Inglis took some more convincing to release the vehicle she needed, and there was some discussion as to whether or not the area was free of Vetch. She agreed to take her handheld, so that she could send for help if she hit any difficulty, and be located if the need arose. She tried not to think about what would happen if some Vetch did find her out in the wild. She was surely unlikely to survive long enough for any help to arrive.

On the morning of her departure she looked around to say goodbye to Palmer, but she could not find her anywhere. She was disappointed—she would have liked to grieve for Vincenze with someone—but Palmer was still avoiding her, and O'Connor was not entirely sure why. Sometimes, she knew, if people revealed too much of what mattered to them, they had to withdraw in order to save face. O'Connor was sorry that the friendship was drawing to a close, but it was not in her power to force Palmer to talk to her, and so she had to be content to leave matters as they were. Still, she would have liked to have seen a friendly face.

Once she was on the road, she felt a great weight lift from her shoulders. The death of Vincenze had hit hard, and there had been nobody willing or able to answer her questions. Woodley, in fact, had come to see her and told her straight that she should put what had happened behind her. "He's dead," she said. "He was a clever man, but he wasn't clever enough not to hide his dislike of the military. That wasn't just stupid, it was suicidal."

"You can't just shoot someone for saying they don't like you!"

"Eileen," said Woodley, softly, "that is *exactly* what they can do."

Woodley had not said goodbye to her either. Vincenze would have. O'Connor did not know, she realised, whether he had been religious or not; she doubted it. Neither was she, despite her mother's best efforts. But as she drove along, she found a few fragments in her memory from her childhood, and she prayed for the repose of the soul of Paul Vincenze.

She reached the river late in the afternoon. She was, if she had only known, taking the same route that Delia Walker had taken, almost a year ago, when she had gone up into the mountains searching for the Weird portal, chased by crimopaths. At the river, O'Connor found puzzles: a ruined bridge, a makeshift crossing. She forded the river and headed for the feet of the mountain range. Here she decided to leave her vehicle behind, and walk the rest of the way. She spent one last night sleeping in its warmth, and started her walk up through the pass early the next day. There was a pathway here; not much used, but clear enough. Well into the afternoon, the path came to an end, near the entrance to a cavern. She peered in and saw a dark, narrow passageway snaking away into the mountain. She took a deep breath, and then walked inside.

The passage was narrow, just wide enough for one. O'Connor proceeded slowly. She could hear nothing other than her own breathing, but couldn't shake the sense of being watched. Superstition, she chided herself; foolishness. She was the most alone she had ever been. At length, the passageway opened out into a wide cavern. She stepped inside, gazing around in awe at the huge, cathedral-like space. And then she saw what was lying shimmering before her. The Weird portal, mirrored as glass, and silent.

She stood for a while in awe, like someone who has come suddenly to a sacred grove in the woods, and found the shrine of some ancient god. She had seen footage of other portals, and she had been expecting the same kinds of horrors: the blood-clotted surfaces, rippling, suggestive of something alive but incomprehensible and voracious beneath—but this was still. It gave nothing away.

After a while staring into its mirrored surface, O'Connor came back to herself. She walked around the edge of the portal as far as she was able, taking pictures on her handheld and taking readings. Ultimately, however, the place was too eerie for her to stay there very long. When she came back out onto the mountainside, the light was disappearing. She put as much distance as she could between her and the cavern, walking in darkness for some time. At last, she made camp.

When she had eaten, she lay looking up at the starry sky, sleepless and excited. She kept sitting up to examine the images she had taken, terrified and compelled at this glimpse even of the silent Weird. Most of all, she was awed. The portal, the gateway to another dimension. She had found it, had *seen* it.

So what next? Here, away from everything, in the peace and silence of this alien night, she could admit to herself that Paul Vincenze's death had frightened her in a way that nothing ever had before. Whatever her dead friend might have said, O'Connor was not a fool. She knew she lived in a policed state; like many others, she accepted it as the price she paid to carry out her work in peace. Out in Satan's Reach, murder and slavery were commonplace; the weak suffered at the hands of the strong; people were prey and targets. Not so in the Expansion. Fleet protected the borders; the Bureau protected the interior; and everyone else, more or less, got on with their safe, comfortable lives. As long as you stayed within the law, as long as you kept your job, you weren't bothered, on the whole. Yes, the politicians were on the make—but that was true of all times and all places. But they kept enough money moving around that ordinary people did not suffer unnecessarily from disease or want. This had always seemed a reasonable enough bargain to O'Connor—until now. All that Paul Vincenze had done was to show less than complete enthusiasm, and that, it seemed, had been enough to sign his death warrant. She should choose carefully who to tell about the portal...

She woke abruptly, filled with fear. She was sure she had heard something move. Animals, perhaps? She knew very little of the fauna of this world. Perhaps, she thought in horror, the portal was waking. Perhaps even now the Sleer were growing, forming, getting ready to creep down the passageway and find her...

The reality was somewhat prosaic, if still frightening. Two Vetch loomed suddenly in front of her. She thought she recognised one of them, but before she could place him, someone slipped up behind her. She thrashed about in their grasp and cried out, but her arms were grabbed and a cover was put over her head. A rough Vetch voice said, "Be quiet! There's nobody here to help, and you'll only hurt yourself if you struggle! We will not harm you, but you are coming with us!"

She decided the best thing to do was obey, for now, and try to find a way out later. They evidently weren't about to kill her.

She let herself be led—uphill, it seemed—until eventually they passed inside, judging from the change in the quality of sound, and came to a halt. "We're going to take the cover off your head now," said the Vetch. "Try not to do anything stupid."

The cover came off and O'Connor blinked. She was in a large cave, and all around her people were gathered—about thirty, she reckoned. She looked round fearfully. There were humans here, but there were Vetch too, and that made her scared. Were these escapees from the settlement? She thought everyone was accounted for. "I don't know who you all are," O'Connor said, "but I am a citizen of the Expansion—"

One of the humans moved forwards. She was young, younger than O'Connor, but she seemed tired, as if she had lived through a great deal, and recently. "I'm a citizen of the Expansion, too," she said, and shrugged. "It makes no difference. If they found me, they'd murder me, and my little girl, the way they murdered my husband."

O'Connor stared at her. "Who are you?" she said.

"My name's Maria," the woman said. "You won't have heard of me. I'm not anybody special. I didn't work for anyone important, and I didn't do anything important. I was a wife and mother. I'm still a mother, but not a wife. My husband was in Fleet. And then he had to run away, and he died, and the people who killed him came after me."

"Your husband went AWOL? Well, no wonder he was chased. That could be considered treason, given our state of near war with the Weird—"

"And perhaps it might have been, if it had ever come to a court-martial. They killed him first, though. The last thing they wanted was Kit in front of a court-martial." Maria shook her head. "I'm not here to talk about that. I want to know who you are, and why you're here, up in the mountains. I hope you'll answer me. Many of these Vetch are eager to get their hands on you, after all that's happened."

O'Connor shuddered. "You don't need to threaten me. I'm happy to answer your questions. My name is Eileen O'Connor. I'm here with the scientific expedition from the Expansion. We're came to look for the Weird portal, to study it and explore it, and with luck to communicate with it."

"You know about the previous mission?" asked Maria. "I experienced it at first hand. My adopted son was shot and wounded by one of that team."

O'Connor looked at the faces around her. Some were angry, some were impassive, but all were suspicious. "Look," she said, "I know nothing about that. I'm a scientist. I'm here to learn about the Weird. If there's a chance we can communicate, there's a chance we might be able to stop a terrible war."

One of the Vetch stepped forwards. "I know you," he said. "You were one of the people running the clinic at the settlement."

She blinked at him. Had they met? All the Vetch looked so similar to her: frightening, and so fierce. "Yes," she said. "I helped set up the clinic."

"Were you one of the people who faked the outbreak of the fever?"

"What?" she said.

"The *teltis* outbreak. I'm a medic," the Vetch said. "There wasn't any *teltis* fever in the settlement. And yet it was found, and that gave the excuse for the soldiers to imprison the Vetch."

"If that was the case," said O'Connor, slowly, "I knew nothing about it. We were there to help. That's all we wanted to do—to help."

Maria studied her thoughtfully. "I *think* that you don't mean us any harm," she said. "But as for the people who have brought you here—they're a different matter. I'm afraid you won't be going back to the settlement."

O'Connor began to tremble. "I've done you no harm—"

"No?" said Maria. "You've come with ships and weapons, and torn the settlement apart. You've separated friends and colleagues. You've turned half the settlement into a prison." She gave O'Connor a canny look. "I think it won't be long before you turn on yourselves—if you haven't already."

O'Connor thought of Vincenze, and kept quiet.

"The people of Stella Maris will be caught in the crossfire when that happens," Maria said. She looked around the small group. "We are the only ones free on Stella Maris right now. We intend to remain that way. You won't be returning to the settlement," she said again, "we can't let you give us away. Or give the Weird away either." She sighed. "The portal might be dead, but we must still protect it."

"It's not dead," said O'Connor.

Maria looked at her sharply. "What do you mean?"

"I mean, it's quiet, but it's not dead. The Weird aren't active. But they're still there, just behind the surface."

There was a rustle of talk around her, and then some laughter—relief, she realised. *I've brought good news*, she thought. *Let it be enough to protect me...*

CHAPTER EIGHT

IN THE WEEK it took the *Baba Yaga* to reach Capital Station, Yale took the time to do a little research. The Reach was an intelligence officer's nightmare and a runaway's dream: information was easily bought and usable currencies easily created. Soon Yale was up to speed on which ships would be heading into Expansion territory over the next few weeks from Capital Station and how much Cassandra's passage would cost, and she had set up an account and stocked it with some of the more reputable currencies that could be spent within Expansion space. She started to flesh out a cover for the girl too: creating a mother, an Expansion citizen who had married a businessman from the Reach, who was now sending her daughter home for schooling. It needed detail, which would mean more money, but she thought she could make it work. Cassandra proved a quick study at learning the story, and embellishing it with details of her own imagining.

"You're good at this game," Yale said.

"I like making up stories," said Cassandra.

"Don't get too wrapped up in that part of it," Yale said. "Remember it's there to serve a purpose—to conceal, to misdirect. Not to entertain."

"I know," the girl replied, simply.

"Normally I'd say stick as close to the truth as you possibly can. It's easier to keep the lies straight. In your case, perhaps that's not the best idea."

"Yale," said Cassandra, "I *know*."

And if she had taken lessons from Delia Walker, then Yale was talking to an expert. "Okay," she said. "But sometimes you *don't* know, do you?"

"What about me?" said Failt. "What's my story?"

"I'm still thinking about that," Yale lied. She flushed under Cassandra's watchful eyes. Cassandra must surely have worked out by now that Yale wasn't going to let Failt go with her into Expansion space. "There's something else I want to get for you first, Failt. Something I think you'll like."

"What's that?" said Failt.

"You'll see," Yale said. "In fact, I've got quite the shopping list for when we arrive at Capital Station. While I'm there, and happen to have cash to hand."

Yale had chosen Capital Station as the crossing point into Expansion space because she had been there many times before, and she knew she could, with enough money, get everything she wanted. They paid the docking fees (few people were ever refused, and the *Baba Yaga* had no serious weapons to speak of), and berthed at the station's main docking area. They passed quickly through the security checks: the temporary IDs she had created were good enough to get them through. The combination of two humans and a Vetch was enough to raise a few eyebrows and earn a second look, but the fact that two of them were minors was enough to get them through.

At a pinch, Yale thought as they made their way through the docking area, she could have come up with a convincing cover story for Failt. Something about being almost a family pet: a slave to whom Cassandra had taken a fancy, and who had been released from hard labour to act as her bodyguard. Close enough to the truth to be an easy lie; convincing enough to get them past prying eyes. She put the idea firmly aside. Under no circumstances was she going to allow Failt to enter Expansion space.

Capital Station was much as Yale remembered from the last time she had passed through: a beautiful, calm, and luxurious space, which promised discretion. It was quiet, too, orderly and ordered. It had to be, to operate so close to the Expansion without being brought into the fold. All empires have their limits, and while it suited the Expansion to have places like this where business could be done off the record, any hint of trouble would quickly lead to increased Expansion presence and, most likely, annexation. The brotherhood that owned Capital Station had no intention of letting their lucrative operation be closed down, and they kept order here as carefully as the Expansion would have done itself, and in full cooperation with them. Yale needed to tread carefully; keep herself off the radar, avoid unwanted attention, and move on as quickly as she could.

Failt seemed stunned by the place. This was the closest to the Expansion he had ever been, Yale realised; he knew nothing of the lives of most Expansion citizens. He was used to the chaos of Reach worlds, and the poverty of Stella Maris. Capital Station was the opposite of poor. Like a great luxury hotel spinning in space, it welcomed discreet and wealthy patrons, and it offered them quiet corners where they could buy and sell, and, when the day's business was done, indulge themselves in whatever ways they saw fit. Yale had done a lot of business here, once upon a time, on behalf of her former employers. She'd indulged herself a few times too, truth be told, although right now her goals were nothing more decadent than a hot shower, a stiff drink, and a quick getaway. She marched the two goggling teenagers along gilded arcades, past tinkling fountains and lush foliage, bringing them at last by dropchute to a particularly pristine area in the upper sector.

Coming off the main arcade, Yale led her charges along a quiet corridor. It zigzagged here and there, so that even as one walked along, one had the sense of being in a private space. It also, unfortunately, meant that you couldn't see what was coming. Yale hurried her little party along, coming at last to the offices she had been looking for. In a small quiet anteroom, she made her purchase, and then a woman came out of the inner room. "We can start at once," she said, and glanced round. "Which one of you is it?"

"Failt," Yale said, "your moment has come."

"What?" he said. "What are we here for?"

Cassandra laughed. "Implants, silly! We're here to get you jacked in."

"You said you wanted to fly," said Yale. "Well, soon you will."

Failt nearly fell off his chair. "Me?" he said. "Me? Get implants?"

"If you want them," said Yale. She was nearly laughing herself. He was so easy to please. But part of her was ashamed. The gift was chiefly for her own benefit and it would serve people other than Failt at least as much as the boy himself. She remembered, guiltily, what Maria had said when they were fleeing the settlement. *We use that boy. I hope he doesn't suffer for it.*

But Failt, at least, was delighted, even at the prospect of

minor invasive surgery. Yale left him in the capable hands of the surgeon, and took Cassandra clothes shopping, in order to give their cover story some verisimilitude. It was a brutal few hours. Neither of them had an aptitude for it. After some increasingly surly encounters with sales assistants who earned every single penny of their commission that day, Yale dragged Cassandra off to a plush bar where the girl stared in bewilderment at an ice cream and Yale had her first decent gin and tonic in what felt like a lifetime. The ice clinking against the glass was possibly the sweetest sound Yale had ever heard, and she nearly burst into tears at her first sip. She would happily stay here forever, she thought, but it was too close for comfort to Expansion space, and, besides, she had made a commitment to the people of Stella Maris. They had taken her in, asking no questions, and she owed them for that. But first, there was another problem.

"Eat the damn thing before it melts," she said to Cassandra, pointing at the ice cream. "It's supposed to be nice. It's supposed to be a treat."

Uneasily, the girl took a spoonful. She licked tentatively, and then smiled.

"See?" Yale watched the girl tuck in; she liked Cassandra considerably more when she did normal things. Then she said, quietly, "You need to talk to Failt. Explain that he can't go with you."

Cassandra looked up at her, and again Yale had the feeling of her whole self being put under scrutiny. "Why would I tell him not to come with me?"

"You know why," Yale said roughly. "Because you'll get two minutes into Expansion space and they'll take him. The border is practically sealed as it is—"

"The Expansion and the Vetch are no longer at war."

"No, but everyone is jumpy, and nobody likes anything out of the unusual. A teenage girl and a Vetch boy travelling together—yes, very sweet, very Romeo and Juliet, but it's unusual. It's more than unusual; it's unheard of. We've got some funny looks coming here, and it's only because I was able to flash around money that we were let in. I don't know why you want to go to Hennessy's World, because you haven't bothered telling me, but I bet you want to get there unobtrusively. Taking Failt with you is the quickest way to getting you noticed, and the quickest way to getting him arrested." She frowned. "I'll bet you good money that boy isn't registered as a Vetch citizen. He was born on Shard's World. So that's where they'll send him. And I bet every single fake credit in my fake bank account that there's someone on Shard's World prepared to make the rest of his life miserable for having the nerve to think he could ever be free. If you take Failt into Expansion space, Cassandra, you're consigning him to a lifetime of misery."

Cassandra's head fell forwards, hiding her face behind a sheet of her long hair. After a few minutes, she murmured something.

"I can't hear you," said Yale.

The girl looked up. Her eyes were very sharp, very clever. "I said, I agree. Failt can't come. It's not safe for him, and it's not safe for me."

"Sense at last," said Yale. She knocked down the rest of her drink, and reluctantly decided against another. "All right," she said. "Finish up your ice cream. They'll be done with Failt soon. We'll go and get him, and then I'll take you both back to the *Baba Yaga*. I have some things to do, and I don't want you two with me. While I'm away, tell him—" She frowned. "Oh, I don't know. What are you going to say to him?"

"Don't worry about it," said Cassandra. "He's my brother. He'll be angry with me, and then he'll do what we need to do—because he loves me."

Yale sighed. Whatever delusion this pair were under, it delivered what was needed. "Okay, you do what you need to do."

"Where are you going, Yale?"

"You don't need to know."

Cassandra took a spoonful of ice cream and tilted her head. "Are you going to buy arms to take back to Stella Maris?"

Yale looked around them. "For Christ's sake, Cass!"

"It's not illegal, is it?"

"No, but..." She shook her head. "Jesus Christ!"

"What if you don't come back?" said Cassandra.

Yale frowned. "Why wouldn't I come back?"

Cassandra shrugged. "I don't know. But it's not entirely safe here for you, is it?"

"It's not ideal, no. But I'm keeping a low profile—or trying to. And, as you said, we're not doing anything illegal. He's having implants put in, you're waiting for him, and I'm, well, shopping. As long as you two sit tight on the *Baba Yaga*, we'll be absolutely fine."

They paid and left. Failt was waiting for them in the anteroom when they arrived, and he showed off the new jacks with delight. "I'm gonna fly," he kept saying. "I'm gonna fly."

Yale took them back to the ship and went on her way. In a quiet red-and-gold booth on the fourth level, she found someone who could provide her with what she wanted. Sidearms, ammunition, missiles. Everything you might need, if you were trying to liberate your world from invaders. She arranged for delivery to the *Baba Yaga*. She and Failt would take these back, and they would get rid of the Expansion for good.

She ran a handful of other errands and then, pleased with her afternoon's work, she stopped for another quiet drink at a beautiful bar on the second level. It had marbled walls and floors, and fountains with little statues in it. She took her time, thinking about how she had once been a frequent visitor to this place, and how squalid and dirty Stella Maris was in comparison. Squalid and dirty and precious. When she had finished her drink, she went on her way, back to the ship, ready to leave behind the luxury of Capital Station and return home.

They were on her before she knew what was happening, coming up from behind around one of those damn corners. Both her arms were held behind her before she could do anything. She kicked out, pointlessly, and twisted her head. She just had enough time to recognise the uniforms before she felt a pinprick on her neck and started to become drowsy. She faded into unconsciousness. They had her.

The Expansion had her.

THE NEW RULES about routine telepathic scans had come in at the Bureau the previous year. They'd been contentious—everyone knew that there had been a battle about it upstairs—but the general feeling was that if you had nothing to hide, you had nothing to worry about, and if there was a Weird mind-parasite lurking around inside you, it was better to get you sorted out sooner rather than later, before it had a chance to do the Bureau some serious damage.

Oh, yes, and to drive you mad.

Still, you didn't have to *like* it. The process was often deeply distressing, dislodging old memories that any sensible psyche kept firmly at arm's-length. For these reasons alone, Lee might reasonably dread having a scan, and going into one knowing she was trying to conceal information was terrifying, to say the least.

An hour before her appointment, sitting at her desk reading, she took a bite of apple and then, under the pretext of dealing with a piece of peel lodged in her tooth, reached a finger into her mouth and gently pressed the tiny ampoule hidden under her upper lip. She felt something sharp, like a pinprick, and a little sourness, quickly covered by the sharp flavour of apple. That was all. She had serious doubts that the drug would work—Mercy Grey had a fervent belief in the power of pills that bordered on the superstitious—but this was all Lee had under the circumstances.

The scan took place in one of an anonymous suite of rooms on the fifteenth level that had once been used for break-out meetings, and were now completely taken over by the sheer volume of scans required by the new regime. Lee went there ten minutes before her appointment, as instructed, and sat in the corridor along with six or seven other anxious-looking Bureau employees. At last she was called in. The telepath was a rather tired-looking woman in her mid-twenties who didn't introduce herself or even look Lee directly in the eye. Lee suspected that like many others in the Bureau these days, the woman didn't particularly like her job. She probably hadn't liked it before Adelaide Grant took over. You didn't *apply* to become a government telepath; you did it to pay off your college bills, or to pay off the fees for being registered as a telepath and trained to use your talents. Who would want the job? If you weren't poking around in the heads of twitchy spooks like her, you were delving into the minds of criminals, murderers, paedophiles, assembling the evidence to put them behind bars. Perhaps the new assignment was a blessed relief. Unless you found one of the Weird mind-parasites. Lee wouldn't want to be on the receiving end of that. If the *pictures* of the Weird were enough to induce nightmares, imagining experiencing what it was like to *be* the Weird, in real-time, with all your emotions...

Did telepaths come back from that? When had this woman last taken leave?

The telepath gestured to Lee to sit, offered coffee (refused; Lee didn't know if it would interfere with whatever was in this drug Mercy had given her), and then sat with her hands folded in front of her. No small talk. Better that way. Lee didn't want to know anything about her, but she couldn't help wondering. How many of these scans did she do in one day? What did she do on her off-hours? Did the telepaths socialise with each other, or did they just go home and watch bad entertainments to blot out the memory of the working day, like everyone else? Did she drink herself to sleep, or take a pill, like Mercy?

Lee knew when the scan had started, of course. Some people talked about peeling an orange or the layers of an onion, but for Lee it always felt as if someone was tap-tap-tapping at the crystal of her mind, and feeling minute cracks emerge in the surface... You were told to relax and to let the telepath in, but that went against every instinct, to protect whatever integrity of identity that you had managed to construct in your life. You were told too not to worry if memories came back to you, as they did now; memories of college, when there had been three of them... Maxine Lee, Mercy Grey, and... Lee gritted her teeth and tried to push those memories back down into her unconscious. It was because she'd just seen Mercy, she knew, and if she thought too much about Mercy, she might think about...

She saw the telepath frown slightly. "Don't push back," she said. "It's easier on you if you relax."

Lee nodded, and tried to think about the work that must be accumulating on her desk while she was down here... But she couldn't stop thinking about college, about the good times, about her best friend and partner, who had died...

The telepath sat back and sighed. "We're done," she said, and pushed a box of tissues forwards. Lee grabbed a handful. After a couple of minutes she wasn't crying any more.

"You'll be pleased to hear that you're parasite-free," the telepath said.

"Thanks for that." Lee stood up and walked towards the door.

"You're the eighth today," the telepath called after her. "Since you were wondering. Twenty-two more to go. I'm here all week, and then I've got a week's leave."

Rules dictated that all staff who had undergone a telepathic scan were required to take two days' leave, so Lee left the building directly afterwards. Staff were also barred from using personal transport afterwards, so she stood in the crush on the lower walkways, slowly inching her way home through tourists gawping at the huge glass-and-steel towers of Venta. For a while she found herself behind a family—two mums and a dad and three boys—and idly listened to their conversation. From their accents she guessed they were from one of the quieter worlds, amazed and humbled to be here. What would they think, Lee wondered, if she told them about her morning? *Hey, everything you are afraid of is true!* She would sound crazed.

She got home after a couple of hours, falling exhausted onto the bed, and into uneasy sleep. She dreamed of home: a quiet world probably not much unlike the one that family had come from, and which she had gladly left behind many years ago. She dreamed about a Weird portal opening there, the hideous Flyers and Sleer emerging, consuming everyone in their path. She saw her mother and father (who still lived at home and pottered about in quiet retirement and spoke proudly of their clever daughter) succumb, and schoolfriends too, and then she saw Mercy eaten, and then... Then her dream took her to the Greenway, in the heart of the political district of Venta, and the

Sleer were there too, and there was nothing she could do to stop them...

She woke to a persistent alert from the companel on the desk. It was Mercy.

"Hi, Maxie. Hope you kept that headache at bay. Did what you asked. Files coming through. No, I haven't looked. Hope it's good news, or if it's bad news, you know what to do."

Lee read and watched the files two or three times. Then she went and sat on the edge of the bed, her head in her hands and her heart pounding in her chest.

No, it wasn't good news. And no, she didn't know what to do.

Everything I am afraid of is true.

And I'm in serious trouble.

Yes, she was most certainly in trouble—because what she had read and seen was the proof that the Weird had not been on Braun's World when the order was given to attack. That alone would have been enough to fill her with terror. But she had also seen evidence to suggest that the head of the Bureau, Adelaide Grant, had known it when she called for the attack.

Adelaide Grant, Lee's boss, was guilty of mass murder.

She didn't know what to do. She knew one thing, though.

My days are numbered.

Lee fell back on her bed, exhausted, but not eager to fall asleep. Her mind raced with her new knowledge. What was she supposed to do with this? Who could she tell? Who could she approach? As she lay there, staring at the shadows the blinds cast across the ceiling, she heard a soft chime from her handheld. Another message.

EVERYTHING YOU ARE AFRAID OF IS TRUE.

The message disappeared from the screen, vanishing without a trace like all the others. Suddenly angry at the situation she found herself in—the situation in which this elusive *someone* had placed her—she nearly threw the handheld against the wall. She had the strong suspicion that whoever it was was enjoying all this. Who was it? Why were they doing it? And why of, all people, had they picked *her?*

The handheld chimed again. "I'll tell you something for nothing," Lee muttered, as she grabbed the damn thing from the floor, "I'm starting to get pretty pissed off."

But it wasn't another message from the stranger. Still not good news, though: her calendar at work alerting her that she now had an appointment for the morning of her return. With Adelaide Grant.

Lee checked the time. Thirty-seven hours. She rubbed her eyes. She was tired, she was scared. She needed to start thinking of a plan, and she didn't dare ask anyone at work. Mercy, she thought, could help her—but she was loath to bring Mercy into this any deeper than she was already. So whatever she did next—she was on her own.

THEY HADN'T KILLED her, and, to O'Connor's intense relief, they didn't seem to have any particular interest in killing her. She sat for a while on a mattress on the floor, conscious of the eyes of several Vetch upon her, while the human woman, Maria, and the Vetch man, Ashot, talked together quietly. At length, Maria came back over.

"Come with me," she said. O'Connor stood up, slowly, her muscles cramping from the long wait, and followed Maria to the back of the cave. There was a little alcove there, curtained off, affording some privacy. A low bed, a table with a glass of water, nothing else.

"I'm sorry," said Maria, "but you're going to have to stay here for a while."

"You're holding me prisoner?"

"We're wanted people. We can't let you reveal our location."

"I don't know the location," said O'Connor. "You blindfolded me, remember?"

"We can't risk you bringing them anywhere near us. And besides," said Maria, "you know where the portal is."

"It's only a matter of time before the people down there work that out too," O'Connor pointed out. "I just followed your tracks."

"I know that," said Maria. "That's one of the things we'll need to talk about."

O'Connor began to tremble. "You're going to interrogate me?"

"*Interrogate* you?" Maria stared at her. "What kind of people do you think we are?"

"You're holding me prisoner!"

"You've come here with people carrying guns!"

"Which they needed when the Vetch *attacked!*"

"They put the Vetch behind wire!"

"There was an infection!"

"If there was a single case of that fever on Stella Maris, it was brought by your people," Maria said. "They're already responsible for murdering millions of humans! Why would they stop at infecting a few hundred Vetch?"

O'Connor stared at her. "What do you mean?"

Maria leaned her shoulder back against the wall. She really wasn't very old, O'Connor thought, but she looked extremely tired. "Do you know happened on Braun's World?"

"Everyone knows what happened on Braun's World," said O'Connor "A portal opened. Sleer and Flyers. Hideous. They had to blanket bomb the planet to destroy the whole place before they took ships and got loose." She shuddered at the thought of all those dead people—but, really, it would have been better than being consumed by the Weird. O'Connor was just glad she didn't have to make those kinds of judgement calls.

"A portal?" Maria smiled, sadly. "There never was a portal. That was a lie. People in the Bureau faked it. They wanted to put their own people in charge."

"That's rubbish," O'Connor said. "That's the kind of thing you hear on blacklist channels."

"I would have thought the same thing, only a few months ago." Maria's voice went very quiet. "I told you my husband was a soldier. He was stationed on Braun's World. One night—in the middle of the night—he came to get me. Me and our little girl; you saw her, back there. She'll be five soon. Kit came home and made us leave with him. He knew the attack was coming, and he came to get us before it happened."

"He knew the Weird were coming? I didn't know we had an early warning system. It must be experimental. I'm glad it works—"

"Dr O'Connor—listen to me. There *were* no Weird. That's what Kit discovered. He brought the proof with him, died trying to get it into the hands of people would do something about it. People who would bring the murderers to justice." Maria leaned in. "They came after us, Dr O'Connor: me, my husband, our little girl. They murdered him, and they would have murdered me and Jenny if they'd had the chance. But we got away. We brought the proof here to Stella Maris. I've seen it."

"I've seen footage from Braun's World too," O'Connor said. "The Sleer, the Flyers. It was horrible—"

"Faked. The images were from another attack on Rocastle. They superimposed it over footage of urban centres on Braun's World."

O'Connor shook her head. "This can't be true—"

"I left Braun's World as the bombardment began," Maria said. "Have you seen a world catch fire, Dr O'Connor? I hope you never see that. I hope you never have to run for your life. I hope the government never sends crimopaths to hunt you and your little girl down, as if you were nothing better than rabid dogs—"

She stopped, and wiped her hand across her eyes. *Crimopaths*, thought O'Connor. She had heard, vaguely, of such things, but she hadn't believed in them either. She thought back to her arrival at the settlement. Hadn't one of the people they'd met said something about an attack on the settlement? Could the government really have sent killers after this woman? Certainly Maria believed this was true. You couldn't fake distress like this.

"This is what happened, Dr O'Connor," Maria said. "You can deny it as much as you like, but it all happened, and my husband died to prove to everyone that it did. My poor Kit!" She looked about to cry again, but she reined herself in. "People are lying to you, and you need to think carefully about whose side you're on." She looked around the space. "Get some sleep. I'll talk to you again in the morning."

O'Connor watched her go. She thought about trying her luck and making a break for it, but when she twitched at the curtain, the dark shadow of a Vetch loomed across the wall. Of course there would be a guard. Besides, how would she get through the cave unnoticed? And if she did, what then? She had no idea where she was going, and these people knew the land. Without any other immediate options available, she went and lay down on the bed, and thought about all that Maria had said. It was nonsense; some kind of mad conspiracy. The woman was grief-stricken, that was true, and grief-stricken people looked for someone to blame. Her husband, for some reason, had decided to go AWOL, and Maria needed to blame someone else, rather than accept his guilt.

O'Connor shut her eyes. Sleep was miles away. She listened to the night sounds: the gentle rustle of quiet conversation, the rush of the river. Then, from within her pocket, she heard a soft *chirrup*.

Her handheld! She had completely forgotten about it. Here was a means to contact the base. They could pinpoint where she was, come here to collect her, stop these people and bring them to justice. She knew the location of the portal now. They could start doing the real work of contacting the Weird; start running tests and make the portal open again...

Again, the device made its soft, friendly *cheep*. A message had arrived. With clumsy, urgent fingers, she silenced the device before it give her away. She looked to see who the message was from, expecting Palmer or, more likely, Woodley, checking in on her. She nearly gasped out loud when she saw Vincenze.

"*Hi Eileen,*" he said. "*If you're receiving this message, I'm dead, and I have been for a while. Sorry about breaking the news this way. Sorry, too, if it isn't news and my presence is rather disturbing. I assure you that I am quite dead, and that this is a pre-recorded message. I am not a ghost or unseemly messenger from another dimension.*" He looked back over his shoulder. "*Dear me, it's all become very complicated. The truth is, I wasn't sure what else to do. Wasn't sure who else to turn to. I'm not sure about much right now, but I'm sure of you, and of my responsibility to you. You're in danger, Eileen. You need to be careful.*"

She realised there were tears rolling down her face. He didn't—would never—know the half of it.

"*The first thing you need to know—in case you haven't worked this out—is that I'm not simply a scientist. I am without* doubt a scientist—a very good one—and an expert on Weird mind-parasites. There's probably nobody in the Expansion who knows more. But I am also—in case you haven't worked this out yet—from the Bureau." He smiled. "I wonder if you did guess. You have an enviable talent of ignoring what's going on right in front of you."

She hadn't, of course. Not at all. Everything around her was bewildering and uncertain, as if the first tremors of an earthquake were shaking the ground beneath her feet.

"*So why am I here on Stella Maris and why am I now dead?*" He laughed. "*These are two separate things, albeit connected. First, let me tell you why I was sent. The Bureau—well, we're good at showing the rest of the Expansion a united front. That's part of why we seem so powerful. But the truth is, we're not particularly united these days. The people at the top—they're not my people. They've committed some terrible crimes.*" He frowned. "*You could say that about the Bureau at the best of times—the telepathic scans, the interrogations. There are some places in our headquarters that you don't want to know about. We accept a great deal when we take this job. But some things are unacceptable.*"

And O'Connor listened as Vincenze confirmed everything that Maria Emerson had just told her: that there had never been a Weird portal on Braun's World, and that someone at the top had ordered the murder of millions. By the time Vincenze had finished his account, she was weeping.

"*So. That's why I'm here. I'm here because some of us in the Bureau are still trying to get to the bottom of this. They sent me on this mission to make contact with whoever sent the message from here about the cover-up. They told me to protect them, and to work with them. I won't be able to do this now. I'm asking you to do it. I don't know where else to turn.*"

"What about your people back on Hennessy's World?" O'Connor murmured.

"*The problem is—well, the problem is something else.*" Again he seemed to glance back over his shoulder. "*The problem is the reason that I'm dead. I'd assumed that the people here were part of the cover-up. Certainly they were sent here to find out where Delia Walker and Kay Larsen are, and they're here to kill everyone who knows the truth about the massacre. That means you, now, of course.*"

At least, O'Connor thought, he had the decency to look embarrassed.

"*But as I worked with them at the base, I began to suspect something else. And I remembered why else I was here. To learn about the mind-parasites.*"

O'Connor wrapped her arms around herself.

"*Yes. Many of the people at the base—they're infected. Mostly the administrators and the military personnel. The scientists— not so many. We were all on that separate ship, weren't we? Anyway, I came to the settlement not just to see you, but to see if the infection was there too. I collected samples, and ran some tests.*"

O'Connor was beginning to feel very sick.

"*You'll be very frightened now, I imagine, so let me say at once then when I tested you—you were fine. I don't know how long I've been dead, and I don't know what might have happened since, but you were fine. So was your friend, Palmer, and so was Woodley. But most of the military personnel were infected. I ran the tests when I got back to the base. I was going to come and see you—but, well, someone has accessed my files. Which means that they're onto me, and are going to kill me. So I'm telling you, Eileen, and I'm putting you in grave and immediate danger.*"

"I'm glad, you brave old bugger," she said. "I'm glad you knew you could trust me."

"*I'm really sorry, Eileen. This is way things go sometimes. We try, in the Bureau—we really try to keep people like you out of these things, so that you can be safe, and get on with your work, and not have to worry about anything of this. But sometimes...*" He sighed, and she saw a man near the limit, frightened and tired, trying his best to do the right thing. "*Sometimes we have to ask for help.*" He smiled at her. "*You're a good person, Eileen. I know you'll do the right thing.*" And then his face disappeared, for good, and when she tried to play the message back, she couldn't.

She sat for a while thinking through everything he had said. Then she stood up, and twitched the curtain. The Vetch was beside her straight away, and she looked at him fearlessly. "Please, could you ask Maria to come and speak to me? I'm ready to help now."

CHAPTER NINE

YALE WOKE WITH the taste of blood in her mouth, a splitting headache, and a feeling of real dread. She opened her eyes a crack, not wanting to alert anyone there that she was awake. There was a bright light shining straight at her which threatened to make the headache worse, so she closed her eyes tight again. The last thing she remembered was walking down the corridor, on her way back to the *Baba Yaga*. The sudden assault, the glimpse of familiar black uniforms, and then a pinprick on her neck. After that: nothing. Yale therefore had a number of questions arising from her current situation. Firstly, where was she? Secondly, how long had she been here? Thirdly, was anyone going to speak to her?

She opened her eyes. Someone said, "She's awake."

"Is she? All right, let's have a word with her."

The light was very bright. Yale closed her eyes again. "I'm happy to talk," she said. "Just turn the bloody light off, will you?"

The light dimmed somewhat. Slowly, Yale opened her eyes and, blinking, tried to get her bearings. The light hadn't been switched off, just moved away. She was able to look round, but she couldn't see who was speaking to her.

"Happy now?" the first voice said.

"Oh yeah," she said. "Ecstatic."

Slowly, trying not to jar her head too much, Yale surreptitiously took stock of her surroundings. To her immense relief, she recognised the expensive if tasteful décor of one of Capital Station's smaller living spaces. She allowed herself to feel slightly better. Her chief fear, on waking, was that she had been under for days—weeks, even. However long was needed for her to be back within Expansion territory and unequivocally under their jurisdiction. While she remained here on Capital Station, she had a chance of getting away. It also told her her captors were on a budget. They'd have picked a nicer room otherwise.

"Nice room," she said.

"Sounds like we've got a live one here."

"I'd like to think so," Yale said. "The alternative would be pretty depressing."

She wriggled about in her chair. It was, all things considered, a fairly comfortable chair (nowhere on Capital Station was particularly uncomfortable; at least, nowhere that a paying guest would ever visit, even on a budget). Her hands were cuffed, which was perhaps the most uncomfortable thing happening to her right now, and (she tested) her legs were secured too. She wasn't making a run for it any time soon. She felt too queasy, anyway; standing up would probably be too much. The best thing all round to do right now was to try and find out exactly how deep the mess was that she was in.

"You said you wanted a word," she said. "Go on, then. Can I ask what the hell is going on?"

"Isn't that clear?" said one of the voices. She'd counted two so far. Was there anyone else here, lurking in the darkness?

"Well, no, actually," said Yale. "I was going about my business and the next thing I know I was waylaid and drugged. I'm assuming you're responsible for that." She peered into the gloom. "Whoever you are."

One of them came into view. Definitely an Expansion uniform, the usual black they seemed to favour, and something else that gave her pause: a badge. Not Fleet, and not regular police either. These people were patrolmen. She'd come across them before; had made use of them, sometimes, in her previous line of work. They weren't bounty hunters as such, but a kind of border police that operated outside of the Expansion's borders. Their jurisdiction was fluid, although certainly they had a remit to pick up individuals whom the Expansion would like to have brought back. Capital Station allowed them to operate here: the station took a small fee, and, in general, turned a blind eye to their activities. It was the best way to keep the Expansion happy.

So she wasn't quite in the hands of the Expansion—yet—but as good as. Yale allowed herself more cautious optimism. She was pretty sure that if they knew who she was, she wouldn't have been allowed to wake up on Capital Station. Probably someone would have come to collect her and take her home. But she needed to make sure. She said, "I don't suppose you want to introduce yourselves?"

"We're asking the questions!" the second voice said. "What's your name?"

Yale's heart lifted. Her guess had paid off. They didn't know who she was. She hazarded a further guess at what had happened: her biosigns had come up on their handhelds, and they'd gone after her without stopping to find out anything more. Chances were that information about her was classified, anyway. She found herself oddly grateful for the secretiveness of her former employers. So what she needed to do now was make sure that they didn't get a chance to work out who she was or, more importantly, what she was worth.

"I'm really sorry," she said, "but that drug you gave me—I don't think it's been good for me. I'm feeling really sick. And I can't remember a thing about anything since I woke up here. That's unlucky, isn't it? Are you sure you've even got the right person?"

One of them belted her across the face. She tasted blood on her lip, and thought: *I'll make you pay for that, you sadistic little shit.*

Quite how she would do that was another matter. She was trussed up like a roast dinner, and these two charmers didn't look particularly set on letting her go. How long would they keep her here? At some point, she thought, Failt and Cassandra would start to worry about her, and they would come looking for her. Or else they would do the ostensibly sensible thing, and contact the authorities about her disappearance. That wouldn't help; even if they didn't know who she was, these patrolmen could presumably show that she was wanted back in the Expansion, and that would be enough to satisfy Station. And if Failt and Cassandra *didn't* contact the authorities, what would they do? Come looking for her? What could two teenagers do to stop this pair? Would they even find her before they were due to leave?

"Losing your memory," said the first voice, "is very convenient for you, don't you think?"

"Not much else about all this is," Yale pointed out.

"And that's a problem for us, since we can't find out any information about you."

Yale almost smiled. Christ, though, these guys were useless. Giving away information like they were handing out sweeties.

No wonder they weren't allowed to operate inside Expansion borders. If she could keep them talking for a while, perhaps she would turn up something useful.

"I'm sorry about that," she said. "That must be a real nuisance for you. Like I said—memory's on the blink. Never did get on with drugs. I'm afraid I can't help you."

"Oh," said the first man, in what Yale assumed was meant to be a sinister and threatening tone of voice, "but I think you *can*."

Yale swallowed down a laugh. The speaker stepped into view at last: a tall man, mid-forties, scowling; pretty fit, but not as fit as Yale. Not tied up, though. He was lucky in that respect. "I'm not sure I'm following you," Yale said.

"We can make you talk," he said.

Oh, God, don't let me laugh out loud. It would not work out well for me if I laughed out loud. He sounds like he's watched some pretty bad vids in his time...

The other patrolman moved into view. Shorter. Sandy-haired. Slouching. One of nature's followers. *If only I could get my hands on them. I'd be out of here in no time.*

"My friend here isn't the nicest of people," said the slouchy one. "Heart of stone. You might want to think carefully about what you say next."

There was a knock on the door. Yale said, "Did either of you order room service?"

Scowl scowled. "Don't be funny," he said.

"So I *am* funny?"

His hand went up, threateningly. "I mean it."

"Honestly," said Slouch. "He can be a real bastard."

Yale subsided. Probably better if she kept quiet. These two were pretty amateurish, but she was tied up, and Scowl looked like he had a lifetime's misery to take out on the nearest victim. Slouch looked as if he'd like it to be someone else's turn. Her moment would come, she thought. Then: *Who are you kidding? You're tied up, and they'll take you off station soon enough. If they find out who you are, they'll have you sedated all the way back to Hennessy's World...* Desperately, fruitlessly, she tugged at the cuffs. The knock came again at the door.

"Were you travelling with anyone?" said Scowl.

"What?"

"Were you travelling with anyone?"

Good God, they were clueless. As if she would tell them that. They were hopeless, and she was too trussed up to be able to take advantage of the distraction. "No, I'm here by myself." *What do you think I'm going to say? That I've got ninety Vetch commandos ready to bring back-up?*

Scowl nodded to his colleague. "Go on, then."

Slouch looked back uneasily. "'Go on, then' what?"

"See who's there."

Slouch slouched back further. "Can't we just ignore them? They might not like what we're doing here. Two men, a woman tied up—how do you think that looks?"

Scowl snarled at him. "Answer the damn door!"

God, thought Yale, *get me out of here.*

Slouch slouched over to the door, and hit the comm. "Who's there?"

A voice crackled back. "*Yeah, we've had a report of reduced pressure in this area. We're checking all the rooms along this corridor.*"

"Can't you come back later?"

"*Yeah, yeah, we can do that, if you want to be unconscious when we come back. Or dead. You want that?*"

"We're leaving soon."

"*You won't be going anywhere if we don't check out your room.*"

Slouch looked back at Scowl. Scowl, scowling, nodded. Slouch hit the control and the door opened.

What happened next was slightly confusing, and Yale only had a few moments to take it in before she was unfortunately unconscious again. The door opened—yes, that definitely happened—but nobody came in.

Slouch peered out. "Hello?"

Then there was a flash. No, not a flash: it wasn't light— definitely not light—but it wasn't sound either. It was somewhere between the two: how a sonic boom might look if it went off inside your head. Yale's headache became immediately worse. But her overwhelming sensation was not pain, but a sudden shudder of sympathy for the two men there in the room with her: two slightly sad, unlucky men who didn't like each other very much, but had nobody else in the universe willing to put up with them. This shock of their being—their reality—was suddenly too sad and furtive for Yale to bear. She fell back into her seat. In the doorway, she thought she saw two figures: two small figures, a human girl and a Vetch boy, hand-in-hand. She told herself that she was imagining things. Then she passed out.

WHATEVER O'CONNOR HAD assumed about her significance to the refugees, she was quickly disabused. Maria did not come to speak to her at once. She was sleeping, the Vetch guard said, and he would not wake her, however much O'Connor insisted. "That woman," he said, "has too much on her mind. I want her to sleep as long as she needs."

"But I have to speak to her!" O'Connor said. "It's important!"

The Vetch put his big body between O'Connor and the rest of the cave. "You'll wait. She'll speak to you when she's ready."

He was big, and powerful, and he had no reason to be kind

to her. There was nothing to do but wait. O'Connor sat on the bed, her mind racing. Eventually, she lay down, and, soon enough, she dozed off into an uneasy sleep. She woke thirsty, with a muddy head, when her Vetch guard came into the alcove and shook her. He was a horrible sight to wake up to: huge bulging eyes, quivering tentacles. O'Connor shrank back—she could not help herself—and then realised that the Vetch was holding his head to one side so that the tentacles did not brush against her. Was that for her benefit, she wondered, or for his? Perhaps humans seemed as repugnant to the Vetch as they did to her.

She sat up. "Can I speak to Maria now?"

"She's awake and she's ready to see you," he said. "You can come now."

She followed him through the huge cavern, looking round. There was daylight coming in, but the place was cold. One or two braziers had been lit, and people were huddled round them, busy with tasks or simply sitting on the ground or mattresses. Her first impressions that most of the people here were Vetch was confirmed: they outnumbered the humans by at least two to one. Almost everyone seemed dispirited. Her Vetch guard led her over to the entrance of the cave, where Maria was standing with another Vetch, the one who had accused her of lying about the *teltis* fever. Maria saw her approaching, and nodded. There was a little girl at her feet, playing with a pile of stones. O'Connor heard the river in the near distance, and licked her dry lips.

Maria looked at her, with calm, tired eyes. "Jashis said you wanted to speak to me."

Jashis? That must be the Vetch guard. Yes, they would have names. All of them would have names. This one with Maria, he was called Ashot, wasn't he? He was the one that had accused her of lying about the *teltis* fever. O'Connor rubbed her eyes. The sound of water was tantalising. "Could I have a drink of water, please?"

"Of course." Maria led her to a low table, where a pitcher of water stood. There were several cups, plain, but carefully and beautifully crafted. O'Connor drank thirstily. "Was that all you wanted to say?" Maria said, gently.

"No," said O'Connor, with a sigh. "No, it wasn't." She reached into her pocket and took out her handheld. "You forgot to take this from me."

Ashot, who had followed them, muttered something under his breath. Maria closed her eyes for a moment. "And have you done anything about that?"

"I was about to," O'Connor said. "I was angry enough. I wanted to bring down a whole Expansion unit on your heads."

Maria and Ashot exchanged a look. "And yet here we stand," said Maria, "alive and well on what promises to be a fine if cold winter's morning. What happened?"

"I got a message," said O'Connor. "It doesn't matter from whom. You wouldn't know the name. But he mattered to me. He told me something, and that made all the difference." She took a deep breath, to prepare herself for saying it out loud. "I believe you. About Braun's World."

Ashot gave a low growl. "Forgive me if that seems very convenient. Can you show us the message?"

"I can't," said O'Connor. "I watched it and then it was gone. The friend who sent it to me must have set to delete after viewing, I guess."

"Again," Ashot said, "that seems very convenient."

"I wish he hadn't," O'Connor said, wretchedly. "It would certainly make my life a lot easier right now, wouldn't it? But I know why he did it."

"What was on the message?" Maria said. "Why do you suddenly believe us?"

O'Connor took a deep breath and then, as quickly as she could, explained about Vincenze and his message. Ashot frowned. "I think I remember him from the settlement. There was an older man who came up to the wire a few times. He wanted to come inside and speak to us. They wouldn't let him near us."

"That would be him," said O'Connor. "He wasn't much in awe of the military. But he had other reasons too. He was from the Bureau." She glanced at Ashot. "That's the Expansion's intelligence agency."

"I know what the Bureau is," said Ashot. "Its reputation precedes it. I don't see why this should commend your friend to us. The Bureau was, as far as I understand, responsible for the first attack on our world."

"Delia Walker was from the Bureau," said Maria.

"Delia Walker," Ashot said gently, "was not universally admired on Stella Maris."

They smiled at each other, and O'Connor wondered what she was missing. "As far I can make out," said O'Connor, "Vincenze was from a part of the Bureau that isn't in charge any longer." She looked straight at Maria. "You told me the truth about Braun's World. Vincenze said that was what happened, he described it exactly as you said. I believe him. I'm sorry that I couldn't believe you when you told me, but, well..."

Maria nodded her understanding. "Why should you? I'm glad you believe me now. Because it's the truth, and it's important that as many people as possible know it. Otherwise whoever did this will think they can get away with doing these things, and they'll do it again, and worse." She sighed. "Delia was forced out of the Bureau because she wanted to find a way to work with the Weird. That's why she came to Stella Maris. I thought she was the last, but it sounds like there are still people trying to work to her agenda... Oh!" Maria cried. "I'm so glad!"

O'Connor knew what she meant. Not all was lost within the Expansion.

"*If* we believe what this woman is saying," said Ashot.

"They shot Vincenze," said O'Connor.

"We only have your word for that," said Ashot.

"How could she have known about the split in the Bureau?" said Maria.

"Maybe she's playing us," said Ashot. "I don't know!" Bitterly, he turned to O'Connor. "Why should we trust you? You opened that clinic and said you wanted to help us. And then you sat and watched while we were all interned and then murdered!"

"Yes," O'Connor said. "I did. I was afraid. I thought you were all infected with the fever. I thought you wanted to kill us. I was wrong. But, please—listen to me! This is important! Vincenze thinks that there is infection down there—"

"There has never been a case of *teltis* fever on Stella Maris!" said Ashot. His huge fists were clenched beside him and he was trembling. "How often do I have to say this?"

"No, no, not that!" said O'Connor. "Please, listen! I don't mean *teltis*! Something else." She lowered her voice. "Vincenze was an expert on the Weird mind-parasites. The whole time he was here, he was running tests on our people. And he detected an infection—"

She was aware that both Maria and Ashot had moved back from her.

"Yes," she agreed, "that means that I might be infected too." She gave a nervous laugh. "I don't think so, though, for two reasons. First, from what Vincenze said, the infection seems mostly to be amongst the administrative and military personnel. The scientists all came to Stella Maris on a separate ship."

"I suppose it's possible," said Ashot, slowly. "As I understand it, the parasite can cause strain, exhaustion. People become confused and don't work as well. If they're here to find the portal, they might want the scientists to be working at full capacity. Perhaps you were intentionally left free of the infection."

O'Connor shuddered. It wasn't much consolation given she had been living and working alongside the infected, and serving the Weird while thinking she was doing her own work.

"You said there were two reasons," Maria prompted. "What's the other?"

"Vincenze ran a test on me and I came up clear," O'Connor said. "I'll be honest, that was a few weeks ago now, and a lot has changed in that time. Who knows what might have happened since? Still... I *feel* all right," she said, but she caught the question in the eyes of Maria and Ashot. How would she know? That was the curse of the parasite infection. You served the Weird without knowing, until your mind broke under the strain.

"You *look* all right," Maria said dubiously. "Although how we would be able to tell that you weren't all right, I don't know."

"Do you have a telepath here?" asked O'Connor. "A telepath can scan me."

"Yes," said Ashot, "we do have a telepath, but I'm loath to ask her to perform a task like this. To look into a potentially infected mind? She would not see that part of the Weird that sustains us, but the part that wants to consume us." He shook his head. "We should not ask her to do that."

"I can run tests," said O'Connor.

"Here?" said Ashot, doubtfully.

"No," said O'Connor. "Back at the base. On me, and on others. I've got Vincenze's notes, and I've got access to equipment." She thought of Palmer and Woodley, and the other scientists back at the settlement. "There's a chance that some of my friends aren't infected," she said. "I can't just leave them there. Please! If there's even the slightest chance that they're still not infected, I have to warn them! I have to get them away!"

"You're asking us to let you go," said Maria.

"We can't do that," said Ashot, shaking his head.

"If I *am* infected," said O'Connor desperately, "then the longer I stay, the greater the chance that the infection will spread." She saw Maria glance quickly, involuntarily, at her little girl, sitting playing on the floor nearby. "And if my friends are still clear? Ask yourselves: would you condemn them to that?"

Maria sighed. She nodded to Ashot, and they moved away to speak in private, a whispered but obviously spirited discussion. O'Connor watched for a little while, and then her eye fell on the little girl, still sorting stones and singing to herself. After a few tense minutes, Maria and Ashot came back.

"It would be madness to let you go," Maria said. Ashot nodded vehemently. "But if what you say is true, it would be madness to let you stay here. If you *are* infected..." Maria looked again at her daughter. "Well, that doesn't bear thinking about."

"There's a strong case simply for killing you," Ashot said. "But we are not the monsters on Stella Maris."

"You've seen us now," said Maria. "You've spoken to us, you've met us. We are people—yes, even the Vetch! We're not faceless. All we want is to live in peace, the way we did before you arrived. We're not trying to harm anyone. There are children here..." She put her hand to her forehead. "There are children here," she said again. "I'm trusting you, Dr O'Connor. If you are infected, there's nothing we can do, and you won't be able to help yourself. If you're *not*—you have a choice. Please don't betray us."

"I won't. I promise." Awkwardly, O'Connor offered her hand to Maria, who looked down at it for a moment, and then shook it. "I just want to make sure that my friends are safe," O'Connor said. "If they are, I'll get them away. I won't bring them here. We'll take some supplies, go somewhere else. Try to get help. That's all I want to do. I want to live in peace too. I won't do anything to harm you, or your daughter. Or your friends."

Ashot growled. "Let's hope these are promises you can keep."

FOR THE SECOND time in less than half an hour, Yale found herself opening her eyes to uncertainty, and checking herself for damage. Her hands were free: good. She reached up to rub her temples. Her legs were free too, but she didn't intend to try standing up yet. She shook her head. She had the vaguest memory that she had seen Failt and Cassandra, but that couldn't be true, could it? She blinked a few times, trying to clear her head, and then found herself with a face full of tentacles. She fell back into her seat, repulsed. "Jesus Christ!"

"Hey Yale! They hit you hard, huh? You okay?"

Yes, that was Failt, leaning over her, jiggling his tentacles around in excitement. She peered up at him. "You know, Failt," she croaked, "you're an ugly little bugger, but right now you're a sight for sore eyes."

"You want a hand to stand up, Yale?"

"You know, I think that would be very helpful."

Failt helped her up from the chair, holding her elbow until she got her balance. Yale took a deep breath, then took stock of her surroundings. She was still in the same room. "How long was I unconscious?" she said.

"Not long," said Failt. "Couple of minutes."

The two patrolmen were lying at her feet on the floor. They

were both unconscious, as if something—or someone—had gassed them. Yale thought she knew who that someone might be. Standing in the doorway, fists clenched by her side, was Cassandra.

"All right," said Yale. "First things first. What the hell just happened here?"

Failt shook his head. "No idea. But sister Cass here—she knew what she was doing." He gave a hoot of laughter. "Did you see them fall over, Yale? No, I don't suppose you did. They fell right over! Like someone had hit them!"

Yale took another look at Cassandra. Her face was chalk-white and she was swaying from side to side. Still feeling somewhat unsteady herself, Yale weaved her way across to her. She put her hand under the girl's elbow and guided her into the room, closing the door behind them. She pushed Cassandra into a chair. "All right," she said quietly. "I won't ask anything yet. Just get yourself back together again. But at some point I want to know what you just did."

Her voice thin and soft, Cassandra said, "I don't think I know..."

Yale grunted. Add that to the long list of questions that was Cassandra Walker. With a sigh, she started to deal with her more immediate problems. First of all, she checked on the two patrolmen: still out cold. Whatever Cassandra had done had been thorough—and directed. More questions... With Failt's help, Yale trussed them up with their own cuffs and dragged them over onto the beds. Then she went through their gear. She found their IDs: yes, as she had suspected, they were patrolmen, licensed by the Expansion to operate in and around Capital Station, and with the security clearance of a gnat. She left their IDs on one side: they'd be no use. She picked up their weapons and hesitated, gun in hand, glancing over at the bed. She realised that Cassandra was standing next to her.

Softly, the girl said, "Don't. We aren't the bad guys." She stared down at them. "I don't think they are either."

"Tell that to my head."

"They're nothing, not in the great scheme of things. They're pathetic." Cassandra looked down at them. "There's something sad about them." She gave Yale her back-of-the-head stare. "You know what I'm talking about."

Yale looked away. "Whatever they are, they could still cause us trouble."

"Murdering them would cause more. Didn't you say that we hadn't done anything illegal on Capital Station?"

"*I* certainly haven't," Yale said. "I've no idea what you just did, or whether or not it's a crime."

"But they don't like trouble here on Capital Station, do they?" Cassandra seemed almost to be pleading. "And killing them—wouldn't that lead to trouble?"

Yale sighed and put the weapon down. She searched through their packs for the sedatives they had used on her, and gave them each a hefty dose. "Okay, Cass. That should keep them out for as long as we need. Are you happy now?"

"Yes," said Cassandra. "Thank you, Yale."

Yale grunted. She went over to the drinks dispenser and mixed herself a stiff gin and tonic—*oh, God, how I have missed all this on that bloody planet*—and sat down in the nearest chair. She had no idea what the mixture of drink and sedative would do, and she didn't care. She needed fortifying for the conversation she was about to have. "Right," she said, looking at her two charges. "Explanations. Why weren't you two on the ship, where I left you, and where I told you to stay?"

The two teenagers looked shiftily at each other. "Never been anywhere like this before, Yale," Failt said, in a guilty voice. "Apart from Shuloma. Wanted a look round. Sister Cass did too."

"I see." Yale smothered a smile. She was almost glad it was something so ordinary. Something so teenaged. "You were playing truant. So how did you know where to find me?"

"That was me," offered Cassandra.

"Could you be more explicit, please, Cass?"

Cassandra frowned. "You're hard to miss, you know."

"What do you mean?" Yale looked at her in horror. She thought she was pretty nondescript, and she'd been trying her best to keep a low profile. Was everyone on Capital noticing her?

"Oh, I don't mean that you stand out," said Cassandra. "Not in a crowd, nothing like that—"

"Thanks."

"I mean... You're like a beacon, aren't you? Like someone has switched on a white light. Focused. Bright. You're..." Cass held up her hands. "You're hard to miss."

And now they were back in the realms of the inexplicable and creepy. "Whatever it was, I'm glad you turned up when you did. I was about to make them their fortune."

Failt looked at their sleeping prisoners. "Those two really took against you, didn't they? What did you do to them?"

"Thanks a lot, Failt! I get beaten up and sedated, and it's my fault!"

"You have done something, though, haven't you?" He gave her a canny look. "Something that made them interested. Something that means you won't come with us to Expansion space."

Yale didn't miss that 'us.' So Cassandra had said nothing yet. She frowned at the girl, who blushed.

"Whatever I did," said Yale, loftily, "it remains my business."

"Bet you were a bank robber," said Failt.

"Or a drug baron," said Cass.

"Or an arms dealer."

They were yanking her chain, the heartless little bastards. Yale rubbed her temples.

"Or a contract killer," said Cass.

But getting too close for comfort. "All right," Yale said, "thanks for your input. I'm not going to tell you. But, yes— there are people within the Expansion who would like to speak to me, and I would rather not speak to them."

"And you ran away and wound up on Stella Maris," said Failt.

"And you won't go back to the Expansion," said Cass. "But you won't tell us why, even though it got you into trouble and we were the only ones who could help."

"You should tell us out of gratitude," said Failt.

"We've earned it," said Cass. "Only someone without *shame* wouldn't tell us."

"Trust me," growled Yale. "It's a pretty compelling reason." She looked at her shameless charges. "Which one of you came up with the story about the air pressure in the room?"

Cass looked proud. "That was me. I told you I was good at thinking up stories."

"Yes, well, nice work."

Failt was looking thoughtfully at the men on the bed. "You still in danger here, Yale?"

Yale shrugged. "I don't know. Probably. I didn't want to come this close to the border, remember? But I've made up my mind. I'm going to take you across the border personally, Cass."

The girl smiled beatifically, and Failt gave a little mutter of triumph.

"Hold your horses," said Yale. "I'll take you there, on one condition."

She looked pointedly at Failt. His tentacles began to quiver in frustration. "That's not fair, Yale! That's not bloody fair!"

"You're being an idiot," Yale said, bluntly. "You'd be a liability and you know it." She nodded at Cass. "She knows it, too."

Failt turned to Cassandra and made a low, sorrowful sound. The girl reached out and took one of his big furry hands in her own.

"She's right, though, isn't she?" Cassandra said, sadly. The Vetch boy moaned. "Listen to me, Failt," she said. "You're my brother. Brother Failt. Sister Cass. You know I love you, don't you?"

He nodded.

"And Mama... Missus Dee. She loves you too, Failt. She asked you before, didn't she, not to come with her somewhere dangerous? Because she needed you to be somewhere else. That's what we're asking again. We need you to be somewhere else. But it doesn't mean we love you any less."

Failt had buried his face into her shoulder. Yale sat watching, awkwardly, as the boy shuddered and tried to control himself. Cass held onto him. "We won't forget you, Failt. We promise. But we have work to do first. We're not done yet."

At last, Failt sat up again. He sniffed. "All right," he said, his voice thick. "I won't come." He shook his head, sending his tentacles waving. "Would have looked after you wherever you went, Cass."

"I know."

"Anyway," said Yale, "I have a job for you, Failt." She pointed at his implants. "The *Baba Yaga*. Someone has got to fly her. Someone has got to take the shopping back to Stella Maris."

Failt began to laugh, a deep throaty chuckle. "All right," he said. "I'll do it." He gave Cass a tentacled kiss, and then shoved his paw into Yale's hand. "Deal?"

"Deal," she said.

"But how are we going to get into the Expansion?" said Cass. "You can't just come on board the cruiser with me, can you?"

"No," Yale said, and smiled. She nodded towards the bed, where the patrollers lay in deep slumber. "But these two have a ship. And that ship will come with authorisation codes." She smiled brightly. "They're all mine, now."

Cassandra frowned. "Yale," she said. "That's *stealing*."

CHAPTER TEN

LEE SAT OUTSIDE Grant's office and waited. Time passed. She stood up and walked around, doing discreet stretches to relieve her cramping muscles. The slim young personal assistant who controlled access to the head of the Bureau signalled his disapproval of even this small activity with a slight thinning of his lips, so Lee sat down again. And waited. Commander Adelaide Grant, Director of the Bureau, was an extremely busy woman. Yet still she had found time in her schedule to speak one-to-one to Maxine Lee...

Eventually the door opened, and Grant's assistant led her in.

"Maxine Lee, ma'am," said. "From the Information Task Force."

The door slid quietly shut behind her, and she looked around the room. It was white and bare. A glass desk stood at the far end. Grant sat behind it in a large black leather chair, working away at her personal viewscreen. Without lifting her head, she gestured to Lee to come towards her.

This office, in its prior incarnation, had been the subject of much mythologizing. Lee had never visited it when the previous occupant—Andrei Gusev—had been in place. She had been far too junior. Gusev had been a legend in his own right. Well into his seventies, and still going strong; avuncular, easy-going, sharp as knives. And everyone had heard stories about Gusev's court: the comfortable shabbiness, the professorial demeanour, the unruly debates and free-flowing drinks. Everyone hoped for an invitation to one of these sessions, and an opportunity to impress themselves upon the real powers at the Bureau.

But all that was in the past. Andrei Gusev had been toppled, almost overnight, and his heirs expunged from the Bureau. Gusev had died not long afterwards; heart-broken, some people said. These days, nobody wanted an invitation to this room. It was chilly, and controlled, and did not invite discussion. It was the kind of place where you received instruction, or were brought in to give an account of yourself.

Lee stood uneasily in front of the desk. Grant continued to work for some time at her personal viewscreen, mouthing her words to herself in concentration. After several minutes, she closed the screen with a decided click.

"Sit down," she said. Lee, as directed, perched herself on the edge of a moulded orange plastic chair, and waited to be grilled—possibly after being filleted and seasoned.

Grant observed her for a few moments in silence. She was an enviably healthy-looking woman. She'd had a long career in Fleet, and obviously took the trouble to maintain a high level of fitness. Lee wondered, madly, whether Grant was also a runner. She certainly had the physique. Under other circumstances, she might have been a role model at least as good as Delia Walker. But under circumstances like these...

At last, the Director spoke. "You have doubts about me, don't you, Lee?"

"I beg your pardon?" Lee said.

"I said, you have doubts about me."

Lee considered what her best tactic was here, and settled on deference. "I'm sorry, ma'am, it's not really my job to have doubts."

"No, it isn't." Grant opened her viewscreen again. "According to your contract, you're part of a team dedicated to tracking and analysing information pertinent to any and all evolving threats to the security and integrity of the Expansion. Nevertheless, you do have doubts about me." She clicked the viewscreen shut. "Tell me what you think happened on Braun's World."

Lee took a moment to recover from the question, and to collect her thoughts. Cautiously, she said, "I only know what I've been told." Which covered her from lying, whilst not exactly telling the whole truth. Grant, of course, was on top of such equivocations.

"What you've been told," she said. "Well put. I can see why we hired you. I wonder what you have been told. Turn around, please."

Lee swivelled round in her chair. The wall opposite was covered in viewscreens, four by three. At the moment, they all showed different feeds. Grant, coming to stand beside Lee's shoulder, pressed the control in her hand, and the twelve small screens suddenly became one huge black screen. At the press of another button, footage began to play.

It was a city street, lively and busy. Lee recognised it at once.

"Dentrassa," confirmed Grant. "The largest urban centre on Braun's World. Do you know what's coming?"

"Yes, ma'am, I do." Lee lowered her head. Of course she did. These images had haunted everyone in the Bureau since they had first been seen, only a few short months ago. She'd seen them only a few days ago, courtesy of Grant, when Lanyon had finally been tipped over the edge. And she had seen the footage again, only this morning, but in a very different way...

"Watch again," ordered Grant. "Just to make sure."

Lee raised her head. A couple of years ago there had been a craze in the flicks for zombies. She hadn't understood it then, and she definitely didn't understand it now. The Weird had come and consumed hundreds and hundreds of people. Why watch something that brought to mind the real horrors that could happen at any moment?

But it hadn't happened like this on Braun's World, had it? Lee realised that something had changed: she knew this footage so well, but now she was seeing what the other films she had watched had shown her: the cuts, the edits, the overlays. The lies. And it helped. As she sat through the footage again, she found she was able to distance herself from what she saw—see the fiction, and direct her anger towards the real perpetrators. The people who had authorised the bombardment of Braun's World. People like Grant. If Grant was hoping that this would cow her, Lee thought, the plan had thoroughly backfired. Her resolve was hardened. To do what, she didn't yet know. But watching that film, and knowing the lies it concealed, Lee knew she wasn't going to let the bastards get away with what they'd done to the people of Braun's World.

"Dentrassa. Braun's World," Grant said. "The most vicious Weird assault on us yet. There was nothing we could do to stop it." The footage played on, and Lee sat and watched, the two realities playing out at once. "All we could do was contain it," said Grant. "And I did that. I contained it."

The footage stopped. Even with the distance she had achieved, Lee still sighed in relief as Grant came back to sit behind her desk again. She swivelled round to face her.

"I pushed for the assault on Braun's World," said Grant. "I

pushed for that order to be given, and it was given. Millions died; millions of ordinary people who had done nothing wrong and who deserved better. Life is cruel, Lee. But it was the right decision. It was hard, and cruel, but it was right. Because if anything had got away from Braun's World—that would have been the end of us. The end of humanity. What I did was necessary for the safety of us all. Anything else is a lie. A plot. A conspiracy."

"I wouldn't believe a conspiracy theory," said Lee.

"I didn't say a theory," Grant said. "I said a plot."

Lee was now starting to feel very uneasy.

Grant caught her expression. "Yes, a plot," she said. "I'll stand by that. You need to understand what this story of the fake portal is all about. It's a lie originating with Delia Walker, and passed around by her people, those who were still here when she was dismissed. That's all this story is: a lie put about by a disgruntled former employee trying to discredit me."

"I heard," Lee risked, "that Walker was fired because she was pregnant."

"Another lie. Walker was angry she didn't get Gusev's job when he resigned. She thought it was hers by right. It wasn't. And Gusev resigned because he couldn't face the new realities of our situation. Walker wanted to *talk* to the Weird—can you credit that? Talk, to *that?*" She gestured back at the bank of screens. "And Gusev would have given her resources to do that, pulled them away from where they were needed. Gusev had gone soft. He couldn't give the order to contain the Weird when they attacked Braun's World. And he was wrong."

Lee said, "I don't disbelieve you—"

"Good. You'll forgive me if, in these uncertain times, I cannot take you at your word. I'm going to make sure of you," said Grant. "We'll do another scan as soon as we possibly can. A deep scan, this time. Once you're medically fit." She opened up her viewscreen again and began to read. "You can go."

Lee stood up.

"By the way," said Grant, still looking at the screen, "your asset is dead."

"I'm sorry?"

"Your asset. Mercy Grey. She's dead." Grant looked up, dispassionately. "A shame. I understand she was a clever young woman. Go home, Lee. Go home at once. Don't go near your desk, and don't speak to any of your colleagues on the way out. I don't want you back in this building until I've seen the results of the deep scan. If you're implicated in spreading this lie, we'll find you out. If you're implicated in the death of your asset, we'll find out. And if you're infected—we'll find that out too."

Lee left, reeling, and stumbled out of the building, handing in her passes on her way out. She stood in the sunlight, blinking back tears.

Mercy...

Was it true? Had Grant simply wanted to wrong-foot her? It was not the kind of power-play Lee associated with the woman: Grant was harsh, but judicious. She was not cruel or sadistic, she was hard. Trembling, Lee pulled out her handheld and thumbed open her contacts. "Mercy," she whispered, "whatever you're doing, it doesn't matter. Just answer me..." But there was no answer. As she put the handheld back into her pocket, it chimed again.

EVERYTHING YOU ARE AFRAID OF IS TRUE.

"Fuck you!" she said, much louder than she intended, and several people, passing by, gave her odd looks and a wider berth. She went on her way quickly, leaving the Greenway behind, and taking the first of the many barges she needed to catch to get to Mercy's home. It was a beautiful day, the kind of day that made Venta gleam, and Lee put on her sunshades, glad to have a reason to hide her tear-stained eyes. Since there was nothing she could do about Mercy for the moment, she tried to steady herself by thinking through what else she had learned in her bruising encounter with Grant.

Everyone had known that Gusev and Grant had been opponents, but the junior ranks had mostly assumed that with Grant in command, the old guard had been defeated, and the pro-Fleet faction was now in control of the Bureau. It seemed that was not quite the case. Someone sympathetic to Walker and her wider aims was clearly working to undermine Grant, and for some reason they had chosen Lee as a person who might potentially be drawn to their cause.

"You're going the wrong bloody way about it," she muttered to herself, thinking of the messages, their almost playful nature, and poor Mercy, a victim of the game...

There was something else troubling her too. *Infection*, Grant had said. Could it be true? Infection loose in the Bureau? Could some of her colleagues unknowingly be in the control of the Weird and working against humanity? Could it be happening to *her*? Lee shivered and wrapped her coat around her. Surely her last scan, even one so apparently perfunctory, would have revealed some infection? That was the point of them, wasn't it? She shook herself. Yes, Grant had been trying to scare her, to make her doubt herself. The purpose of the new scan was to get other information from her. It would work. Would the drugs that Mercy had given her cope with a deep scan? Lee doubted it.

And Mercy...

The boat pulled into its berth. Lee jumped out and dashed along the pier until she reached the side street where Mercy's building stood, and came to a halt. The road was barred; there was no way through. Two police officers, standing on the corner, saw her and came over.

"I know someone who lived there," she said. She reached into her pocket to pull out her Bureau pass, her shortcut to information—but of course she had handed it over when leaving the building. The officers, politely but firmly, ushered her on, asking her not to disturb a crime scene. Walking along the pier, she saw one of Mercy's tenants. He waved her over when he saw her.

"Maxie? It's Maxie, isn't it? Do you have any idea what's happening? We were all woken up in the middle of the night and asked to leave."

"Is Mercy with you?" she said.

He shook his head. "Not seen her since."

Lee looked back down the street. "I don't know what's going on," she admitted. *And I have no way of finding out...* And that was something else she was afraid of, Lee realised: being beset by enemies, and not knowing where to turn.

YALE DIDN'T WANT to linger around the scene of her nearly-crime, so they left the two patrolmen to their deep, drugged sleep. Cautiously, she ushered her charges through Capital Station to the docking area. Yale quickly identified the patrolmen's ship and reset the access codes. Even if the men did wake up before she and the others had left, and Yale was pretty sure they wouldn't, they would have trouble getting back into their own ship.

"All right," said Yale. "It's time for us all to get going. I don't want to hang around here for much longer. Particularly"—she patted the ship's hatch—"when I've finally done something less than legal." She turned to Failt. "I don't need to tell you that people are depending on you," she said. "I know you're disappointed not to come with us, but what you're doing now—

it matters. I know how much Stella Maris means to you, Failt. They're in trouble back there, and what you're taking back to them in the *Baba Yaga* will be the difference between life and death for them."

Failt nodded solemnly. He turned his big sorrowful eyes to Cassandra, and they pulled each other into an embrace. "I promise you," said Cassandra, her head pressed into his shoulder and her voice muffled, "that we won't forget you. Me and Mama. You're part of us, Failt. We're part of you. You are part of the whole. Mama promises that she won't abandon you. She's coming back for you, Failt. She'll never forget you, and she'll never let you suffer."

Yale looked around anxiously. Gently, she put her hand on Failt's shoulder, and drew the two young people apart. "Good luck, kiddo," she said. "Give my love to Stella Maris. Tell them..." Yale screwed her face up into a smile. She wasn't in the business of making promises. "Tell them good luck, and thanks for everything."

The boy nodded, and ran on his way through the docks towards the *Baba Yaga*. Yale watched him go with a heavy heart. *We use that boy. I hope he doesn't suffer for it...*

"Mama has promised we won't abandon him," Cassandra said. "In the meantime, we have to go, Yale. We have work to do, and not much time."

Yale watched until the Vetch boy was no longer in sight. "Yeah, Cass, I know. There's always work to do. Come on."

Together they boarded the patrolmen's ship, and Yale appraised her new vessel. It was all paid for by Fleet, and while they didn't spend a fortune on this branch of their operations, they didn't skimp either. Yale had inherited a decent little flyer. The phase technology was bang up-to-date, and Yale was relieved that she wouldn't need to jack in. Between that, the gin, and the sedatives, her head had taken enough of bashing the past few days. Yes, this wasn't a bad little ship, she thought, as she made her way to the pilot's sling. Border patrol must have gone up the agenda, since the emergence of the Weird threat. Vetch were easily identifiable as enemies; infected humans and refugees from the Reach less so. In the pilot's sling, she confirmed that the deliveries had been made to the *Baba Yaga*, and sent a message to Failt: *Shopping's arrived. Good luck, flyboy.* Then she and Cassandra listened in as Failt communicated with Capital Station's traffic control, and the *Baba Yaga* began her slow, stately progress out into the black.

"Out of our hands now," Yale said. She began to make preparations for their own departure. They passed easily through traffic control and out of Capital Station, and Yale put the ship into phase. Their flight time to the border was only a few hours, so they ate a makeshift meal and worked their way around the systems. Yale put some more work into securing them a credit account when they arrived in Expansion space.

At last they came out of phase and approached the border. Yale tried to relax, putting herself and the ship on automatic. These little patrol ships came in and out all the time, and all they really needed to do was supply the right answers and make everything seem routine. There was a tense moment when border control asked them to send their authorisations for a second and then a third time; Yale glanced over at Cassandra and saw the girl's look of intense concentration. And then they were given permission to cross the border and set in their course for Hennessy's World. Yale put the ship back into phase and fell back in her sling.

"Did you do something back then, Cassandra?" she said to the girl.

"What do you mean?"

"When they asked for our codes again. Did you do something?"

Cassandra looked puzzled. "I wished very hard that they would believe us. Is that what you mean?"

"Not really, no." Yale sighed. "All right," she said. "I've had enough of all this cloak-and-dagger stuff. It's just you and me now, and I so think it's time for us to share a few of our secrets. Here's the deal. I'll tell you something about me, and then you can tell me something about you. How does that sound?"

"I'll do my best," Cassandra said, doubtfully. "I might not be able to."

"All right," said Yale, "let's see how far we get. You wanted to know why I didn't want to come back into Expansion space. It's straightforward. Well, it's complicated, but not in the main issues. I was in the Bureau once. I think you've probably guessed that."

Cassandra gave a non-committal shrug.

"Special operations. Black book stuff. Lots of running around, getting myself into and out of trouble. It was brilliant. I loved every minute of it. And then..." Yale frowned at the memory. "Then I was given some orders that I didn't like, and I refused to comply. And you don't do that. You don't get to pick and choose; you're there to do what you're told. People insisted, and I refused again. This happened several times, and then everything went quiet. I didn't get any orders for a while. And I started to get frightened, so I ran away. Refusing orders is one thing, but they *really* don't like it when you run away. They're afraid that you'll pass on their secrets. So I found a place to hide. Stella Maris. It wasn't the most luxurious place, but it was safe. And then your bloody mother turned up and bang went my bolt-hole." She looked at Cass. "But enough about me. What about you? What's your story, Cass? What's your *real* story?"

"I've told you," said Cassandra. "My mother was the Walker. Delia Walker."

"Sticking with that line, huh? At least you're consistent. Straight out of the handbook, too. But do you really think I can believe that?"

"No," said Cass miserably, hiding behind her long hair. "But it's the truth."

"I know she was pregnant when she disappeared—"

"She didn't disappear," Cass said. "She went into the portal."

Yale raised her eyebrows. "Wow, if true. But you weren't with her. She was pregnant, yes, but, you..." She stared at the girl, wondering. "Go on then—what's it like?"

"Being Delia Walker's daughter?"

"Don't be ridiculous. You know what I mean. The portal. The Weird. What's it like?"

The girl shrugged. "It's hard to say."

"You do realise that this is part of what makes it difficult to believe you?" Yale pointed out. "The absence of any details?"

"I mean," Cassandra said, "that it's what I knew. Like fish swimming in water. Could they tell you what it's like? It's just how it is. It's what I knew—*all* I knew. But when I came out— it slipped away. It's not like here and I wasn't like this." She pressed her hands against her chest. She meant her body, Yale realised; she meant having a body. "It's hard to remember what it was like. What *I* was like. I was part of the whole. I was many. We are part of the whole. We are many... And then when I came out, I knew so much, but didn't know how I knew it. Anglais, for one thing. How to speak human speech. I knew where to find the settlement. Other things came back the more I was here, and there's more and more the longer I'm here. And I know I've forgotten things, so many things..." She looked up at Yale, suddenly, piercingly. "She doesn't remember you, you know."

"What?"

"My mother."

"Doesn't remember you. From the Bureau."

"I was pretty unimportant. Until I wasn't."

Cassandra laughed. "She likes that. That's made her laugh."

There was a pause.

"Cass," said Yale, "are you talking to your mother now?"

"Sort of," said Cass. "She speaks to me. You know? Telepathically. We have a link, I guess."

"Your mother speaks to you telepathically."

"Yes."

"You hear your mother's voice in your head?"

"Yes."

"Constantly?"

"What?" said Cass, and she looked at Yale in horror. "No! That would be awful! Just sometimes. Quite a lot. But not all the time." She shuddered. "Eeuw!"

"Oh, well," said Yale calmly. "That's one up on the rest of us."

"She doesn't tell me *everything*, you know," Cass said, defensively. "I told you that. It's on a need-to-know basis. She said—she *says*—that's safer."

"Well, yes, if we accept the basic premise that you're communicating via telepathy with your mother who has taken up residence in another dimension, that's very sensible policy," Yale agreed.

"She knew you would understand," Cass said. "She said you'd have been a bloody awful operative if you didn't."

"Thank her for that." Yale pondered all this. Best not to worry, she thought. She'd come this far; she might as well roll with it. "So, does she have anything to tell me now? Anything you haven't told me yet? It would be helpful to have a proper briefing."

Cass sat for a while, playing with strands of her hair. Yale waited, patiently, and watched her. The girl was certainly hearing *something*, that was for sure. Her look of concentration; her occasional nod, or tilt of the head as if she hadn't quite understood something... *What am I doing, risking my life to this?* Yale thought. *Why I am going back, with only this girl's word?* Then she reminded herself: *Roll with it, Yale.*

"The thing is," said Cass, haltingly, "it's like this. The Weird—they're on the verge of a terrible schism. Like nothing that's ever happened to them before. They are whole, you see. They are many, but they are whole. Part of the whole. That's how it's always been—whole and part and whole, all working together. But the whole is breaking apart. And half-the-whole—more than half—it wants to come through here. It wants to open portals and consume as many humans and Vetch as possible. And the other half—not half, really, less than half—it doesn't want that. It wants to understand us. That's why it—they—came to Stella Maris, long ago. That's why they wanted Mama. Because she wanted to understand too."

"I see," said Yale. "A schism. A war—"

"Not quite a war," said Cass. "Not yet."

"Why do they want to wipe us out?" said Yale. "The bad Weird, for want of a better name."

Cassandra looked at her. "Why does anyone ever want to do that? Fear? Distrust? Revulsion? All of that. Some of it. I think, Mama thinks, that they look at our dimension and see nothing of value. They see only something that might be dangerous. And perhaps they're right, in a way. Because entering our dimension in the first place is what seems to have caused the schism." She frowned. "This is hard. I don't really understand what happened. But being on Stella Maris—the others don't like that. They think that's what caused the trouble in the first place. Being in our dimension for too long. Like the Weird has been infected."

"So there's a split. Your mother is with the good guys—the guys who don't want us for dinner. Next question: why are you here, Cass? What have you been sent to do?"

"Mama hasn't said, yet. All she said was to get into Expansion space." Cass frowned. "Well, I've done that, haven't I?"

Yale nodded. "Yes, we've done that."

"Mama says 'thanks.' She knows you didn't want to come, and she's sorry those patrolmen hit you."

"You're welcome, ma'am," said Yale. "All in the line of duty."

"Oh, I see," said Cass. "There's going to be a portal. A portal is going to open on Hennessy's World. Hey, Yale," she said. "That's big news, isn't it?"

Yale closed her eyes and swallowed. "Yes," she said. "That's big news." A portal opening on humanity's chief world. "I'm guessing it isn't going to be one of the good kind."

"No, definitely not. Anyway, we need to go there. That's what Mama says."

"Hennessy's World." Yale turned to the controls "We're on our way."

"Yes."

"And what do we do when we get there?"

There was a pause. "Mama won't say."

"Well, while your ma is on the line, could you remind her that Hennessy's World is the most policed, best defended, most surveillance-heavy world in the Expansion?"

Cass gave an embarrassed cough. "Mama says she knows more about that than you do."

"I'm sure she does. I'm just checking I've got my orders straight."

Cass smiled sweetly. "Mama says you can do it. She says you'll love the challenge."

"Does she?" Yale turned to the displays. "You know what, Cass? She's not wrong."

*   *   *

THIS TIME, O'CONNOR accepted being blindfolded with good grace. *If I am infected*, she thought, *I won't be able to stop myself giving them away. And if I'm questioned or interrogated or scanned, it's better that I know as little as possible...* After walking for some time, the blindfold was removed, and O'Connor found herself back near where she had left her ground vehicle. Only a few days had passed, but her world had changed irrevocably. She had learned secrets about her own people that she could never forget, and she had seen the Weird portal, as serene and silent as the grave.

Maria watched her climb into the driver's seat of her vehicle. "You understand that you can destroy us very easily," she said. "I hope you'll remember that we did you no harm, and that we're trusting you. We've done no harm to *anyone*; we only want to live in peace and harmony."

O'Connor nodded. "I know. I won't do anything to hurt you." She shuddered. "Not willingly, at any rate."

Maria nodded her understanding. "Goodbye," she said. "Good luck."

O'Connor started the vehicle and began her long journey back. She took her time, driving slowly back down the mountains and crossing the river at the shallow ford, near the ruins of the bridge. She camped that night under the stars.

She lay awake for some time, wondering what it would feel like, if she were infected. Would she feel the parasite there, shifting around her mind? She felt no different, as far as she knew; but how would she know? If she *were* infected, would she *ever* know? Would there always be something inside of her, telling her to fight, pleading with her to understand that she was being controlled? Would it be a struggle until the very end, or would she never realise that she had been taken and used against her own will?

The next morning she woke tired and unrested, and not eager to return to the settlement, where she knew some of her fellows were now her enemies. She tried to think of her friends, of Palmer and Woodley and the others. If there was anyone still there who was not infected, she owed it to them to bring them to safety.

She bypassed the base and went straight on to the settlement, where she returned the vehicle and went straight to her desk. She opened the console, and began, slowly and systematically, to destroy the logs of her search for the portal.

"Any success?"

O'Connor turned to look back over her shoulder. Palmer was standing in the doorway. *How would I know if you were infected? I wouldn't. I couldn't.* There wasn't a mark or a brand; people didn't come out in spots or run a fever. They just changed, slowly and imperceptibly. People who had been your friends were turned into your enemies.

"Success?" she said.

"Looking for the portal," said Palmer. She took a step inside.

"No," O'Connor said with a smile. "But I saw some lovely countryside!"

Palmer didn't return her smile. "You were gone longer than I expected. Woodley was getting worried. You know there might still be Vetch out there. I think she was about ready to send a search party out for you."

"I'm sorry about that," O'Connor said. "I couldn't raise a signal on my handheld. I'll go and see Woodley in a minute and apologise. Everything was fine. I didn't see anyone. Certainly no Vetch—I think I would have noticed them!"

Palmer didn't smile. "You couldn't raise a signal?" She frowned. "That doesn't seem likely."

O'Connor shrugged. "Well, that's what happened."

"You must have been a long way out. Where exactly did you go, Eileen?"

Slowly, the hairs began to prickle along O'Connor's arm. "Along the river," she said. Why all these questions?

"Up into the mountains?" Palmer said.

"I couldn't get the vehicle up that high," O'Connor said, truthfully enough, but she offered no further information.

Palmer looked at her thoughtfully. "Is this going to become a common occurrence?"

"Is what?"

"Driving around the countryside. Camping out under the stars. Holidaying."

"I'm not holidaying," O'Connor said. "I'm mapping the area—"

"We can do that from orbit."

"I think I can do it better, and more quickly."

"You're not a cartographer," said Palmer, "you're an anthropologist. You should be here, working with the locals."

"I'd love to be working with the locals," said O'Connor. "But they're not really interested in talking to us any longer, are they?"

"They'll talk," said Palmer. "They'll talk in time."

"I'm not an interrogator," said O'Connor. "And since when did how I went about my job become your concern? You're not my superior. If Woodley doesn't like what I'm doing, she's welcome to come and talk to me about it. But she was happy to see me on my way, the last time we spoke."

Suddenly Palmer looked very sad, and O'Connor regretted her tone.

"I'm not trying to pull rank on you, Eileen," Palmer said. "There were a lot of comments after you went off, and I thought you'd appreciate a warning." She lowered her voice. "I don't know what's happened between us, but I really did like it better when we were friends."

O'Connor stood up and went over to her friend. "I liked it better too. I'm sorry if I was defensive. I'm tired. I've driven a long way today. I misunderstood what you were saying and that was wrong of me. I appreciate you telling me."

"That's okay, then," Palmer said, and gave her a rueful smile. "I'd better go."

"I'd better check in with Woodley."

"One other thing," Palmer said, stopping halfway out to look at her again. "We all know you were friends with Vincenze." Then she left and closed the door behind her.

What the hell was that supposed to mean? Shaken, O'Connor rubbed her hand across her face. "I can't live like this," she murmured to herself. "I can't do it."

But she did, for the best part of a fortnight, quietly going about her business, making sure she was seen at team meetings, and was available for routine tasks, while all the time she was collecting samples from her colleagues. She tried to tell herself, that she was imagining things, when she saw colleagues gathered together whispering in corners, or saw what she thought were hostile looks thrown in her direction. She told herself that they were no different from how they had been before, or that this new mood was a natural response to all that had happened since they had arrived on Stella Maris. And surely she had misheard, when lingering for no real reason outside someone's office one days, the words "portal" and "destroy"? Who here would want to destroy the portal? It was known to be friendly. Had that always been the point of the mission? Why bother to send so many scientists, in that case? And if everyone was infected, then why would the Weird want to destroy one of their own?

O'Connor had no answers to these questions, but at least as concerned the extent of the infection, answers were on the way. When she had collected samples from everyone—herself included—she began the process of running the tests on them, working from Vincenze's notes. And in the meantime, she considered how she would get a message up to the people in the refuge in case of the worst, and started to think about what would be the best—the least painful—way to end her own life. If she was infected—if there was a parasite in her mind worming its way into her and turning her against everything she loved and believed in—she would not let it live. She would do whatever was necessary to stop it in its tracks.

CHAPTER ELEVEN

YALE BROUGHT THEM out of phase well inside the Hennessy's World system. They were scrutinised immediately by the automated defence systems, and she fed out the required codes until they were given authorisation to make planetfall. She had picked one of the smaller, more remote spaceports, partly because their security systems tended to be a little less on the paranoid side, and partly for cover. Landing the patrol ship was one thing; having a plausible story to come through customs was another, and Yale couldn't think of anything convincing to explain why she and a teenage girl might be in possession of this ship. So she synchronised their landing with an incoming cruiser and, once it docked, added their names to the passenger list. Then she and Cassandra left their little ship behind, and joined the fast queue to enter Hennessy's World proper.

She'd made Cassandra dress for the occasion, in one of the expensive outfits they'd bought for her on Capital Station. Yale knew she looked scruffy, but it was the accessories that counted, really, so she grabbed an expensive bag and shades for herself at the shops lining the way to customs. The rest was attitude.

"Look like you're supposed to be here," she whispered to Cass.

"I *am* supposed to be here," Cass replied.

Given the level of security, and the ever-present military, passing through customs at Hennessy's World could be a nerve-wracking experience even when you weren't trying to come through on fake ID. But it was lovely weather outside, and this was the only cruiser landing that day at this remote port, so the officials were keen to hurry them all through and get off to wherever they were planning to spend the rest of the day. And that it was it—they had made it onto Hennessy's World. Yale took off her shades, and breathed the air of home. Unlikely many of her friends, she had been born here, a true river rat, and she realised now how much she had missed the place. "Welcome home, Yale," she said to herself, then: "All right, Cass, let's get going. We've a long journey ahead."

The downside of coming down at one of the smaller ports was the time it then took you to get to Venta. Even to reach the outer suburb islands was going to be a journey of several hours, and then they would have to slog through the commuter boats to get to the city proper. Not that Cassandra had revealed their ultimate location yet. Yale planned to get them to the city, find somewhere to stay, and then find out what the last part of their mission was going to be.

They bought tickets for a big shuttle boat heading into towards the main archipelagos. "Do you get seasick?" said Yale.

Cassandra shrugged. "I don't know."

"We'll stay on deck just in case," said Yale. "It's a nice day. Enjoy the sunshine."

So they sat out on the deck, watching the water whip past. Cassandra was silent, and Yale thought she looked tense.

"You okay, Cass?"

"Yes," she said. "Fine. I'm fine."

"It's been a busy few days. And Hennessy's World..." Yale looked out across the blue water. "There's nowhere else like it."

"I've never seen anything like it in my life," said Cassandra, which was pretty high praise from someone who had spent their formative years in another dimension. But Yale knew what she meant. Years on Stella Maris had narrowed her horizons down to a speck. A few thousand people, and a handful of hard-worked fields. You got up, you worked, you ate, you worked some more, and then you fell asleep and got up the next day and did it all over again. That had been her life on Stella Maris. Now she was home again, and home seemed changed. Had Hennessy's World always been so *big*, so busy and full of life? Yale thought of all the quiet days, doing the same things and seeing the same faces, the weird silence that could fall upon a mostly uninhabited world. They were not even near the centre yet, but even here, in one of the less populated parts of Hennessy's World, Stella Maris felt like the back of beyond.

They disembarked on an island near the north-eastern edge of the metropolis. Yale didn't mention to Cassandra that the boat could have taken them right into central Venta as the girl would probably have wanted to try; but Yale wasn't happy yet their credentials could get them that far. She had been away too long, and she was too uncertain of her own capabilities. She wanted some help.

And she wanted to see a friendly face. All those years on Stella Maris, concealing herself, trying not to give away too much, had taken a toll. Yes, she had made friends in her long-house, had proved herself worthy of respect over and over, but she was back home now, and she wanted someone to welcome her back. Someone to say, "Yale, I've missed you." Strange, she thought;

she had never felt homesick on Stella Maris. She had not expected that coming back would fill her with such a sense of loss.

"I'm getting hungry," said Cassandra, and Yale realised that it had been some time since they'd eaten. They wandered along the pier until they found a small café: something of a greasy spoon, but cheap and anonymous. Yale ordered breakfast, and sat tapping away at a handheld she had taken from the patrol ship. She sipped from a mug of hot coffee, something else she had missed, and then forgotten, and now found herself missing all over again.

Lost in her work, she didn't hear Cassandra at first, and had to ask the girl to repeat her question.

"What's the Greenway?"

Yale looked up. Cassandra had made short work of scrambled eggs on toast, but she hadn't touched the milkshake that Yale had also ordered for her. Yale pointed at it. "Are you going to try that?"

"Mm. So what is it? The Greenway?"

"Well, it's probably one of the best known places in Venta. It's the central political district. Parliament's there, when it's in session, which isn't that often, and most of the big civil service departments have their headquarters there. The Bureau is located there."

"Sounds busy."

"Yes, it is."

"Why is it called the Greenway?" said Cass.

Yale put her handheld down on the table, and started drawing a picture on it for Cass to see. "There are three main islands, see? Together they're shaped like a big diamond. People call them Wayland Island, but that's a bit of a misnomer, because, like I said, there's three islands, really. They're joined by these huge wide walkways, big bridges, covered in grass and with flower beds—it's beautiful in the summer. And the walkways all head towards a central point, where there's a big park. That's the Green. People call the park the Greenway too, but that's the name for the district, really. The Greenway. The heart of Venta. The heart of the Expansion."

"I see."

Yale looked around. She'd assumed Cass had seen a poster or something, but there wasn't anything. "What makes you ask?"

Cass tried her milkshake. "Hey, this is nice! Mama says that's where the portal's going to open."

Yale stared at Cassandra in horror. The Greenway was exactly as she had described it—but it was much, much more. The spires and towers and parks of the Greenway were the chief symbol of the Expansion, the biggest empire that humanity—a species of empire-builders—had ever created. Thousands upon thousands of people worked there, and the work they did kept the Expansion running. The Weird couldn't have picked a more significant target for their assault if they'd tried. The thought of a portal opening there...

Yale swallowed to quell the sick feeling rising up in her stomach. She ran her hand across her mouth. "You know, Cass, you might have mentioned this sooner."

"I didn't know until now," she said defensively. "I keep telling you that I only know what Mama tells me!"

Since she couldn't glare directly at Delia Walker, and it wasn't fair to glare at Cassandra, Yale glared at the map she had drawn on her handheld instead. Where would the portal come, exactly? Next to Bureau HQ? By MiniPax? Near the Founders' Fountain, by the Exchange? "Well, like I've said before, your mama needs to start doing a more thorough job of briefing me."

There was a pause. Then, in a polite voice, Cassandra said, "Mama would like to draw your attention to two facts."

"Oh, she would, would she?"

"Firstly, if you had full information, and were captured, that would not work to the benefit of the mission. She says you know that, full well, and you've used it as an excuse to withhold information yourself, so you're a fine one to talk. Secondly, she would like to remind you that she is working against a powerful enemy, and that her own information is perforce dynamic and subject to constant change—"

Perforce? Yale glared at her map and then, with a thump of her thumb, deleted it. "Not to use you as a comms channel, Cass, but could you tell your mother to shut up? I'm trying to concentrate."

After a while, she became aware once again that Cassandra wanted to speak to her. She wasn't quite sure how the girl did it, but somehow Yale always knew when Cassandra had something to say.

"If you're doing some telepathic jiggery-pokery, Cass, knock it off," she said. "What's the matter?"

"I just want to know what you're doing."

"Not your mother again, then?"

Cass smiled like the girl she was. "No! I think she's sulking." Her eyes danced at Yale, who thought that perhaps Cass had enjoying their exchange. "So, what are you doing?"

"Well," she said, smiling back at the girl, "much as I like the breakfasts at this café, we can't stay here indefinitely. So I'm trying to find somewhere for us to stay. We need a credit history if we're going to do that, one that reflects our cover story, and that will keep me in a lifestyle to which I would like to be accustomed." She glanced up towards the counter and lowered her voice. "We also have to pay the bill here at some point before we leave. For which we *also* need credit. And for a credit history, we need credible personal histories..."

"I thought we'd come up with a cover story?"

"Yeah... I'm just fleshing it out and turning it into money..." She was distracted again by her efforts. After about ten minutes, she said, "Is it nice being an heiress, Cass?"

The girl smiled at her. "It's okay, I suppose. I'd rather Daddy was still alive."

"Yes, it's been a sad time for us, daughter of mine," she said. "Your daddy—my beloved husband—died last year. He was a mining magnate on one of the fringe worlds. The very definition of filthy rich. We've had a suitable period of mourning, and now we're here on Hennessy's World to put that behind us and do some shopping. I guess I'll check out schools for you at some point while I'm here... Do you fancy a finishing school, Cass? Make you presentable? Here, we've got some appointments lined up next week."

Cass eyed her suspiciously. "Where's the money coming from really?"

Yale gave a wicked smile. "My old employers have near-limitless funds," she said. "I'm tapping into them."

"Is that allowed?"

"Worried about stealing again? Think of it as back pay. I'm owed about five years." Yale stood up. "Plus expenses. Come on. Time to go."

Cass jumped up from her seat. "Where?"

"Our new place. You'll like it. It's got a great view."

They left the café and went out onto the street. Yale strode off towards the pier.

"We need to get to the Greenway," Cass said.

"I'm sure we should. But we can't," Yale said. "Not with these IDs. I need to do some more work, and I want to be comfortable while I do it. So we're going somewhere else where I can work in peace. It's safe, and it's secure."

"Okay," said Cass. She glanced back over her shoulder. "Did you pay the bill?"

"Pay the bill?" Yale smiled at the thought of the hole that had just opened in the Bureau's accounts. "Cass, I paid their *pensions*."

OVER THE YEARS, the beauty and glamour of Venta had not exactly faded in Lee's eyes, but they had become familiar. This morning, however, Lee saw the capital city of the Expansion again as if for the first time: an improbable, almost magical place, built from glass and steel, light and water. Its high towers stretched to the sky, and its great bridges and causeways crossed the seas, linking hundreds of tiny islands to make a great, cosmopolitan whole.

She had been awake since before dawn, curled on the window-seat of her apartment, looking out across the lights of the city and the glimmer of the sky. The stars above and the lights below had merged into one. When dawn came with a low golden haze that slowly crested the horizon and broke into glorious flame, the city stretched and yawned, and began to come to life. Flyers emerged from their hatches like insects crawling out of their nests, and the white sky was picked out with black dots that, by rush hour, had become a swarm. Lee sat watching, her life on hold as she tried to work out what to do next.

Somewhere across the city, she heard the peal of a clock tower chiming ten, and then the news came all in a rush, her handheld suddenly cluttering up with new messages. The first was from a medical centre she had visited after leaving Mercy's island. She hesitated for a moment before opening the message, but ultimately there was no point delaying, so she tapped the screen and scanned through quickly. Reading between the lines of the report, she was able to put together the facts that she needed to know. There was no infection. She looked out of the window. Venta had never been so beautiful in that moment; never so vital or beloved. She was not infected. She was here, and now, alive, and she would continue to live and be her own person—for a while yet.

The handheld still contained some surprises, however, not all as welcome. The next message was automated, from the office, confirming her appointment for a deep telepathic scan at the end of her week's leave. She filed it away and contemplated her options. Mercy might have had some means to counter it... Lee rubbed her eyes. There were devices—ferronnières—which were able to block out telepathic scans, but nothing that she could get her hands on easily, and certainly nothing that she could use in the Bureau without attracting notice. She could hardly sit there in front of the telepath with a blocking device on her head. The next couple of days might deliver something, but in the meantime she was going to have to assume that Grant would soon know that Lee held incriminating evidence against her. Lee's choices were increasingly narrow: she could pass on her information, but the scan would be surely be deep enough to reveal everything she had done, and Grant's people would go after whoever she told. Information was a curse.

She could run, she thought. Run away. She had never been a field operative, but she knew a trick or two, and perhaps she could buy an identity good enough to get her offworld, or hire a ship with a pilot who knew how to get away. Delia Walker had managed it, hadn't she? Lee sighed. She was not even remotely in Delia Walker's league. She knew what would happen. She would get to the spaceport, and they would be there waiting for her. And then? Interrogation, scan after scan, and then a small room in a prison somewhere. Her parents, too, would find themselves under scrutiny, and perhaps even arrested. She thought of them, quietly pottering about in retirement, and knew she couldn't do anything that would bring harm on those two gentle souls. She'd jump into the ocean first. No, running was not an option. So she would have to come up with something clever.

She was still pondering what that might be when her handheld buzzed again. Without particular enthusiasm, she opened the message. She had to read it a couple of times before she realised what it was: an invitation, anonymous, of course, to come to an address on one of the more exclusive residential islands. The people behind this conspiracy were going to make themselves known to her—and not before time. Perhaps they could explain why nothing had been done to save Mercy Grey. Perhaps they would have the means to help her block the scan. If all else failed, she would make them help her get away; help her mum and dad to escape and join her in safety somewhere...

Lee shook herself. It hadn't come to that yet. It *couldn't* come to that. The Bureau pursued runaways mercilessly even before the new regime. She didn't want to think what forces would be sent after her once Grant's people realised what she knew. There would be nowhere in the known worlds remote enough.

Quickly, she showered, dressed, and headed out into the street towards the pier. It was strange to be out mid-morning, when she was usually at work. Her district was mostly professionals like herself, mostly young or not yet middle-aged; the accommodation was pricey enough to exclude most, but within reach of enough, and a mark of achievement and aspiration. You didn't see your neighbours during the day, locked as they were in their offices on the central islands. Sometimes you didn't see them during the working week either: like the Bureau, many of the big corporations offered their staff the convenience of sleep cells rather than their long commute. As she walked onto the pier, Lee saw a handful of new mothers gathered at a café on the corner, falsely breezy, chatting about their children's achievements, the dark circles under their eyes giving the lie to the good cheer. So this was the island when she wasn't here; something she'd never seen. Everything and everyone seemed to lead a double life.

The message had come with an address, but this time without explicit directions, so Lee followed her own instincts and trusted her rudimentary tradecraft, slipping on and off public barges, taking shortcuts by foot on small back islands where the paint on the walls was peeling and even the narrow waterways seemed sluggish. At Fatima Pier, a busy intersection between central Venta and the western island suburbs, she hired a small barge to take her out to a small islet just inside the western suburbs.

Miriam Island: a byword for luxury. A complex of residential apartments had been built there a few years ago. There had been some kerfuffle over the planning permission, but it was very exclusive and expensive, and so the kerfuffle had come to nothing. Lee, like most people on Venta, was dying to get a peek inside. She was dropped off at a pier on the island adjacent to Miriam, where she was picked up by a private shuttle-ship operated by the company that managed the apartment complex. Automated security devices scanned her to make sure her presence on the boat had been authorised by one of the residents. When the authorisation was confirmed, she was on her way.

After about half an hour, the boat began to make its approach to Miriam Island, slowing down and passing into a narrow tunnel. It eventually came to a halt by a small jetty, and Lee got out. There was a single locked door ahead. Lee's credentials were checked again, and then the door opened directly onto a dropchute. Lee stepped inside. More credential checking, and the dropchute started, taking her directly to the correct floor. When she got there, Lee stood patiently while, once again, an arsenal of security devices checked that she was who was expected, before finally letting her into the apartment. After a minute or so, a soft electronic arpeggio hummed, something clicked, and the door slid open. Lee walked into a penthouse well beyond her salary, if not beyond her dreams.

Light flooded the space, as if stars shone within. The room was long, and very high, painted white, and the furniture was minimal, pale wood, with a few bold, arresting patterns on the soft covers—red and orange, green and gold. There was soft music playing, something jazzy, laid-back. Lee thought she knew the tune, but couldn't quite place it: something she had known a long time ago and not listened to in years. She stepped forwards, walking slowly, the heels of her shoes echoing on the hard wooden floor. At the far end of the room, in the shade of a huge green palm, a woman lay stretched out upon a lounger. She was entirely at rest, like the effigy upon the tomb of an ancient warrior, the remains of a cocktail in a glass beside her.

Seeing her, Lee's heart nearly stopped, as if she had seen a ghost.

"Yale," she said.

The woman on the lounger opened her eyes. She looked extremely relaxed, for someone who was officially dead. "Hello, Maxie," she said. She waved a lazy hand around her. "Do you like it? Better than that flat share on Cherry Blossom Island back in the day, huh?" Like a corpse rising from the grave, Yale rose from the lounger. "How's Mercy? You guys still in touch?"

Lee walked slowly forwards. Yale was smiling at her; she seemed completely at ease. Lee came up close and studied the face of her dead friend. Up close, and behind the relaxed smile, Yale looked older, much older, as if she had been through rough times—although right now, she looked like she was on holiday. She was also more than slightly drunk. No change there, then. Yale smiled, and Lee thought about kissing her. Instead, she slapped her, hard, across the cheek.

Yale swayed perilously. "Ow," she said. Then, after touching her fingertips against her cheek, "*Ow!* Maxie! What the hell was that for?"

Lee exploded. "I thought you were dead!"

"Yes, well, I think I might be, now."

"Where the hell have you been?"

"Busy... Ow! Stop doing that! Stop *hitting* me!"

Lee was punching her repeatedly on the upper arm. Then she stopped and pulled Yale into an embrace, which Yale readily returned.

"That's more like it. Good to see you too, Maxie. How's work?"

"You stupid, impossible... Jesus *Christ*, Yale! Where have you been all this time?" Lee pushed her friend back to hold her at arm's length. "I thought you were dead! Instead, you're—here. And *drunk!*"

"Well, of course I'm drunk."

"Where have you *been?*"

"I took a sabbatical. On a gin-free world. It's been good for me, I think. I feel fit. I feel strong. I feel drunk."

"I thought you were dead!"

"You keep saying that. Sorry to disappoint you." She gave Lee a jaunty smile. "Anyway, I'm back now. Back from the dead, no less! And I'm here to fight demons. Fancy joining me?"

* * *

ONCE SHE HAD some time to reflect upon the test results, O'Connor had to admit that they did not really come as a surprise. She had known, weirdly, that her one-time friends and colleagues were no longer who they had been, *what* they had been. The snubs from Palmer, Woodley's hesitation: it was all part of a pattern. A part of her still hoped, too, that the merciless occupation of Stella Maris was down to the Weird, but she knew that she was deluding herself in this respect. The Weird had not killed those millions on Braun's World and sent murderous assassins to hunt down a young mother and her child. Humans had done that, without any infection or parasite to excuse their actions.

What did surprise O'Connor was her own results. She, at least, was still parasite-free, for the moment. How long this would last, she had no idea. She knew that people were keeping an eye on her; Palmer, superficially friendly, seemed always to be hanging around. Did Palmer have even the remotest idea that she was in the service of the Weird? O'Connor doubted it. The woman she had known would have hated it, would have begged for O'Connor to put her out of her misery. They'd discussed it once, late one night, on the voyage over, after learning about Vincenze's area of expertise. Palmer wouldn't want to live this way. There were questions, too, from Woodley: How was O'Connor's mapping going? What area was she studying now? When would she be going out on another recce? O'Connor made vague noises; hinted that perhaps the project was too much, that it was a dead end, that it wasn't much use. But the place was full of eyes and whispers. She had to get away.

O'Connor knew her time was up when she received a message from Inglis, asking her to come and see him over at the base camp. The base, according to Vincenze's final message, was completely infiltrated by the Weird. She had no intention of going there. She knew that most people did not know when they became infected, but she was sure that if she went to the base that would be the end for her. She would soon be infected, and the only future for her would be one of agony: a mind splitting under the strain of unwillingly serving a vicious, hostile intruder.

It did, however, give her a pretext for leaving the settlement, and for taking one of the ground vehicles with her. She drove off late one afternoon towards the base, switching route when she was safely out into the desert to head out towards the mountains. She took the route she had taken before, but halted after crossing the river. Maria had given her a code to use, should she need to contact them, and a password: *Venta*. O'Connor sent the code, and a message with her location, asking to be met. Then she waited.

Night fell. O'Connor sat inside her vehicle and looked across the river and down into the valley, where the base and the settlement lay, wholly under the control of the Weird. She had no idea if she had been followed. Perhaps they would not try to capture her and, instead, keep following her until she brought them to the refuge and the portal. She sat and worried for a long time. Eventually she fell asleep.

She woke suddenly to someone knocking on the windscreen. Shielding her eyes, she peered outside to see the now-familiar face of Ashot. She smiled. Who would ever have thought she would be glad to see a Vetch? She slipped out of the cabin and greeted him.

"Were you followed?" he said.

"I don't know. I don't think so."

They hid her vehicle in the undergrowth. She slung her pack across her back and they set off, climbing up towards the mountain pass. They walked the whole of the next day. She told him about the extent of the infection; he told her that their numbers had grown to almost fifty. Eventually, they came to a place where he asked if he could blindfold her, just in case, and she allowed him, trusting him to lead her to the hideaway. Soon enough she heard the echo of the cave, and the soft voices of the other refugees, and she knew that she was safe.

Ashot removed the blindfold, and O'Connor rubbed her eyes. Maria was there, looking less tired, but no less resolute.

"Welcome back," Maria said. "Are you all right?"

O'Connor burst into tears. "I'm sorry!" she said, getting herself back under control, grateful for Maria's arm around her. "It's been awful! I'm not—you know what I mean. Infected. I'm not infected."

"Thank goodness," breathed Maria.

"I wouldn't have come back if I was."

O'Connor didn't miss Maria's doubtful expression: that there was very little O'Connor could have done about it, if the Weird had wanted her to come back.

"I have the test results in my pack, if you want to check." She shivered. "It's been dreadful. All my friends down there—I know you all feel they betrayed you, stood by while bad things happened, but they were good people. They came to get to know you, and to learn about the Weird and the portal, and now they're all... It's worse than death, isn't it? A quick death would be merciful. This is going to hurt, it's going to be agony, and then they'll die."

Maria held her. "I'm sorry," she said. "All of your friends. I hope there'll be a way out for them—a cure, or something."

"Vincenze was the one who would have found a cure. They've shot him." O'Connor stifled a sob. "In a way, I'm glad to know it was the Weird that did that. Not friends or colleagues. Something that's replaced them."

Maria took her arm and led her further into the refuge.

O'Connor gladly accepted the offer of something to eat and drink, and they sat together on mattresses at the far end of the hideaway. Ashot came to join them. "I'm sorry to hear about your friends," he said. "I'm glad you're all right." He glanced at Maria. "Maria tells me that you ran tests. Were you able to find out whether the infection has spread out across the settlement?"

O'Connor shook her head. "I'm sorry, I didn't dare do too much. Once I knew that the infection had taken hold among the scientists, I had to get away."

Ashot nodded. "It was the right thing to do. Staying longer might have led to you being infected, and that would have revealed our location to soldiers. You did the right thing. But I wish," he said sadly, "that we could know for sure that all our people are safe."

The mention of the soldiers reminded O'Connor of the piece of conversation she had overheard, and her belief that the Weird had infiltrated the mission to Stella Maris in order to use the humans to find and destroy the portal located here. "That's what I don't understand," she said. "Why would they want to destroy one of their own portals?"

Maria frowned. "We heard that there was a schism within the Weird. That the portal here was friendly towards humans. Not just humans—towards all people in this dimension. Certainly it's been friendly to the people of Stella Maris—it's been the only way the community here has been able to survive. But perhaps that schism has turned into something closer to open war." She shook her head. "We have no way of knowing. But we must make sure that the portal remains safe."

"Have you had any news from the Weird?" O'Connor said. "Anything at all from the portal?"

Ashot shook his head. "The telepaths—we have three now— keep trying to make contact, but nothing." He glanced at Maria.

"What do you want to do next?"

"There's not very much we *can* do right now," Maria replied. "We'll send some scouts off down the river, to see whether Eileen has been followed and if anyone is coming."

"And if there is?" Ashot said. Maria did not answer, and he pressed her. "How would we defend ourselves, Maria, if they came?"

"We have some of the weapons the crimopaths brought with them," she said.

"It won't be enough against a serious assault," he said.

"It might be enough to delay them," Maria said.

"Delay them for what?"

Maria sighed. "We said we'd fight. Perhaps we should plan for that." She glanced at O'Connor, whose eyes were starting to close. "Come on. You ought to get some sleep." She led O'Connor over to a quiet corner and a comfortable mattress. "I'm grateful you didn't give us away," she said.

"I'm grateful that you gave me the chance to prove myself," O'Connor said.

Maria patted her on the arm and left her to rest. As she drifted off to sleep, O'Connor could see, on the far side of the cave, Maria and Ashot, and a few others, deep in conversation. She watched how they all deferred to Maria. Had she expected, this young woman, to find herself leading these desperate people? Perhaps not, but she had stepped up when the need arose. And that, in the end, was what counted.

CHAPTER TWELVE

LATE IN THE afternoon of the day after O'Connor's arrival at the hideaway, the scouts returned to report that Expansion soldiers had been seen near the river ford. Ten of them altogether, forging through the countryside in two armoured vehicles. Maria received the news with equanimity: she had been expecting it. O'Connor, however, was distraught.

"I brought them," she said. "I tried my best, but I brought them after all. I am so sorry!"

Maria tried to console her. "We don't know that this is because of you. They could have been lucky. They could have been carrying out the same searches as you, without your knowledge. What matters is that we defend ourselves—and the portal—against them. The Expansion can't be allowed anywhere near the portal." She sighed. "I keep thinking of them as Expansion, but they're not, are they? They're the *Weird*. The ones that want to destroy us. I suppose that might help—when the time comes."

When the time came to kill somebody, she meant. O'Connor

was looking at her fearfully. "Do you think you could kill someone, Maria?"

"If it meant the only way to save myself? Or to save Jenny? Of course I could." She gave O'Connor a rueful smile. "If you'd asked me that question a year ago, I would have told you not to ask me such a stupid question. When would I ever have to think about something like that? That kind of thing was Kit's business. But when they come for you, when they come for those you love..." She nodded, sure of herself like never before. "I'll kill," she said. "And I think you'll defend yourself too, Eileen."

But it wasn't quite clear that any of them would get the chance. They took stock of what they had to defend themselves, and it didn't amount to much. Some weapons had been salvaged from the crimopaths, but there were no more than a handful of personal weapons, enough to defend the passageway leading to the portal, should the parasite-soldiers get that far.

"And if they've got that far, we're in big trouble," Ashot said. "Because we'll be down to our last few people. And even if we see them off—there are many more of them back at the base. They can keep coming. We might see off one concerted attack, but I doubt we'd be able to deal with a second."

The ground weapons they had taken from the crimopaths' ship were of limited use. They didn't have the manpower to mount a serious attack on the base, much as they would like to. The base was staffed with well-trained soldiers. Besides, Maria sensed there wasn't much stomach yet for a fight. Not after the failed uprising. She was still pondering their next move when a message came through on the comm. "*Stella Maris. Calling Stella Maris...*"

"It's Failt," said Maria, excited. "Failt!"

They crowded round the comm, trying to catch his message. It repeated a few times before it stopped, and they were able to piece the gist together. The *Baba Yaga* was coming home to Stella Maris, with Failt at the helm, and a hold full of shopping.

"Shopping?" said Maria.

"I think he means weapons," said Ashot. "Although some new farm equipment would come in handy. I wonder if Yale thought of that."

"I knew she wouldn't forget us!" said Maria, in delight. "I knew she'd come back!"

"I'm glad to hear that Yale filled you with confidence," said Ashot, dryly. "You'll notice Failt didn't say that Yale was with him."

"He didn't mention Cassandra either. Perhaps she and Yale have gone together."

"Or Yale has gone off on her own at last." Ashot frowned. "Some part of her never entirely committed to life here. She always kept herself separate. We all felt it."

"She committed enough to send us the means to defend ourselves," Maria pointed out. "And I don't believe she would have abandoned Cassandra. Yale wouldn't abandon a child to make her own way through the Reach."

"We'll find out the truth when Failt gets back," said Ashot. "If we live that long. Our problem now is these parasite-soldiers might find us before he gets here. Weapons will be no good to us if we're all dead."

"I've had an idea about that," said Maria. "We talked about taking the fight to them. So why don't we?"

"What do you mean?"

"I think some of us should go down to the base and fire a few of those missiles at the Weird there."

Ashot shook his head. "It's a waste of resources. We'll be spending people, and weapons, that we need here. And there would surely be reprisals against the people in the settlement."

"But it will frighten them, make them think they're fighting a much better equipped enemy than they realised. Might even make them think that our own Weird have come back and are fighting for us."

"That," said Ashot, "might make them even more anxious to find the portal."

"But if they think the base is at risk, they might pull people back away from us. Who knows—it might even stir our own people to start defending themselves."

The debate went on for a little longer. Eventually Ashot agreed it was worth a try. It was certainly better than sitting waiting for the Weird soldiers to come and find them. He looked at Maria and said, "Did you think you were going to end up a general?"

"A *general?*" She shook her head. "I'm Jenny's mum," she said. "That's what this is all about."

"DEMONS," SAID LEE slowly.

Yale took a step back. "You're not going to start hitting me again, are you?"

"Not immediately."

"Good."

"But I want some explanations," Lee said. "Not least as to how and why you're not dead."

Yale frowned. Yes, she did look older, Lee thought, and it was not all down to the five years since they had last seen each other. Yale had not been living the high life for most of that time, she guessed. "Where have you been, Yale? What have you been doing? You've not been in Expansion space, have you? Did you head out into the Reach?"

Yale sighed. "It's a lot more complicated than that, Maxie." She waved to her friend to follow her. "Come on, come on through.

Come and have a drink."

Lee followed Yale through the beautiful apartment. They went via the kitchen—picking up more drinks.

"Haven't you had enough to drink already?"

"Christ, Maxie, if you knew where I'd been the past few years... I haven't even started catching up!"

"I don't know where you've been the past few years because you haven't told me," Lee said, patiently. "Stop faffing around with the cocktail shaker and start talking."

Yale piled a plate full of snacks—"Don't *start*," she said, catching Lee's expression—and led them out to the terrace. Bright sunlight washed over them, and they stood for a while looking out over the magnificent view of downtown Venta. The city was beautiful, Lee thought: spires and towers, glass and light and dreams. They had both of them worked so hard on its behalf. Had it been worth it? Taking a sip from her cocktail and wincing (Yale mixed them strong), she said, "Mercy's dead."

Yale turned to her in shock. "What?"

"Mercy Grey. She was helping me with something. Something big. I went out to the house. Sealed off. Police."

"God," said Yale. "Poor Mercy."

"She never hurt anyone," Lee said.

Yale gave her a sharp look. "You were always romantic about Mercy," she said. "But she was in the thick of it, too, as much as we were."

"What do you mean?"

"Oh, come off it, Maxie! Who do you think she worked for?"

"Big business, I thought. Banks. That kind of thing."

"Maybe a little. Not so much later on—at least, not before I left. Oh come off it, Maxie, surely you knew! She was Bureau, the same as us. But they gave her a lot of leeway. No long commutes for Mercy. No stupid madcap missions without proper back-up."

Yale frowned. "You must have known?"

"I didn't," Lee said. "Really."

"Chances are whatever's happened to her has nothing to do with what she was doing for you. If that helps. She was probably up to her neck in something you can't even imagine. Something much bigger than your problem."

"I doubt that any of her problems were as big as mine," Lee said. "I really do. But I'll tell you about that soon. I want your story first, Yale. I want to know what happened."

Yale put her glass down on the terrace wall. "I guess you heard the last mission went wrong."

"We were told that. We were told you'd died."

"Yeah, well, they say a lot of things, don't they? Tell a lot of lies. So I was on Shuloma Station. It was getting messy, so I asked for back-up."

"Things usually got messy for you, as I recall. I sometimes think you like it that way."

"Well, it was worse this time. And the back-up they sent made it worse." Yale dropped her voice—unnecessarily, secure as the room was. "They sent a crimopath."

"*What?*" Lee stared at her. Crimopaths were the Bureau's dirty little secret. "I thought they'd all been decommissioned."

"Me too," said Yale. "I think the Bureau was starting to get wind of the Weird threat. They were testing them out again. I said I wouldn't work with her; they said I had to. We went round this a few times. Then they gave me some sort of device to control her. It was sick. I was supposed to hold her back by threatening her with pain. I used it once or twice..." Yale's face screwed up in revulsion. "I'll never do anything like that again. Anyway, it became moot. Their clever little device stopped working. Maybe she sabotaged it. I bet they hadn't thought of that. So she was uncontrolled, and uncontrollable. She started killing..."

Yale's expression was unreadable. "You don't need the details of that," she said. "Suffice to say that it's not numbers that count with crimopaths, it's how they go about it. Anyway, it was a mess and it ended with me killing her, and after I'd done that I thought, 'I'm sick of this. I've had enough.'"

She stopped talking. Lee reached out to touch her friend's hand. "I'm sorry, Yale."

"Yeah, well, it's okay now," Yale said. "It was a long time ago. Anyway, there was someone on Shuloma Station who knew a place where I could hide, even from the Bureau. A planet called Stella Maris—"

"I've heard of it," said Lee.

"I bet you have. Everyone has." Yale's eyes narrowed. "What have you heard?"

In a virtuous voice, Lee said, "I can't discuss Bureau business with an outsider."

"Fuck off, Maxie!"

"All right. Stella Maris. There's a Weird portal with unusual properties there. And there's an scientific expedition there right now, led by Fleet—"

"Not Fleet," said Yale. "I've seen them, remember?"

"All right," said Lee. "The Bureau's there."

"Certainly is," Yale said. "And we're up to our usual tricks."

Lee frowned. "What do you mean?"

"When I got to Stella Maris, I found something out of the ordinary there. Human and Vetch living together, side-by-side. Working together. The Weird helped, somehow. But the community is under threat. The Vetch have been locked up. The Weird have gone silent."

"I see." The Bureau *was* up to its usual tricks.

"There's more." Yale took a long slow drink. "What do you know about Delia Walker?"

Lee sighed. Delia Bloody Walker. "I'd love to speak to Delia
Walker right now," she said. "I would ask her if she realised
exactly how much trouble she had caused."

"You might get your chance yet," said Yale.

"What?"

"To tell her that."

"What do you mean, Yale?"

Yale gave a smile. "I'll come to that in a minute. Walker came
to Stella Maris, looking for the portal. Crimopaths came after
her. We saw them off. But Walker went into the portal."

"Good God!" said Lee. "Is that even *possible*?"

Yale burst out laughing. "If you can't cope with that, you're
really not going to like the next bit! Walker was pregnant when
she went in. A few weeks later—her daughter came out. Aged
fifteen." She must have caught Lee's expression, because she
smirked and said, "No, I didn't believe it either. Now—I'm not
so sure."

"Her *daughter*?"

"Yeah. Cass—Cassandra. She's upstairs right now. Do you
want to meet her?"

Lee watched in amazement as Yale headed back indoors.

"*Cass!*" she called upstairs. "Cass, come and meet my friend.
The one I think can help us get where we want to go."

There was a pause, then a thump from upstairs and, a minute
or two later, a small, plain girl came down. She stood by the
open door, neither in nor out, and looked at Lee.

"Hi," she said. "So you're Maxie?"

"Yes," said Lee. "Hi. So you're Cass."

"Mm-hm."

"Delia Walker's daughter."

"Mm-hm."

"Teenagers, Maxie," Yale said. "Remember what it was

like?" She nodded to Cassandra. "There's snacks," she said, and pointed over to the table where she had left the plate. Cassandra shuffled over at speed, and stood by the wall, eating and looking at Lee.

"So," said Yale. "Here I am, back in Expansion space, *in loco parentis* for a teenage girl who wants to get to the Greenway because she thinks a Weird portal is going to open there."

Lee burst out laughing.

Cassandra looked at her in fury. "It's *true*," she said.

Yale said, "I think it probably is true, Maxie. Not very funny."

"And why not?" Lee said, shaking her head. "I've had to believe so many impossible things in the past few weeks that what's a few more? But that's why you're here? That's why you got in touch? You're not behind the messages?"

Yale looked at her blankly. "What messages?"

"'*Everything you are afraid of is true.*' Bit melodramatic, Yale, even for you."

Yale shook her head. "Sorry, Maxie, that doesn't mean anything to me."

"Someone has been sending me messages. Information."

"Yes, well, I've been in the back of beyond until the start of this week. Information about what?"

Lee sighed. Braun's World was going to take some explaining. "A Weird portal opened on Braun's World—"

"Oh, right, yes, that." Yale waved her hand. "Yes, I know all about that. The portal that wasn't there. There's been a top-level conspiracy to cover up a mass murder."

Lee pursed her lips. "Not quite the back of beyond, then."

"Delia Walker passed our way, plus a couple of friends. Yes, she had friends, amazing as it seems. And one of them brought files proving that the footage of the portal on Braun's World had been doctored."

"You believe the story?" Lee felt her world slowly coming apart.

"Well, they sent crimopaths to Stella Maris to kill everyone who potentially knew, so, yes, I'm inclined to believe it's true. Plus I've seen the original footage." Yale nodded. "Yes, it's true." She glanced at her friend. "If you're thinking that there's nobody in the Bureau who is enough of a bastard to do such a thing, think again. Anyone who can order the use of crimopaths can do something like that."

Lee rubbed her hand across her eyes. The relief she felt—to be with someone who knew what she knew, who wanted to work with her, who was focused on getting to the truth, was vast. She was so grateful that she thought she might even forgive Yale for being dead and then not being dead. For turning up here, in this ridiculous place, alive, and so very drunk.

"Who do you think was responsible?" said Yale. "For the cover-up, I mean?"

Lee sighed. "The information I have implicates Adelaide Grant."

"Wow," said Yale. "Up to the top. Probably beyond. Wait, can you go beyond the top, or were you just not at the top to begin with? God, I need to sober up soon."

"Mama didn't like Grant," put in Cassandra. "She didn't like her at all."

"I didn't like Grant much either," said Yale. "But I don't think she'd do that kind of thing. She was..." She struggled to find the right word. "She was hard, but she was honest. You know, we should follow the money. Isn't there some 'superweapon' they've been building?"

"You really are very well informed." Lee shook her head. "No. I've seen the evidence about Grant—"

"Yes, but who sent it to you?" Yale said.

"I don't know. I thought I was coming here to find out—but instead I stumbled over an old friend who I thought was dead, soaking up the sun and knocking back cocktails—"

Yale gave a broad smile. "Maxie," she said. "You know you've missed me."

"We'll see about that. But the point is that I still don't know who's got me involved in all this," Lee said. "And I don't know why. Why make it up if it's not true?"

Cassandra, who had been standing looking out across the water, turned and said, in an impatient voice, "To discredit Grant, of course—what else? She's Fleet—or ex-Fleet. There are plenty of people who don't like the Bureau becoming a division of Fleet. And enough people who remember Andrei Gusev to know what it was like before Grant." The girl twisted round. "None of this matters, you know. Yes, the *truth* matters, and it'll come out eventually. But if we don't hurry, there'll be nobody around to care." She clenched her fists. The sunlight behind her was white, almost blinding, and her face was in shadow. "They're coming, you know. The Weird. The bad Weird. They're coming to the Greenway. I have to get there somehow. Can you help me or not?"

Lee turned to Yale in shock. "How the hell does she know all this?"

"You'll love this bit," said Yale. "She hears her mother's voice in her head."

"Don't we all?" muttered Lee.

"Not all the time," said Yale. "Just some of it."

"Oh," said Lee. "That makes all the difference."

"If it's any help," said Cassandra, "Mama says she would have done much the same thing if she was still here. She would have got something together to sideline Grant for a while. But she's asking you to understand that there are more important things at stake right now." Cassandra stared at Lee. "I have to get to the Greenway. Can you help me?"

"She's persuasive, isn't she?" said Yale. "I mean, I know it's ridiculous, but somehow I still end up helping her." She shrugged. "Roll with it, Maxie. That's what I've been doing. What have we got to lose?"

WHEN THE PARASITE-SOLDIERS crossed the river, the refugees started to harass them. It was a game of cat-and-mouse: armed with the few weapons they had, the settlers would ambush them, harry them, then all back into the scrub. They had the advantage of local knowledge, but the soldiers had the advantage of armour and heat-seeking equipment. Maria and her people had to keep constantly on the move, and they were slowly in retreat—delaying the enemy Weird, but not halting their advance.

After three days, the soldiers had reached the mouth of the pass. On Ashot's advice, Maria sent a message back up to the refuge, instructing everyone who had remained behind to leave and head up further into the mountains. They were mostly the old, the wounded and the few children, Jenny included.

"This is the endgame, isn't it?" said Maria to Ashot. "We can slow them down, but we can't stop them. They'll pick us off, and they'll get through, and they'll find the portal..." She sighed. "I guess this is what happened to Delia and Mother Heyes, in the end," she said.

"But they did enough," Ashot reminded her. "They did exactly enough."

That afternoon brought bad news, when a couple of scouts who had gone down to the river reported the arrival of a further dozen parasite-soldiers. They would soon surely be heading this way. Maria was close to desperate, but only let Ashot see it. And late that afternoon, the end came. There was a huge gravelly noise overhead, and a great rush of wing. "It's a ship!" Ashot yelled, over the noise. "A ship's coming in to land!"

Reinforcements, Maria thought; *more parasite-soldiers. Will they kill us? Or will they infect us, and make us fight our friends? Are the Weird cruel that way?*

And then she realised that she knew the ship. She knew its squat shape. It was the *Baba Yaga*, coming straight down into the narrow pass, cutting off the parasite-soldiers from the band of refugee-fighters, blocking the way through to the portal behind. Maria thought she had never seen as beautiful a sight as that ugly old boat.

The soldiers nearest to the ship fled back down the pass, fearing whatever weaponry it might have. Maria and Ashot waited until the engines had stopped, and then came forwards. The hatch opened, and Failt popped out. "Look at me," he said. "Look at me, mama Maria! I flew her. I flew the *Baba Yaga* all the way back home!"

"You did more than that," said Maria, embracing the boy. "You saved our lives."

The hold revealed its treasures. They set up defences along the pass, and left people there to guard it. Then Maria and Ashot took Failt back to the refuge to hear all that had happened since he left.

"Where are Cass and Yale?" Maria said.

Failt looked sad. "Gone," he said, waving his hand upwards.

"Dead?" said Ashot fearfully.

"No, no! Gone to the Expansion. That's where she wanted to go—to Hennessy's World. Not sure how they'll make it. Yale—she's wanted in the Expansion."

Maria turned to Ashot in surprise. "Did you know that?"

He was clearly as startled as she was. "I did not. I knew she was from the Expansion—but I didn't know that."

"Patrolmen tried to take her on Capital Station," said Failt. "We got her free."

"Do you know *why* they were after her, Failt?" asked Maria. "She wasn't telling."

"That's like Yale," said Ashot. "Never gave a straight answer to a straight question."

"Probably better we didn't know," said Maria. "But if she's gone into Expansion territory with Cassandra..." She sighed. "I don't think we can expect more help from that quarter."

"She's done pretty well by us," Ashot pointed out. "She's even remembered to put in a few tools in case we make it through."

"Don't write Yale and Cass off yet," said Failt. "Cass—sister Cass—she's got something special up her sleeve. Some kind of power. When Yale was in trouble—Cass saved her! She walked in and all she had to do was look at those men who had beaten up poor Yale and they fell over like that. She's amazing. Like an *assassin!*"

"An assassin," said Maria, and her heart went cold. The notion had too much of a ring of truth about it, she thought. Was that why Cassandra had been sent? Was that why she wanted to go to the Expansion? Delia Walker had been a hard woman, and one willing to take risks and make hard choices. But would she really turn her own daughter into a killer? Maria tried to put the idea out of head; whatever plans Delia Walker had, Maria could not offer her counsel, could not influence in any way.

But to use her own child? It ran against every instinct Maria had.

She shook herself. They had the weapons they needed at last. They could defend the refuge and the portal, and now they really could open the battle on two fronts. "We need volunteers," she said to Ashot. "People willing to go down to the base and attack. People ready to go down to the settlement, and get our people fired up. We can't sit up here forever. We have to go back down and show that we're ready to fight."

They sent a party of ten altogether, O'Connor included, down the mountain to do what damage they could at the base, and to try to rouse the settlement. That left fifteen to defend the pathway up to the hideway and the secret beyond. And whatever Walker was doing—and the Weird, too, silent behind the glassy façade of their portal—Maria hoped that they would, at some point, remember Stella Maris, and send a little aid.

CHAPTER THIRTEEN

YALE'S PLAN WAS for them to pose as sightseers visiting the capital for the first time, but Cassandra wasn't exactly living up to her part. She sat on the shuttle-boat a couple of seats away from Yale and Lee, her head down and her face hidden behind her long hair, murmuring to herself. Yale sighed. She struggled to remember, through the dim mists of time, what it had been like to be fifteen. She didn't remember long periods of sulking at the adults in her life, but then the adults in her life had not been particularly present, and not particularly attuned to Yale's mood swings. Yale's had been an unusual childhood—although not, admittedly, as untypical as being brought up amongst aliens in an unknown dimension and sent on a mission to prevent humanity's destruction.

Lee, she noticed, didn't seem too concerned that Cassandra's behaviour might draw attention to them, but then Lee had always been good at presenting a calm front to the world. Perhaps Cass really did look just like a typical teenager, dragged unwillingly on a tourist trip that she hadn't chosen. Certainly none of the other families were paying them any attention, being too busy with their own affairs, arguments, and private jokes.

As the barge drew closer to Wayland Island, Lee nodded at Yale. They both stood up. "Cass," Yale called, softly, and, when the girl didn't reply, she went over and patted her arm.

The girl looked up, and Yale's heart turned in her chest. Cass looked awful. Her face was pale, and she was trembling.

"Hey, kiddo," Yale whispered, her hand upon Cassandra's arm. "Are you okay?"

"I know what I have to do," Cass whispered.

"Okay," said Yale. "Let's get off this boat and get our bearings." Gently, she put her arm underneath the girl's to steady her as she climbed off the boat. There was a tense moment when they all set foot on the island, as Lee's fixes to their IDs were scrutinised, but they passed through the security zone and stepped out onto Wayland Island proper. Human traffic rushed around them: visitors meandering slowly and without certainty; Greenway workers pushing through more purposely and muttering timeless complaints about tourists. Yale, so long away from this heaving crush of humanity, was momentarily overwhelmed by it all, before getting a grip on herself. She felt Cass sway ominously within her grasp.

Lee, close behind, said, "Is she okay?"

"Bit watersick," said Yale, for anyone passing by. "Takes a while to get used to the barges." With her arm still around Cass, she guided the girl out of the barge station and to a quiet spot off the path. "Cass? Are you going to be sick?"

"No," she muttered, then, more robustly, "I'm all right. But I know what I have to do."

"Do you want to tell us?"

"The bomb. The compassion bomb—"

Both Lee and Yale jumped. "Holy fuck!" Lee hissed. "Don't

say words like that around here! *Everything's* monitored round here!"

Cass began to cry, and Yale shot Lee a filthy look. "Don't shout at her," she said.

"Sorry," said Lee. "But, *really*!"

"It's all right, Cass," Yale said. "Maxie's just trying to make sure we get you where we need you. But you have to choose your words carefully. The walls have ears round here. There are automated systems that monitor what people say, and look out for key words. What you just said—well, it might draw attention to us. Can you try explain without saying anything that might attract attention?"

"I'll try," said Cass. "Do you remember when Failt and I came to find you? On Capital Station?"

Yale remembered the bright flash of light; more, she found herself thinking of that sudden sense of being inside the reality of someone else, those two sad, lonely patrolmen, stuck on the border with only their mutual disgust for company. She shivered. "I'm not likely to forget. Is that the plan?"

"Yes, I have to do the same thing here. But that was a practice run. This will be bigger, Mama says. Much deeper and wider in its effects. Everyone will feel it."

"Feel what?" said Lee.

"Feel what it's like. To be part of the whole to be many. To be one to be part of the whole to be many."

Lee shook her head. "That doesn't mean anything to me."

Cass screwed up her face, clearly trying to find another way to say what she meant. "Everyone will feel what it's like to be everyone else."

A compassion bomb. Yale, thinking about those patrolmen, thought she glimpsed what that might mean. Being someone else, while being oneself... The sharp, poignant insight into the undeniable *other*...

"That's it?" said Lee. "That's the plan? What's it supposed to do?"

"It's like a javelin," Cass offered. "A telepathic javelin. Everyone will see the world through the eyes of all the others."

"I still don't see what that's supposed to do?" Lee turned to Yale. "Yale, if there really is going to be something opening here soon, we need to alert the authorities. We need to start getting people out of here."

"What good will that do?" said Yale. "So we move them off the Greenway? The Sleer and the Flyers will give chase—there'll be no corner of Venta that will be safe. There'll be no corner of Hennessy's World that will be safe." She turned back to Cassandra. "Cass, what's this javelin supposed to be doing? What's the big picture? Can your mother say?"

"It's meant to slow them down," Cass said. "The part of the whole that wants to be the whole. Slow them down. Maybe even stop them."

The part of the whole that wants to be whole. The assimilationist Weird. The part of the Weird that wanted to consume this dimension. "It sounds pretty risky," said Yale, mostly to Walker, if she could hear.

"It sounds absolute crap," said Lee.

And once upon a time, Yale would have agreed with her. But Stella Maris, now. Stella Maris, where people had once lived in peace and harmony, because of the Weird. They were whole in a way that humans weren't; they shared minds and experiences in a way that humans couldn't. But could it be glimpsed? Could it be experienced? What would that do?

"Really, Yale," said Lee. "This is the plan? This is a *terrible* plan."

`Yale reached out and took Lee's hand. "I know," she said. "When did that ever stop us?"

*　　*　　*

THE REFUGEES HAD been hard at work throughout the morning, mining the pathway, building what fortifications they could. A party of five remained near the *Baba Yaga* to watch for any advance, and to delay it while they could. Maria and Ashot took Failt further back, to prepare the defence of the portal. Mid-morning, one of the party arrived from the *Baba Yaga*, reporting that while the mines had done significant damage, there were still six parasite-soldiers heading up the path that led to the refuge and the portal beyond. The four of them looked at each other.

"I guess it's time to go and take up our positions near the portal," said Maria.

"Would we be better inside the passage?" asked Ashot.

Maria frowned. "Once we're in, there's no other way out."

"We could bring down the roof," said Ashot.

Maria stood silent for a while, contemplating that option. Yes, that would protect the portal, but it would also cut off the people of Stella Maris from their chief source of support. If this attack was held off—and Maria had to hope, for Jenny's sake if nothing else, that it could be—then a life on Stella Maris without the Weird would be hard. "I'm not keen on that option," she said, slowly.

"We could dig our way back through, eventually..." Ashot's voice faded. Maria guessed what he was thinking. If Stella Maris came through this, and the settlement was able to re-establish itself, neither of them was likely to see that happen.

Failt, listening, said, "Don't do it, mama Maria." There were tears in his eyes. "Don't cut us off from the portal. Don't cut me off from Missus Dee!"

"I think we need to keep our options open, Failt," said Maria.

He grabbed her hand. "It's not right! We need the Weird!"

"But they aren't here, Failt!" she said. "They've gone! We've got to do what we can for ourselves!"

"Missus Dee *promised*," Failt wailed. "Cass said so! She promised that they wouldn't abandon me! Don't cut us off from the portal!"

Maria looked at Ashot. The big Vetch shook his head. "I don't know what to suggest, Maria. Let's lay the mines anyway—and perhaps we won't have to use them."

Before Maria could decide, there was a crackle on the comm, and O'Connor's voice came through. "*There's a party of about fifty coming from the base,*" she said. "*I hope you guys have got some trick up your sleeve, because I think they're heading your way. We'll do what we can, but...*"

The comm went silent. What *could* they do, really? There were so few of them.

"Let's get up to the portal," Maria said. "We'll lay the mines, but I promise you, Failt"—she looked at the boy—"we'll only use them if we've no other option."

The five of them headed up the path, coming quickly to the tunnel to the portal. Maria and Ashot, with Failt in tow, went inside, leaving two to guard the entrance and slow the advance of the soldiers when they arrived. They moved slowly, in single file, along the narrow way, stopping every five or so metres to lay explosives, and coming out at last into the cavern.

Maria looked down on the silent portal. Still glassy and vacant, it showed no sign that the intelligences beyond had any sense of what was happening in the world that they had once succoured. Failt knelt down and reached out his hand. "*Missus Dee,*" he murmured. "*Not long now...*"

Ashot came to stand by Maria. "Anything?"

"Not a ripple."

"Failt seems to think there's something."

Maria looked sadly at the boy. "Failt trusts beyond reason."

Shots echoed along the passageway; someone cried out. The soldiers were coming. Maria shuddered. Here she was, where her friends had stood less than a year ago. This was what had happened to Heyes and Walker, pushed back slowly up this narrow passageway, until the only place to go was...

Maria nodded. She was sure now, completely certain, that Delia Walker had gone into the portal, and somehow found her way to the Weird dimension. She was sure, beyond any doubt, that Cassandra had been sent from her, for some purpose that Maria could not fathom. Maria looked at Failt, standing staring down into the portal, stock still, waiting, waiting, for something... She looked down at the portal again, opaque and unmoving. That route was not an option for them, and besides, there was Jenny, waiting for her mother to come back.

Maria stifled a sob. She heard more shots being fired, and then silence. The soldiers were coming, sent by something that only wanted to consume. Would they kill them outright? Or would they take them captive, infect them, use them against their friends? Against Jenny?

My baby, she thought. *First your daddy, now your mummy. I'm sorry, Jenny. I did my best for you. Perhaps you'll be safe, up there in the mountains. These people are kind, and brave, and they'll look after you as best they can, for as long as they can...*

But she couldn't bear to think of all that, of Jenny—so small—left all alone in the world, and so she rubbed her eyes, and gripped her weapon more tightly, and wondered whether she really would be able to kill when the moment came, even knowing that they were guided by parasites, and half-dead already.

"They're coming," Ashot muttered, beside her. "They're coming. Maria, if we want to stop them, we have to trigger the explosives now."

She felt a hairy hand tug at her own. "Don't do it, mama Maria!" Failt said. "Please! I know she's coming! She promised me! She promised she wouldn't abandon me!"

Maria licked her lips. She began to issue the instruction, but her mouth was so dry that her voice came out as a croak. In that moment, there came a noise behind her, like the tearing of fabric, but louder; so loud that she cried out.

"The portal!" Ashot shouted. "It's opening!"

"I knew it!" Failt cried. "I knew it!"

Maria looked behind her. The glassy surface of the portal was shimmering and shifting. Great dark pink clots were gathering, and bubbling, and rising. The portal was opening. The Weird were coming.

But which Weird?

TODAY ON THE Greenway was just another busy working day. Yale had seen a thousand days like it. She had been part of them—heading to briefings, meeting colleagues, stopping for a hurried working breakfast. Now she was an outsider, but this huge busy space had never seemed so vital to her before, in all the times she had been here on business. She was glad to be back, and if this was the last thing she saw before it was all consumed, she was glad to have come home and seen it at its height one last time.

"Where now?" Lee said to Cassandra. The girl pointed across the park to the huge round swirling face of the Parliament building.

"Of course," said Lee. "It would be. All right, let's see how far we get before these IDs show up as fake."

They walked out onto the Green. Yale was conscious, as she had never been before, of the presence of security devices, armed soldiers, the constant identity checks and verifications that covered the Green like an invisible web. From the corner of her eye, she saw two figures in black uniforms begin to head in their direction, their weapons lazily rising. "Not to alarm you guys," she said, "but I think our cover is blown."

"Not long now," said Cass. "Mama says it won't be long now."

People were moving away from them, like ripples on water. They knew what was coming. One of the armed people said something into the comm on his helmet. Yale guessed they had less than half a minute before they were ordered to lie down flat on the ground. "I never thought," she said, "that I'd welcome the arrival of a Weird portal, but I could do with it now."

Lee raised her arm, and pointed beyond the armed men heading towards them. "Be careful what you wish for," she said.

As Yale watched, something tore open in space and time. Brutal and sudden, for all its weirdness, this was plainly an enemy attack. All around her, she heard people gather their voices: *What is this? What's happening?*

And then the horrors poured forth. Humanity looked into hell, and screamed.

Out came the Sleer, huge humanoid shapes, but formless, without sentience, the mindless arms of a murderous consciousness. Out came hideous winged creatures, descending on the crowd, tearing at them with terrible claws and teeth. People began to run, pushing past each other in a desperate rush not to be consumed. Yale thought: *This is it. I'm living through my worst nightmare. Someone has looked inside my head and seen all the worst things I ever thought could happen, and put the show on for me right here, in the place I love most in the whole world...*

She realised that Lee, beside her, was shielding Cassandra, putting herself between the girl and the horrors spewing forth from the portal's maw. In a shaking voice, Lee said, "All right, Cassandra, it's time to show us what you can do."

"Be careful what you wish for," Yale whispered, and seized Lee's hand. Lee gripped back, hard. Yale looked at Cassandra, small and frightened, and she thought: *Is this girl really all we've got?* In a quiet voice, the voice of a child, Cassandra said, "Mama?" And then, again, more strongly: "Mama? I'm here. I got here, like you told me. Mama, it's time."

Yale heard a *thud* that seemed to start at the nape of her neck, and then pulse through her brain, like a terrible, untreatable headache that threatened never to end. *Oh*, she thought, *am I being eaten?* And then: "Mama!" she heard Cassandra cry. Beside her, Lee gasped: a mixture of pain and pleasure. Yale felt it too: the sudden joy of being at one with the universe. It lasted only a second, before the second wave came: the terrible anguish—the pain of isolation, of being torn away from the whole, of having been part of the whole and then becoming separate... And then, just as suddenly, came the third wave: the rush of desire—the overwhelming urge to connect, to help, to heal...

"Holy hell," Yale said, "this hurts so much!"

Dimly, she was aware of other people around her; that they too were feeling some of what she felt, and that even a small part was enough to throw them into utter disarray. She saw Sleer, halting, and curling in on themselves as if in pain. She saw the Flyers falling from the sky. She turned to look at Lee, now so clearly the most precious thing in the universe.

"Maxie," Lee said, through tears. "Is this love or is this death?"

*　　*　　*

THREE OF THE parasite-soldiers burst through into the cavern. Ashot, turning to Maria, said, "We're too late! We're too late!"

But Maria wasn't sure. "Wait!" she cried. "Look at the portal!"

Something was coalescing on the surface. The clots were pulling together, shaping into a distinct form. A column rose up, and from it arms and legs unfolded, then a head; like watching the formation of a foetus, Maria thought, accelerated beyond reason. Soon what looked like a whole person was there, tall and hard and purposeful.

"Delia?" she whispered.

The figure turned its head towards her. For a moment, Maria thought she saw Walker, the ghost of a smile upon her lips. Then her head was riven with pain. Maria fell to her knees, clutching her hands to her temples. She was aware that Ashot, too, had fallen down. She thought: *Have I been shot?* But the pain wasn't like that. It seemed to come from within, as if the whole of creation had been poured into her body, a vessel too fragile to contain something so big, so beautiful, and so full of love and pain. She heard Ashot whisper, "*Too much... Too much...*" She heard the parasite-soldiers cry out in pain. Down in the valley, if Maria had known it, O'Connor was feeling the same. So were all Maria's friends, and her enemies, and the parasites they carried within them. They could all feel the whole, and the parts of the whole, and it hurt beyond speech and reason. And some of them could bear some of it, and none of them could bear all of it; and some of them curled up and died.

Maria, who was perhaps closer to this source of knowledge and understanding than many, soon began to regain her grip on the world. It was Failt that brought her back to her senses: Failt, standing on the edge of the chasm, reaching out for the figure at its heart. "Missus Dee!" he cried. "Oh, Missus Dee! I knew you'd come back! I knew you'd come back for me!"

Maria struggled to her feet. Failt was learning forwards, waving at the bright figure. "Missus Dee! Over here! I'm over here!"

Maria saw him teetering on the very edge. "Failt!" she cried. "Be careful!" She stumbled towards him, reaching out a hand, still reeling from the blow of the telepathic bolt pulsing across the whole of Stella Maris.

"Missus Dee!"

Failt was perilously close to falling in. Maria reached out her arm, but Failt had *stepped forwards*... "Failt!" she cried. "No!"

He fell. And then, as Maria watched, she saw the bright starlit figure—*Delia? Delia!*—reach out her hand and grab the boy. Delia Walker pulled Failt to her, and Failt held her in turn, his body silhouetted against hers. They were still for a moment, like a pieta, and then Failt laughed in sheer joy, and they fell back, back and down into the embrace of the Weird. The portal rippled madly for a while, and then began to settle, turning still and glassy once again. Silence fell across the world, and even the cold stars seemed to cease their twinkling.

CHAPTER FOURTEEN

SILENCE TOO HAD fallen upon Hennessy's World. Yale, staggering to her feet, reached out to Lee. "Are you okay? Maxie, are you okay?"

"I think so," said Lee. "What happened? What the hell just happened?"

"The bolt," said Yale. "The bomb. The compassion bomb." She looked around. "Cassandra," she said, and then began to call out. "Cassandra! Cass! Where are you?"

Lee took hold of her arm. "I think she's gone, Yale."

"Gone? Gone where?"

"Gone back."

Yale stood in the Greenway, blinking back tears. "Cass? Where are you, kiddo?" But she knew. She had seen, for a moment, as the portal began to ravel back in upon itself, the tall figure of a woman reaching out for her girl, bringing her back home. Walker had come to collect.

Lee, standing next to one of the Sleer, called out. "Yale! Look at this. Do you think it's dead?"

Yale walked forwards. The Sleer, hideously half-human, was unmoving, and already the colour was leaching from it. Yale tapped it with the toe of her boot. There was no reaction. "I think so," she said. "Whatever hit us—it hit the Weird too."

Lee said, "What *did* hit us? Do you have any idea?"

Yale looked around her. People were starting to recover from the immediate debilitating effects of the bomb, but the secondary effects—the *real* effects—were now starting to emerge. Beside her, somebody burst into tears.

"Everything," Yale said. "We've all looked into each other. We've felt what they feel; we know what they know."

"They know," said Lee. "They all know about Braun's World. They all know the truth. What do you do with that knowledge? How do you live with it?"

Yale wrapped her arms around herself. *Welcome home, Yale.* "You do what you can. Or else you give up."

MARIA, KNEELING BESIDE the portal and weeping, felt a big hand upon her shoulder. Ashot knelt down beside her. "What happened?" he said. "Do you know what happened?"

"Delia came," Maria said. "Delia Walker. She brought the Weird—*our* Weird—with her. They sent something—some kind of telepathic blast..."

"Yes," he said, "I felt that. And I think they did too."

Maria, turning to look behind her, saw the corpses of five parasite-soldiers behind her.

"They're quite dead," said Ashot. "I guess that whatever hit them was too much strain on top of the parasite."

"Oh," cried Maria, "I'm sorry! It wasn't their fault! I hope it's not all of them. It wasn't their fault."

"Where's Failt?" said Ashot.

Maria gestured down at the glassy portal. "He's gone. In there. Delia promised, didn't she, that she wouldn't abandon him? And she didn't. We won't see him again, Ashot. He's gone home." Slowly, she stood up, and they both located their weapons. Then they went out into the passageway.

The rest of the assault party was there. Some of them, nearest to the cavern, were unconscious. One or two were sitting, heads in hands, still reeling from the bolt. Maria knelt down next to one of them. "Are you okay?" she said. He looked up at her. He was young. He reminded her of Kit, when they were first married. "I'm Maria," she said. "Are you okay? Can you talk to me?"

He stared up at her. "My head," he said. "My *mind*... I feel like I'm thinking clearly for the first time in ages..."

"The infection," Ashot said. "The parasites are dead, but not the hosts. Whether that's just here, or across the whole of Stella Maris, we'll have to see."

Maria, reaching out her hand, helped the young man stand. "I don't think Delia Walker will have missed anything."

LATER, WHEN THEY were able to make contact with O'Connor, she confirmed Maria's suspicions. "*The infection seems to be gone. People have been cured... 'Freed' might be a better word for it. And nobody seems to be in command. The Vetch are coming out from their long-houses—nobody is stopping them.*"

"What about the humans?" Maria said.

"*There's a lot of grief, a lot of guilt...*"

"So there should be," Ashot muttered.

"*It's going to be a long road back,*" said O'Connor. "*I don't think everyone will be able to live with themselves after this.*"

*   *   *

NOT EVERYONE COULD live with themselves, afterwards. In the days that followed the Weird attack on Hennessy's World, the news was full of what had happened. It almost drowned out the reports of the wave of suicides that followed the attack. Several very wealthy and influential people, it seemed, could no longer live with what they had done. Yale and Lee didn't miss the reports, and they checked off the names one by one. Everyone now knew—*everyone*—who had been involved in the cover-up on Braun's World.

And that, Lee had been surprised to learn, did not include Adelaide Grant. When the compassion bomb delivered full knowledge, Lee had grasped that Grant was innocent. Yes, she had pushed to bombard Braun's World, but her belief in the portal had been complete. She had been exploited as much as any of them. When at last Lee returned to the Bureau, she went straight up to Grant's office, but the room was empty. Grant was gone, resigned, and in this new dispensation of open minds and open secrets, nobody had quite got round to appointing a replacement head of the Bureau.

It wouldn't last: the fullest effects of the bomb would wear off, in time, and become no more than a dream or a memory. But something would linger for a while. No experience, thought Lee, could be entirely repressed.

At her desk, she deleted almost all of her messages unread. Nobody was bothering to track the story about Braun's World now that everyone knew the truth. But one message caught her eye, and as she opened it tears began to run down her cheeks.

There was Mercy Grey, smiling guiltily and very much alive. "Hi Maxie," she said. "Sorry if I gave you a scare. I couldn't help looking through those files you sent me. And I knew I wasn't safe. So I hid... I'm sorry. Come over, will you?"

I will, thought Lee, *and I'll bring a surprise.*

*   *   *

MERCY DIDN'T REACT quite as Lee had hoped when she walked in with the dead Yale. "Oh," said Mercy, peering at Yale, "I guess faking one's death is in, right now."

Later, after they had eaten, they sat on Mercy's rooftop garden and watched the sun set, and they talked about what they would do next. Mercy's skills would be more in demand than ever from the Bureau, after its quite significant security breaches. Lee too was in demand from her superiors, eager to find out what she knew about the Weird. As for Yale...

"Are you going back to Stella Maris?" said Lee.

Yale put her hands behind her head and looked up at the stars. "No," she said. "It's in good hands. Besides, I like it here." She smiled at them both. "It's good to be home."

THERE WAS A long, uncertain road ahead for Stella Maris, O'Connor thought, but it was in good hands. There were good people here, willing to make things work.

The Expansion soldiers were leaving. Most could not cope with staying. Some had no memory of being ordered here; some did not believe the orders they had received were valid. Inglis, without any guidance from Hennessy's World, had decided the mission was over. The shuttles were almost packed, and the ships would be leaving in the next few days.

Most of the scientific mission was leaving too, but not all. O'Connor, of course, was going nowhere. Palmer too, back to herself, was staying, as was Woodley. They knew now that the closure of the portal need not be permanent, and many hoped that one day it would reopen, and that the Weird would return, and allow them to learn about them first-hand. In the meantime, they were prepared to live here, and help the settlement rebuild.

That would be the longest journey. Without the telepathic field the Weird had generated, the people of Stella Maris—Vetch and human—had to learn to live with each other again. Not everyone thought that they could do it. Some of the humans had decided to take up the offer of Expansion citizenship, and go on the ships when they left. The Vetch, lacking the option, were all staying. The long-houses were being rebuilt; some of the old groups were able to form again, but for others, the memories of what had happened during the recent occupation were too fresh. It would be a long, hard road back to trust.

A few weeks after the Expansion ships departed, they received a message from Yale—alive and well and staying put—and heard the news that Cassandra had gone. They sent word back of all that happened on Stella Maris, and sent Yale news of Failt. They all missed the boy, but nobody could blame him for his choice. He had gone to be with the family he had always craved. The only real family he had ever known.

Family, thought O'Connor, *that strange, elastic word*. If you asked her now who mattered to her most, she would say: Maria, Ashot, Jenny. *These people—here, now. These people, around me. These people with whom I am building a new life. Welcome home.*

ACKNOWLEDGEMENTS

GRATEFUL THANKS TO Eric Brown for allowing me such freedom within the Weird Space universe to pursue my own characters and ideas. My thanks also to David Moore for supporting my vision of this universe.

Thank you to colleagues who supported me and my writing through a difficult year.

And most of all thank you to Matthew, for giving me the space and time to write, and to Verity, who makes it all worthwhile. I love you both deeply.

Una McCormack

UNA McCORMACK

Una McCormack is a *New York Times* bestselling author of novels based on *Star Trek* and *Doctor Who*. Her audio plays based on *Doctor Who* and *Blake's 7* have been produced by Big Finish, and her short fiction has been anthologised by Farah Mendlesohn, Ian Whates, and Gardner Dozois. She has a doctorate in sociology and teaches creative writing at Anglia Ruskin University, Cambridge. She lives in Cambridge with her partner, Matthew, and their daughter, Verity.

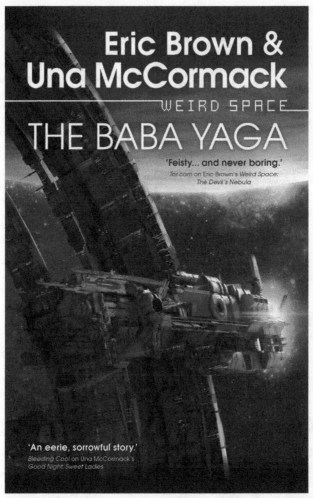

Eric Brown & Una McCormack

WEIRD SPACE

THE BABA YAGA

'Feisty... and never boring.'
Tor.com on Eric Brown's *Weird Space:
The Devil's Nebula*

'An eerie, sorrowful story.'
Bleeding Cool on Una McCormack's
Good Night, Sweet Ladies

The growing threat of the dimension-invading Weird has driven the Expansion government to outright paranoia. Mandatory telepathic testing is introduced, and the colony Braun's World – following reports of a new Weird portal opening – is destroyed from orbit, at an unimaginable cost in lives.

Delia Walker, a senior analyst in the Expansion's intelligence bureau and a holdout of the pragmatic old guard, protests the oppressive new policies and is drummed out. Sure there's a better way, she charters the decrepit freighter the *Baba Yaga* and heads into the lawless "Satan's Reach," following rumours of a world where humans and the Weird live peacefully side by side.

Hunted by the Bureau, Walker, her pilot Yershov, and Failt – a Vetch child stowaway, fleeing slavery – will uncover secrets about both the Weird and the Expansion; secrets that could prevent catastrophic war...

Eric Brown
WEIRD SPACE
SATAN'S REACH

'It's a runaway success.'

Telepath Den Harper did the dirty work for the authoritarian Expansion, reading the minds of criminals, spies and undesirables, for years. Unable to take the strain, he stole a starship and headed into the void, a sector of lawless space known as Satan's Reach. For five years he worked as a trader among the stars – then discovered that the Expansion had set a bounty hunter on his trail. But what does the Expansion want with a lowly telepath like Harper? Is there something in the rumours that human space is being invaded by aliens from another realm? Harper finds out the answer to both these questions when he rescues a young woman from certain death – and comes face to face with the terrible aliens known as the Weird.

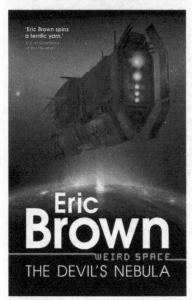

'Eric Brown spins a terrific yarn.'

Eric
Brown
WEIRD SPACE
THE DEVIL'S NEBULA

Ed Carew and his small ragtag crew are smugglers and ne'er-do-wells, thumbing their noses at the Expansion, the vast human hegemony extending across thousands of worlds... until the day they are caught, and offered a choice between working for the Expansion and an ignominious death. They must trespass across the domain of humanity's neighbours, the Vetch – the inscrutable alien race with whom humanity has warred, at terrible cost of life, and only recently arrived at an uneasy peace – and into uncharted space beyond, among the strange worlds of the Devil's Nebula, looking for long-lost settlers.